THE RIGH

Doubt overtook [...] to get the wrong idea [...] ou think I am."

Abraham wanted to kick himself. Yet again, he'd said the wrong thing. He'd meant every word, but a girl like Emma would think he was flattering her, tempting her to be proud. No wonder she looked concerned. But he didn't know what to say. He never did, so he fell silent and hoped she'd forgive him.

She straightened her shawl. "I should go now. Mamm will wonder what happened to me."

"*Jah.* Okay." He barely dared ask the next question. "Is it still *gute* if I come tomorrow to visit your chickens?"

She cracked a smile. Abraham breathed a sigh of relief. "I don't think my chickens have ever had anything so fancy as a visitor before. They'd love it, for sure and certain."

Abraham nodded. "Okay. I will bring them a present."

Her smile got wider. "A present? They'll be beside themselves."

"How is ten o'clock?"

"Wonderful *gute.*"

He really had to go now, or she'd think he was a bother. "Emma, I didn't say what I said to flatter you or tempt your pride. I would never do that. I think you're just the right amount of nice."

"*Denki*, Abraham. I'm going to try to live up to your opinion of me. . . ."

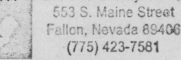

Books by Jennifer Beckstrand

The Matchmakers of Huckleberry Hill

HUCKLEBERRY HILL

HUCKLEBERRY SUMMER

HUCKLEBERRY CHRISTMAS

HUCKLEBERRY SPRING

HUCKLEBERRY HARVEST

HUCKLEBERRY HEARTS

RETURN TO HUCKLEBERRY HILL

A COURTSHIP ON HUCKLEBERRY HILL

HOME ON HUCKLEBERRY HILL

The Honeybee Sisters

SWEET AS HONEY

A BEE IN HER BONNET

LIKE A BEE TO HONEY

The Petersheim Brothers

ANDREW

ABRAHAM

Anthologies

AN AMISH CHRISTMAS QUILT

THE AMISH CHRISTMAS KITCHEN

AMISH BRIDES

THE AMISH CHRISTMAS CANDLE

THE AMISH CHRISTMAS LETTERS

Published by Kensington Publishing Corporation

ABRAHAM

JENNIFER BECKSTRAND

ZEBRA BOOKS
KENSINGTON PUBLISHING CORP.
www.kensingtonbooks.com

ZEBRA BOOKS are published by

Kensington Publishing Corp.
119 West 40th Street
New York, NY 10018

All Kensington titles, imprints, and distributed lines are available at special quantity discounts for bulk purchases for sales promotion, premiums, fund-raising, educational, or institutional use.

Special book excerpts or customized printings can also be created to fit specific needs. For details, write or phone the office of the Kensington Sales Manager: Attn.: Sales Department. Kensington Publishing Corp., 119 West 40th Street, New York, NY 10018. Phone: 1-800-221-2647.

Zebra and the Z logo Reg. U.S. Pat. & TM Off.
BOUQUET Reg. U.S. Pat. & TM Off.

First Printing: December 2019
ISBN-13: 978-1-4201-4772-8
ISBN-10: 1-4201-4772-2

ISBN-13: 978-1-4201-4775-9 (eBook)
ISBN-10: 1-4201-4775-7 (eBook)

10 9 8 7 6 5 4 3 2 1

Printed in the United States of America

Chapter One

Mamm was out to get him. Alfie was sure of it. Why else would she put her two youngest sons to sleep in the cellar and make them walk to church in March? March! In Wisconsin! Alfie's fingers were going to freeze off, even wearing these goofy mittens Mammi had knitted him.

Alfie blew into his hands to warm them, which only got him a mouthful of lint and little drops of spit on his mittens. If any nine-year-old had a harder life, Alfie would sure like to meet him. He'd give him a big hug and feel very sorry for him.

Alfie and his twin *bruder*, Benji, trailed behind the rest of the family on the way to church or *gmay*. Benji often fell behind because he liked to look for birds and he was never in any especial hurry to get to church. Alfie trailed because he was mad at the whole family and they needed to know it, especially Mamm. If she felt she had to turn back seven times to yell at Alfie to keep up, then it was just what she deserved.

Mamm and two of Alfie's older *bruderen*, Abraham and Austin, walked ahead, not looking the least bit cold or caring that their little *bruderen* might fall behind and get lost. Dat had taken Mammi and Dawdi in the buggy and left Alfie to walk, even though there was plenty of room for one more little boy in that buggy.

Alfie slid closer to Benji, who was purposefully shuffling his feet through what was left of the snow on the side of the road. "We need a plan."

Benji made a face. "I thought we already had a plan."

"We did. We need another one."

"But we already got Mary and Andrew married," Benji said.

Alfie smiled in spite of his lint-covered lips and his sour mood. "We totally rocked that plan."

Benji puckered his lips so hard his nose wrinkled. "What does that mean?"

"Willie Glick's Englisch friend Max says that all the time. It means we did a *gute* job."

Benji nodded. "So why do we need another plan?"

Benji was a wonderful nice *bruder*, but sometimes he didn't think things through very well. Alfie sighed loudly enough to scare the birds from the nearest tree. "Benji, we're still sleeping in the cellar."

"So?"

Alfie slid his arm around Benji's shoulders and encountered something sticky at the back of Benji's head. He pulled his hand back. "Benji, what have you got in your hair?"

Benji touched the back of his head, and a grin grew on his face. "That's where that went." He winced and tugged and pulled a half-eaten sucker off the back of his head. He smiled triumphantly and held the sucker in the air. It had hair on one side of it. "I fell asleep eating this last night." He stuck the hairy thing in his mouth. "It still has its flavor."

Alfie growled. "Oh, *sis yuscht*, Benji. This is why we can't sleep in the cellar anymore. We get stuff in our hair, and Mamm doesn't even check."

Benji picked a piece of hair out of his mouth. "We have to sleep in the cellar. When Dawdi had his stroke, Mammi and Dawdi moved into Mamm and Dat's room, and Mamm and Dat moved into our room." Benji frowned. "We need to take care of Dawdi. Mamm said so."

"But there isn't a room for us."

"I like taking care of Dawdi. He calls me Benny because he can't say his *j*'s yet. He's getting better, and he let us borrow his binoculars."

Alfie sighed again, more quietly this time so Mamm wouldn't suspect they were making plans. Mamm was the suspicious type, and sometimes she was very smart. "We thought that if we found a wife for Andrew, he'd move out and we'd get our room back. But Andrew got married, and Mamm turned his room into a sewing room. She'd rather sew things than give her little *buwe* a decent place to sleep."

Benji scrunched his lips to one side of his face. "It's not a sewing room. It's her I-want-to-be-alone room."

"What do you mean?"

"When she wants a break from Mammi, she goes to her sewing room. I heard her tell Aunt Beth."

This was why Alfie needed Benji to help with the plan. Benji noticed things no one else did. He listened to grown-up conversations when the grown-ups thought he was doing his chores. "But even though our plan with Andrew worked, we need another plan because the cellar is no place for two growing *buwe*."

Benji grinned. "Our plan for Andrew was a real *gute* plan. I liked when we stole the cat and used the walkie-talkies."

"We didn't steal the cat. We borrowed it."

A worried look crossed Benji's face. "You got stuck in a tree, and they had to call a fire truck. I thought you were going to die."

Alfie grunted. He'd almost been eaten by a cat and stung by a hundred bees in that tree. His heart still jumped when he remembered how the branch he had been sitting on creaked every time he took a breath. It was wonderful scary, but he'd never tell Benji or he might not go along with the plan. "I wasn't going to die. I just couldn't climb down because Bitsy's cat hissed at me every time I tried." Alfie glanced in Mamm's direction, then pulled Benji to a stop. "We need a new plan. We've got to find wives for Abraham and Austin if we're ever going to get out of that cellar."

Benji shook his head. "I don't want you to climb any trees in our new plan."

"We have to climb trees. It's the best way to spy on people."

"But what if you fall?"

"I won't climb so high next time."

Benji took a deep breath, bit off the last bite of sucker from the stick, and looked up at the sky. "I guess that's okay. But I get the top bunk if Mamm puts the beds on top of each other."

Alfie thought about that for a second. Would he rather sleep in the bottom bunk upstairs or stay in the cellar with the spiders and worms? "Okay. Mamm took the bunk beds down when Abraham and Austin moved into our room. Maybe she'll leave them that way as a sign of her gratitude for getting Abraham and Austin out of the house."

Mamm didn't even look back. "Alfie and Benji, move those feet before the grass grows under them."

Mamm thought she was so smart, but there were still patches of snow everywhere. No grass would be growing today. Still, when Mamm used that tone of voice, it was best to go along with her. Either that or end up cleaning the grease from behind the stove with a toothbrush. Alfie and Benji both hurried their steps but not by much. They had important plans to make.

"So we have to find wives for Austin and Abraham?" Benji said.

Alfie kept his eyes on Mamm and nodded slowly. "And right quick. The spiders get really bad in the spring, and I'm not sleeping with a can of bug spray under my pillow again. It makes a lump."

"Okay. We should find someone for Abraham first. After Andrew, he's the oldest."

Alfie smirked. "Austin would be easier. He already knows lots of girls, and he thinks he's so handsome."

"*Nae*," Benji said. "Mamm says always do the hardest job first—to get it over with."

Alfie rubbed the side of his face where he hoped his whiskers would be someday. "I've never seen Abraham talk to a girl except Mamm and our cousins and stuff. It's like he doesn't even dare."

Benji looked worried. "He's wonderful shy. If we brought a girl over, he might run away and hide. I don't want him to be sad. He always gives me extra butter on my toast for breakfast."

Benji was mostly a *gute* partner, but sometimes Alfie ran out of patience. "Benji, you can't care about people's feelings when you're making a plan."

Benji sucked on his empty stick. "Okay, but Abraham won't get married if he runs and hides every time he sees a girl. We have to be sneaky."

"We're good at being sneaky. Just look at how we got Andrew and Mary together." Alfie nodded in Abraham's direction. "Who should we pick for Abraham?"

"Hannah Yutzy's real nice, and she knows how to make doughnuts."

Alfie shook his head. "Frieda Miller is tall. Abraham needs someone tall."

Benji drew his brows together. "But she's so old."

"So she'll be in a big hurry to get married if she doesn't want to be an old maid. She'd probably settle for Abraham."

"Settle? What does that mean?"

"She's given up waiting for a better offer." Alfie sighed. Sometimes Benji was so thick.

Benji slowed his pace. "That's not true. Abraham would be a *gute* husband. He's tall and he plays basketball and he gives us piggyback rides. And sometimes he tells Mamm not to be mad at us because we're just little *buwe*."

"But if he won't talk to girls, how will we find him a *fraa*?"

"He stares at Emma Wengerd during the sermons."

Alfie stopped short. "Emma Wengerd?"

"*Jah.* He stares at her like he's very hungry and she's a bag of potato chips."

Benji was a *gute* partner. He noticed things. Alfie's

heart felt like it was beating in his throat. "She only lives three houses down, and she's not short. *And* she talks and talks all the time. She probably wants a boy who will just sit and listen to her. Abraham wouldn't have to say anything."

"And she's pretty. Lots of boys like her."

Alfie shook his head. "That's not good. Emma can marry any boy she wants. She wouldn't pick Abraham."

"He plays basketball. Girls like that."

"It's not enough," Alfie said.

Benji scratched his red nose with his mitten. "She raises strange chickens. Maybe Abraham could talk to her about eggs. He likes animals. He wants to be a vegetarian."

"It's veterinarian, Benji, and he can't be one. It's not allowed."

Benji gave Alfie a sour look. "He can't go to school, but he can learn how to take care of animals like Dwayne Burkholder. I heard him telling Dawdi about it."

Alfie couldn't argue with that. Benji heard a lot of conversations Alfie never paid attention to. "Okay. They can talk about chickens. But how do we get them together to talk about chickens?"

Mamm turned around and started walking backward. "Alfie and Benji, catch up this minute or you'll be oiling the buggy every day for a week."

Alfie and Benji glanced at each other and started running. Oiling the buggy made your arms hurt, and Mamm would never let you get away with only doing the parts you could reach from the ground. Making plans was at an end.

But they'd made a *gute* start.

They had a girl, and they had chickens.

Add in the walkie-talkies, and there was no way they could fail.

The whole plan was a total failure.

Abraham would not cooperate, and Alfie was getting very annoyed about it.

It had been a month since he and Benji had made their plan and put new batteries in their walkie-talkies, and Abraham and Emma hadn't even so much as said hello to each other. There certainly wasn't any kissing going on.

Four different times they'd asked Abraham to fetch eggs from Emma, but Abraham always told them to do it themselves. Abraham was not following the plan.

Alfie hated to admit it, but it was time to get help, and Bitsy Weaver was the only person they could trust besides Dawdi. They told Dawdi all their secrets, but Dawdi could barely say Alfie's name, let alone offer advice on how to get Abraham and Emma together.

Alfie and Benji trudged up Bitsy's lane after school. The air was finally getting warmer, and the dandelions had started popping their heads out of Bitsy's grass. That also meant the honeybees on Bitsy's property were flying around, trying to sting little boys. Alfie swatted at a honeybee that came too close.

"Don't hit them," Benji said. "Or they'll sting you."

Alfie scowled. "I know." And he did know. But when he got around a bee, he sort of panicked.

"Bees don't want to sting you. They just want to

get honey from the flowers. If they think you're trying to hurt them, they'll sting."

"I know, Benji," Alfie snapped. "I just don't like them in my face. Don't you think I should try to get them off my face if they land on me?" Alfie marched up Bitsy's porch steps with Benji trailing behind him. "Remember, Benji. We don't have to tell her our plan. We just need to ask her advice."

"Our plan is stupid," Benji said.

"It is not. Abraham's the one who's stupid. He'd rather choke than talk to Emma."

Benji opened the screen, and Alfie knocked on the inside door. The door squeaked open a few inches, and the barrel of Bitsy's shotgun poked out. Bitsy didn't usually answer the door with her shotgun unless she was mad at somebody. Alfie took a step back just in case she accidentally shot him. Mamm would be mad if he got blood on the new shirt she'd just made for him.

Benji was wearing his old shirt. He didn't care if he got shot. He pushed the door open. "*Hallo*, Bitsy. You don't have to be scared. It's just me and Alfie."

Bitsy smirked. "I'm not scared, young man. There's a stray dog wandering my property, and I don't want him barging into the house."

Benji drew his brows together. "Can he knock on doors?"

The gun sagged a bit. "That's a *gute* point. It's probably a good bet that the dog wouldn't knock on my door." Bitsy lowered her shotgun and stepped back so Alfie and Benji could go into the house. She wore a dark blue dress with a normal black apron and a white *kapp*, but her hair was bright blue, like a patch of clover.

"I like your hair," Alfie said. It never hurt to say something nice to the person you needed help from.

Bitsy touched her hair. "*Denki*. It's called Violet Fantasy, but it turned out bluer than I thought." She pulled two chairs from the table. "Would you boys like some coffee cake?"

"*Jah*," Alfie said.

Benji nodded.

They scooted onto the chairs while Bitsy pulled two glasses from the cupboard. "My coffee cake is well known for being moist, but it's still better with a glass of milk."

Bitsy set two slices of coffee cake on the table with the milk. Benji took a huge bite. "Itzzz weally goot, Bizzy."

"Anything you have to say can wait until you've chewed and swallowed, Benji Petersheim."

Alfie decided to eat first and ask for advice later. Bitsy might not be willing to help them if he talked with his mouth full.

"You boys caught me at a *gute* time. I was just about to go into town and report that dog to Animal Control."

Benji took a big gulp of milk. "You mean the pound?"

"*Jah*. He's gotten into my garbage and fussed with my chickens. He's making a nuisance of himself."

Benji stopped eating altogether. "But maybe he's lost."

Bitsy got up and handed each of them a napkin. "He's not lost. He's been abandoned."

"We should help him find his owner." Benji got that familiar look in his eye. He was a *gute* partner, but he got distracted too easy. People who made plans had to be focused. They couldn't feel sorry for anyone, not even a dog. Even if they really, really wanted to.

"His owner is gone," Bitsy said. "The Baxters lived just beyond the pasture across the road. They drove away and left that dog to fend for himself. It's a rotten way to treat the family pet, but I didn't know they'd left their dog until it was too late to show them my shotgun."

Benji worried the edge of his napkin. "Why don't you adopt him, Bitsy? If he goes to the pound, they'll gas him."

Bitsy raised an eyebrow. "Gas him? Wherever did you hear such a thing?"

"Max Burnham," Alfie said. Max's cousin worked at the pound, and he knew everything about everything. Max even knew where babies come from. He had told Willie Glick, and Willie Glick had told Alfie. That was something he wouldn't be able to forget no matter how many times he said his prayers.

Bitsy brushed a crumb from the table. "Well, gas him or not, I can't take him in. I already have four cats, and they are annoying enough. There will be no dogs in this house." Most grown-ups would have tried to smooth things over with Benji to make him feel better, but Bitsy always told the truth, even when nobody wanted to hear it. Alfie liked that about her.

Benji pushed his coffee cake around his plate with his finger. "Maybe we could keep him."

Maybe they *could* keep the dog. Alfie's heart started pounding. A dog could find them if they ever got lost in the woods. A dog could fetch sticks and bring Dat his slippers. A dog would eat crumbs off the floor. Mamm would never have to mop again.

Bitsy shrugged. "That's up to your *mamm*."

Alfie's heart sank to his toes. "Mamm would never let us have a dog. She won't even let me have a goldfish."

"I have a pet spider," Benji said.

Alfie popped a small bite of coffee cake into his mouth. "He's not your pet. He just lives in the corner of the cellar and kills other spiders."

"You tried to spray him," Benji said, "and I saved his life. He's my pet now."

Bitsy nodded. "Spiders are *gute* pets. They feed themselves and don't poop on the carpet."

Benji sat very still before wrinkling his forehead like he did when he was upset. "We need to help that dog."

Alfie wanted a dog as much as anybody, but they had to be sensible. They'd been asking Mamm for a dog ever since they could talk. "Mamm won't let us."

Benji started crying. "But he's going to get gassed."

Bitsy reached over and patted Benji's arm. "He might not get gassed. They might find a nice family that wants to adopt him. People like chocolate labs. I'm told they're cute."

Benji caught his breath and suddenly stopped crying, as if someone had turned off a faucet. "Do girls like chocolate lamps?"

"Chocolate labs?"

"*Jah.*"

Bitsy folded her arms. "Well, I'm a girl and I don't think he's cute, but most girls love dogs. Do you remember Vernon Schmucker? Poor fellow had a face like a potato, and the girls ignored him. One night he brought a puppy to the gathering, and he was surrounded by girls all night. That's how he met his wife."

Benji jumped from his chair and threw his arms around Alfie, making Alfie spill milk down his new shirt. "Hey. Watch it."

"Alfie, girls like dogs!"

Benji was a good partner, but sometimes he made no sense. "So?"

"If Emma Wengerd saw us walking our chocolate lamp down the street, she'd run out of her house to pet him."

Alfie's heart started pounding. Benji was the best *bruder* in the world. "We could bring Abraham with us."

Benji got more and more excited with each word. "And they'd talk about dogs and chickens and maybe start kissing."

Alfie set his milk on the table. "We've got to catch that dog."

Bitsy cleared her throat. "It's none of my business, but what about your *mamm*?"

"It's none of your business," Alfie said, immediately regretting it when Bitsy gave him a look that could have killed all the spiders in the cellar. "I mean . . . we need this dog, but if Mamm finds out, she'll take him to the pound."

Benji nodded. "He'll get gassed."

Alfie tried for his most pitiful face, the one he used on Mamm when she told him he had to muck out the barn. "You won't tell her, will you, Bitsy?"

Bitsy scrunched her lips. "How do you boys plan on keeping the dog a secret? He's big and lively and has to be fed three times a day. And he barks."

Benji chewed on his fingernail. "We can do it. He can live in the woods."

Alfie formed a plan in his head. Of course they could take care of their dog. A real bedroom was closer than ever. "He can come to school with us, and we'll sneak food when Mamm's not looking."

"This plan is getting more and more complicated all the time." Bitsy leaned forward. "Your *mamm* is going to find out."

They had to get Abraham and Emma to fall in love with each other. Then it wouldn't matter if Mamm found out about the dog. A lump caught in Alfie's throat. Of course it would matter if Mamm found out. Alfie and Benji needed a dog, and not just to get Abraham and Emma together. Every boy needed a dog. Willie Glick said so.

Benji put his plate in the sink and walked slowly around the butcher-block island. "Maybe she won't find out." Benji was on Alfie's side. He was the best partner anyone could ever ask for.

Bitsy narrowed her eyes. "I won't have this dog of yours starve to death. What do you plan to do about feeding it?"

Alfie raised his eyebrows. At least Bitsy was considering they might be able to do it. "Leftovers."

"You can't feed a dog leftovers. It's not healthy," Bitsy said.

Benji started working on that fingernail again. "Does he eat eggs? Emma could give us some eggs."

Bitsy groaned as if she was angry and in pain at the same time. She looked up at the ceiling. "Dear Lord, heaven help me, but I never could resist a freckled boy." She stood up and went to the great room where she pulled a Bible from the bookshelf.

She quickly turned the pages. Alfie pressed his lips together. This was no time for scripture reading. If they couldn't catch that dog, Abraham and Emma would never get married. "So, you won't tell our *mamm*?"

Bitsy acted as if she hadn't heard him. She was probably looking for that scripture about honoring your parents. "Please keep in mind, I don't like dogs. I don't like cats or squirrels or hamsters. I don't like most people either."

"Do you like bees?" Benji said.

"I love bees. So don't even think about stepping on my dandelions." She found the passage she was looking for, but instead of reading them a scripture, she pulled a hundred-dollar bill from between the pages and handed it to Alfie. "Use this to buy dog food."

In complete shock, Alfie held the bill in his hand, afraid to move for fear he might bend it. "Dog food?"

"*Ach, du lieva,*" Benji said. There truly were no other words.

She shook her finger in Alfie's direction. "And I won't hear of you buying even one piece of candy with my money. Do you understand?"

Alfie nodded slowly. "We won't let our dog starve, even if we never get to eat another piece of candy for the rest of our lives."

"*Gute,*" Bitsy said. "Candy is bad for you anyway."

Benji rushed to Bitsy and gave her a hug. Alfie shook her hand. He wasn't about to act like a little kid. "*Denki*, Bitsy."

Bitsy didn't smile, but she sure looked happy in her grumpy sort of way. "Take *gute* care of that dog, but don't ever bring him on my property. I'd rather care about him from a distance." She slid the Bible back onto the bookshelf. "Now, did you boys come over for a reason or just to eat my coffee cake?"

"We came over for a reason," Benji said, "but we don't have time to explain now. We need to catch that dog."

Bitsy sighed. "Okay. Then I guess it's time for you to get out of my hair." She led Alfie and Benji to the front door. "Be careful catching your dog, and don't get bit or I'll have to confess to your *mamm* that I'm the one who put the idea in your head."

"Don't worry, Bitsy," Benji said as he walked down the stairs. "We're smart, and we have walkie-talkies. We know what to do."

Bitsy nodded. "A boy with a walkie-talkie is a formidable thing."

Alfie had no idea what all those big words meant, but she'd given them coffee cake and money. Aside from his family, Bitsy was his favorite person in the whole world.

"And please don't tell anybody I gave you that money. I'm already in enough trouble with your *mamm* over the fire truck incident."

"But what if they think we stole it?"

Bitsy nodded thoughtfully. "Tell them an anonymous benefactor wants to make the world a better place. That'll confuse 'em." Bitsy went to shut the door, then threw it open again. "Let me know when the kissing starts. I've paid good money for it."

Chapter Two

Until last summer, Abraham had always liked being invisible. If no one noticed him, he didn't have to talk to girls or try to be interesting or charming. He was neither interesting nor charming, and it gave him a headache to try to be.

He liked making peanut butter, he liked caring for animals, and he liked playing basketball. That used to be enough.

But not anymore. He'd never understood how miserable he was until now.

It was all Andrew's fault.

Abraham finished sweeping the floor, which was his job after dinner now that Andrew had married and moved out. They all had more chores now that Andrew was gone, but Abraham didn't mind. Andrew and Mary were so happy, they seemed to float off the ground whenever Abraham saw them.

Unfortunately, the wedding had made him wish for something like that to come into his life.

And there was his problem.

"Don't miss those crumbs in the corner by the fridge, Abraham. You're getting lackadaisical with your sweeping. We don't want mice." Mammi stood just out of reach of Abraham's broom while pointing out all the spots he'd missed on the floor. Mammi was very particular about the floors, and it didn't matter how carefully he swept. He could have taken a toothbrush to that floor, and Mammi still would have found a crumb.

Abraham had never been able to figure out how Mammi, who needed strength +3.00 reading glasses, could see a cookie crumb from ten feet away. She was truly amazing. No wonder Mamm retreated to her sewing room more and more often now that Mammi and Dawdi lived here.

Mammi had a way of trying your patience that made you feel horribly guilty about it.

Mamm stood at the sink washing bottles for tomorrow's peanut butter batch. Mammi was too focused on Abraham's sweeping to offer Mamm any helpful suggestions on how to wash bottles. Abraham purposefully missed some crumbs so Mammi would focus on his sweeping instead of Mamm's bottle washing. Even Mamm had her breaking point.

Mammi was the dearest woman in the world, and she wanted nothing but the best for her family. Unfortunately, that meant they had to use special soap in the shower, rose water spray whenever they went out, and special cleaning pads for the floors. It also meant thirty minutes of family reading time every night, wheat germ sprinkled in their oatmeal, and cookie sheets for placemats—to keep crumbs off the table.

The front door slammed, and Alfie and Benji ran into the kitchen like their trousers were on fire. "Abraham, we need your help," Alfie said, yelling as if Abraham was in the next county instead of five feet away.

Mammi clicked her tongue. "Now, now, boys, you're getting your dirty feet all over the floor. And Abraham's done such a nice job of cleaning."

Abraham lifted an eyebrow. Mammi had given him a compliment? The twins must have distracted her.

"Did I hear the door slam?" Mamm said, not taking her hands from the soapy water.

Alfie groaned. "But, Mamm, it's an emergency. We need Abraham."

Mamm didn't even turn around. "It's only an emergency if someone is dead or bleeding. Go back to that front door and show me that you know how to close it correctly. Ten times, please."

Abraham stifled a smile at the look on Alfie's face. Abraham didn't know why Alfie was so indignant. Mom made Alfie and Benji practice opening and closing doors at least once a week. They had yet to learn how to properly close a door.

Alfie went back to the front door and gently opened and closed it over and over again. Mamm couldn't even see him from the kitchen, but she could obviously hear every click of the knob.

Alfie trudged back into the kitchen. "Can Abraham come now, Mamm?"

"That was only nine times, young man."

Alfie frowned. "It was ten."

"You're in third grade, son. You should know how to count to ten."

"The last one was really quiet, Mamm. Isn't that what you wanted? Quiet so you couldn't hear it?"

Mamm turned around and gave Alfie a look. Alfie slumped his shoulders and dragged himself to the front door, then opened and closed it twice for good measure.

Benji took Abraham's hand. "Come on. We need to show you something."

"You haven't finished the floor," Mammi said. "I see a piece of broccoli under the table yet."

"Okay, Mammi. I'll get it when I come back."

Benji held the dustpan while Abraham swept his pile of dirt into it. "If we had a dog," Benji said, "we wouldn't need to sweep. Dogs eat everything right off the floor. You don't even have to mop."

"You most certainly would have to mop," Mammi said. "You'd have dog germs all over the floor."

Abraham put the broom in the closet and let Benji pull him out the door. Alfie closed it softly behind them. He obviously didn't want any more of a delay than he'd already been put through. Sometimes the *buwe* learned their lesson.

"Come on, Abraham," Alfie said, taking his other hand and pulling as hard as a nine-year-old could pull. "You're always so slow, like you have to think about every step before you take it."

Abraham resisted both *bruderen* pulling. "If you think before you do something, you make a lot less mistakes."

"And get there ten minutes later," Alfie said.

Abraham didn't want to argue with his little *bruder*. Nothing got through that head anyway. "What is it you want to show me?"

Benji gave him a wide grin. "You'll see."

The grin was a *gute* thing. If they'd set the woods on fire or lost the horse, they probably wouldn't be looking so excited. Probably. You never knew with those two. A forest fire could be pretty exciting to a nine-year-old. Abraham picked up his pace. Should he have brought the fire extinguisher?

The boys led Abraham at least three hundred yards into the woods behind their house. The woods weren't deep. There was a pasture not a quarter mile to the north and another one to the west. Their own pastures lay to the east, where Dat planted corn and soybeans every year.

"Do you boys really want to show me something, or did you just want to go on a walk?"

Benji laughed. "We have to go kind of far. Because it's a secret. We're almost there."

Abraham heard a dog barking wildly just up ahead. It didn't take long to spot the dog, a beautiful chocolate brown lab with floppy ears and a blindingly fast tail. A smooth rope was tied around the dog's neck, and he was tethered to a nearby tree. Abraham's stomach dropped to his toes. The boys had found a dog.

The dog jumped up and down as if he was very happy to see all of them and nearly knocked Benji over when Benji tried to pat him on the head.

Abraham eyed the dog and then his *bruderen*. "You . . . uh . . . you didn't steal this dog, did you?"

Alfie eyed Abraham as if he was a *dumkoff*. "We would never steal." He did his best to pat the dog on the neck while the dog tried to lick his face off. "We found him, and we're keeping him. His name is Tintin, after our favorite book."

Oh, *sis yuscht*. They'd already named the dog. It was getting worse and worse. "Mamm won't let you keep him."

Alfie pulled Tintin in for an awkward, wiggly hug. "She just has to get to know him first, like a new neighbor on the street."

"And you don't name a dog Tintin," Abraham said, feeling like arguing. "You name him Thunder or King or Rocky. Something exciting."

Alfie made a face. "We like Tintin."

Benji nodded. "His owners moved to California and just left him. He was really hungry."

"We fed him two cans of tuna fish from the cellar," Alfie said, trying to get the dog to hold still long enough to be petted. "He ate it, but I don't think he liked it."

Abraham tried to keep his gaze away from the beautiful dog and on his *bruderen*. He had to be firm. Mamm would just as soon adopt a wolverine, and the boys knew it. "Mamm won't let you keep that dog."

"Tintin."

"Tintin," Abraham stuttered. "The minute she sees him, she'll send him to the pound."

Benji's eyes filled with tears. "We can't take him to the pound. They'll gas him."

Abraham tapped his hat more firmly onto his head. "But Mamm won't let you keep him."

Alfie grunted as the dog nearly tripped him. "That's why we're keeping him in the woods. Mamm never has to find out."

Abraham huffed out a breath. "Of course Mamm's going to find out. We have to tell her."

Alfie and Benji both turned to stone and stared at Abraham as if he'd shaved off all his hair. "We're not going to tell her," Alfie said.

A tear rolled down Benji's freckled cheek. Abraham ground his teeth together. "If you tell her, Tintin will die."

Tintin came to rest and gazed at Abraham with big

brown eyes. Maybe he sensed they were talking over his fate. Abraham shook his head. The twins had no right to put this on him. It wasn't his fault Tintin's previous owners were coldhearted. It wasn't his fault Alfie and Benji had decided to adopt a dog they couldn't keep. And it for sure and certain wasn't his fault they'd named him Tintin.

But Benji and Alfie were nine. They wouldn't understand any of Abraham's reasons.

Abraham turned away from Tintin so the dog wouldn't make him feel guilty. "I can't be responsible for this secret. We have to tell Mamm."

A quiet sob escaped Benji's lips, and he grabbed onto Alfie for support. "I wish Andrew was here. He never told Mamm about the fire truck or the smoke bomb. He loved us."

Abraham clenched his teeth even harder and reminded himself that his two *bruderen* were trying to manipulate him. But he couldn't quite convince himself of it. Andrew had always watched out for Alfie and Benji. When one of the twins fell and scraped a knee, Andrew was the one to fix it up. Andrew had often smoothed things over between Mamm and the twins, and if the twins did something particularly shocking, Andrew tried to fix it before Mamm found out.

Abraham had been avoiding it, but it was time for him to step up and take Andrew's place. Alfie and Benji needed a strong and kind big *bruder*. They didn't need another *mamm* or another *mammi*. Especially not another *mammi*, who insisted on spraying rose water on each of them and made them read *Martyrs Mirror* for half an hour every night.

His *bruderen* needed a protector, and Andrew wasn't there to do it.

Just one more way Andrew's marriage had ruined Abraham's life.

Abraham planted his feet and folded his arms. "Tintin can't live on tuna fish. You need to find something else to feed him."

Benji bloomed into a smile, even though his nose and eyes were still dripping. "You mean we can keep him?"

Abraham scrunched his lips together. "At least until Mamm finds out, but I won't tell her."

Benji and Alfie squealed and jumped up and down, and Tintin ran around them until his rope tangled with their feet.

Abraham smiled. Even though Mamm might find the dog tomorrow, it was good to see his *bruderen* happy today. But this was ridiculous. How would they even feed Tintin? They wouldn't. He'd be in the pound by Saturday. At least at the pound he'd eat. "Are you expecting me to hunt for food?" he said, only half joking. These boys had no idea how hard it would be to feed a dog.

"We don't need to hunt," Alfie said smugly, as if he had it all figured out. He pulled something green out of his pocket and handed it to Abraham.

Abraham nearly popped a blood vessel in his neck. "Where did you get this?"

"We can't tell you," Benji said, pressing his lips together as if Abraham would try to pry the truth out of him.

Alfie seemed more confident. "It's from a nominous benedictor."

Abraham frowned. "You mean an anonymous benefactor?"

Alfie thought about it for a second and nudged Benji with his elbow. "I told you he was the smartest brother."

Abraham ignored Alfie's compliment. At a time like this, flattery was lost on him. Well, flattery was always lost on Abraham. The only thing he was better at than any of his *bruderen* was being tall. "Someone gave you this money?"

The twins nodded in unison. Benji seemed especially happy about that hundred-dollar bill. "To buy food for Tintin."

"Who else knows about Tintin?"

Alfie shook his head. "We said it was unanimous."

"Anonymous," Abraham said.

"*Jah*. Our unanimous benedictor asked us not to tell."

"So this benefactor is the only one who knows?"

Benji nibbled on his fingernail. "And Emma Wengerd."

His *bruder* might as well have thrown cold water in Abraham's face. Emma Wengerd? What did Emma Wengerd have to do with anything—except for being the daily source of Abraham's misery?

Abraham cleared his throat and tried to act like Emma was just a girl who lived three doors down, a girl he had no interest in whatsoever. "You told Emma?"

Alfie wrinkled his forehead and fell silent, as if he had to think about it really hard. "We was walking Tintin and decided to take him to see Emma's chickens."

"Emma doesn't like dogs around her chickens."

Benji nodded. "We know. She ran out of her house and told us to please keep our dog away from her chickens. She was a little mad, but then she gave us three eggs and a cinnamon roll."

"She smiled at us after that," Alfie said. "And told us she wouldn't tell anybody about our new dog because Benji started crying."

Abraham could well believe it. Benji's crying worked on just about everybody except Mamm.

Benji looked at Abraham with wide, innocent eyes. "She's real nice and wants you to come over and see her chickens sometime."

Abraham frowned. "She . . . she said that?"

"*Nae*, but she was thinking it. We could tell, couldn't we, Alfie?"

"*Jah*. We could tell she wants you to come over."

For sure and certain that wouldn't happen. Emma Wengerd didn't even know Abraham was alive, and she certainly didn't care.

And he was miserable.

It was all Andrew's fault.

Ever since Andrew had married Mary, Abraham had started feeling itchy and bothered, like something was missing in his life—something like a girl. A girl who could make him happy. A girl he could cherish and love and kiss and bring little presents. Maybe someone he could make happy in return. He wanted what Andrew had with Mary but it couldn't be just any girl. It had to be Emma Wengerd, and that was going to be impossible.

Ever since Andrew's wedding, Abraham had started taking notice of Emma, and the more he saw her, the more he wanted to date her, and the more he wanted to date her, the worse everything got because Emma Wengerd had about ten boys surrounding her at every gathering. She laughed and talked and played volleyball, and Abraham was too cowardly to serve her the ball or ask to be on her team or sit down next to her and start up a conversation. He didn't even dare talk about the weather with her. Boys who talked about the weather were boring.

Emma lived three doors down and they'd been in the same grade in school, but Abraham wasn't even sure Emma knew his name. Emma was well liked by everyone, and Abraham was completely ignored.

Up until last year, that's the way he'd liked it.

Jah. He was miserable.

"Don't let Tintin bother Emma's chickens," he finally said. Whatever else happened, Emma's chickens were very important to her, and Abraham would not allow the boys to do anything to upset her.

"We'll be nice to the chickens. She gave us a cinnamon roll."

Abraham's heart finally slowed to a normal rhythm. "I guess we should go get Tintin some dog food. But a hundred dollars won't last forever."

"It will last long enough," Alfie said, as if he knew something Abraham didn't.

Benji frowned. "We're not getting rid of Tintin, even after the wedding."

"What wedding?" Abraham said.

Alfie looked at Benji and slumped his shoulders. "I want to keep him just as much as you do, but we've only got a hundred dollars."

Abraham didn't have the heart to tell them it didn't matter. It wouldn't be more than three or four days before Mamm discovered the dog and he'd be off to the pound. They'd better save their money and buy a small bag of dog food. But until then, the boys might as well have fun with their dog. Abraham knelt down and gave Tintin a good scratch behind the ears. "Why would anyone leave you behind?" he said.

Tintin licked his face. Abraham laughed. Like his *bruders*, he'd always wanted a dog, but Mamm had been adamant. *I work my fingers to the bone keeping this house clean, and a dog is just one extra mess every day . . . That's all I need is dog doo-doo all over my yard . . . The day you boys learn how to hit the inside of a toilet is the day we'll get a dog.*

She'd never let them keep the dog.

But he was going to buy a big bag of dog food anyway. They could always donate it to the pound. Something told him the anonymous benefactor wouldn't mind.

Chapter Three

"Oooh, look who just walked in," Lizzy squeaked, ducking behind the counter as if she was playing hide-and-seek.

"Lizzy," Emma hissed through her teeth, trying not to laugh at her sister's sudden need to be invisible. "Lizzy, get up. What if someone comes over here and catches you crouching?" Emma couldn't help herself. The laughter just bubbled up from inside her, even though laughing at work was strictly prohibited. At least it seemed that way. The Glicks did not seem to be a very cheerful family.

Glancing around the restaurant to make sure no one was looking, she reached down and tugged Lizzy to her feet. Lizzy's face glowed bright red, but she didn't look all that upset, especially since she was smiling like a cat with a bowl of cream. Emma shook her head and grinned. Lizzy would get used to the job soon enough, and then she wouldn't dive behind the counter whenever a cute boy walked into the restaurant.

"It's only Mahlon Zook and his *bruder* Moses,"

Emma whispered. "His cousin Jethro is much better looking."

"But he's so strong," Lizzy said. "And he said *hallo* to me at the last gathering."

Emma affectionately slid her arm around Lizzy's shoulder. "Which was also your first gathering."

"I know, but only two boys said *hallo* to me, and Mahlon was one of them. Do you think he's interested?"

Emma laughed. "Well, probably."

"Probably?" Lizzy squeaked in delight as if Emma had handed her the moon.

"But he's almost twenty, and you're only sixteen. You should give it a few years."

Lizzy huffed out a frustrated breath. "I hate being sixteen. It's too young, and the *buwe* don't care about you."

"It's better than being fifteen."

Lizzy pressed her lips together. "I guess that's true. Now I'm in *rumspringa*, I get to go to gatherings and flirt."

"Not too much flirting," Emma said. "You don't want to get a reputation."

Lizzy straightened the already tidy menus on the counter. "Not too much flirting. Just the right amount to get the boys thinking about me."

Emma smiled at her sister. "Okay. Just the right amount." She grabbed two menus and some silverware and took them to Mahlon and Moses's table.

Both brothers smiled widely, and Mahlon pulled his shoulders back. "*Hallo*, Emma. I didn't know you worked here."

Unlike Lizzy, who flinched at the very sight of a

boy, Emma loved the attention. Since she had been old enough to understand, she'd often been told how pretty she was. She liked being pretty. It meant the boys paid attention to her and she always had lots of friends. Who wouldn't like that?

Emma handed the brothers their menus. "I started work here about two weeks ago. Erna Bieler quit so the Glicks hired me and Lizzy." Just for fun, she pointed to Lizzy standing behind the counter with her eyes glued to Mahlon Zook.

Mahlon and Moses both waved at Lizzy, and she turned an even darker shade of red. With a sheepishly delighted look on her face, she waved back, turned around, and fled into the kitchen.

Moses might have winked at Mahlon. "We'll have to come in more often now that you're here."

Mahlon squirmed in his seat. "I want the biscuits and gravy."

"I'll have the same," Moses said. "With a glass of milk."

"*Gute* choice," Emma said, taking their unopened menus. "I made the biscuits this morning."

"Then Mahlon might want two," Moses said.

Mahlon kicked Moses under the table. Emma smiled to herself. Mahlon was a very sweet boy, even if he'd just kicked his *bruder* in the shin. She liked him. She liked a lot of boys. And there were lots of exciting ones in Bienenstock. She knew them all. Some of them had asked to drive her home from gatherings. She just wasn't ready.

But she enjoyed the attention. That didn't have to stop.

Emma wrote down the order, took it into the

kitchen, and handed it to Martha Glick. Martha was the matriarch of the Glick family, in charge of the menu and all the cooking at Glick's Family Restaurant. Well, maybe "in charge" wasn't the right way to describe Martha. She did much of the food preparation, but her husband, Raymond, was definitely in charge.

All the Glicks worked at the restaurant or at Glick's Amish Market, which was attached to the restaurant. Martha's daughters were busy with their small children, so each of them came in only one day a week. That was why Raymond hired a few girls to help at the restaurant. Martha couldn't manage it by herself. Emma was just glad she knew how to make biscuits. And rolls. It was why she got the job.

"*Denki*, Emma," Martha said, squinting at the order before locating her glasses and sliding them onto her face. "Biscuits and gravy. I'm glad we made extra this morning."

"Everybody loves your gravy," Emma said. "I've heard people say they come from Green Bay to eat here."

"It's not my gravy," Martha said. "Gotte gave me my hands and my eyes and the talent to make it. I am nothing of myself."

The Amish sought for humility, always giving Gotte the glory for any *gute* they did in the world, but Emma had never seen Martha take a compliment or even be happy about how well a batch of dinner rolls turned out. Did Martha find joy in anything?

Martha was a sweet woman. She really was. But she shuffled around the kitchen like an old lady, keeping her head down and her opinions to herself. Emma felt sorry for her. Raymond was stern and serious, and Emma couldn't imagine he tolerated laughter or lightheartedness in his home. If this was what it was like to be married, Emma might just as soon delay a wedding for as long as possible.

Emma got Moses and Mahlon water and milk while Lizzy helped Martha dish up biscuits and gravy. After she'd served the brothers, Emma helped Lizzy wash dishes while keeping her eye on Mahlon and Moses, who were the only ones in the dining room.

Martha slid a sheet of her famous rolls into one of the industrial-size ovens. "Emma and Lizzy, I need to start another batch of rolls for the dinner rush. Could you bring some yeast and another bag of flour from the storage room? I think the two of you can carry it together."

For sure and certain they wouldn't be able to carry it. Those flour bags weighed a hundred pounds. But it seemed Martha would do almost anything to keep from inconveniencing her husband or her sons, who were right next door at the market. Emma had only been working here two weeks, but she'd seen enough to know Raymond complained loudly when Martha asked him to do anything, and her sons, Paul, Perry, and Peter James, weren't much more help. Paul had always fancied himself too important to help anyone but himself. Peter James broke a sweat stocking shelves, and Perry lurked in the dark recesses of the market aisles playing on his secret phone his *dat* had paid for, probably just to keep Perry out of everybody's hair.

There was a little mover's dolly in the storage room. If she and Lizzy could load a bag of flour onto the dolly, they'd probably be able to wheel it into the kitchen. They'd manage, which was probably what Martha had been doing for years.

Emma wiped her hands, and Lizzy followed her into the large storage room. The Glicks stocked all the food for the restaurant in here as well as everything they sold at the market. Three huge refrigerators lined the far wall along with two freezers. Cardboard boxes of food, candy, clothes, and other merchandise filled the shelves.

Emma took a deep breath. The room smelled of freshly ground wheat and oregano—earthy and substantial.

Lizzy started giggling the minute they stepped inside. "What did Mahlon say to you? Did you tell him to wave at me? I thought I was going to die."

Emma pressed her lips together to hide a smile. "I think he'll wait for you to turn eighteen."

Lizzy gasped. "Did he say that?"

"Not exactly."

Lizzy cuffed Emma lightly on the shoulder. "Don't tease me. I'm going to die of embarrassment."

Emma laughed. She loved Lizzy's infectious enthusiasm. "You'll probably die of old age. Embarrassment never killed anyone."

"It could kill me if you're not careful."

Perry Glick shuffled into the room, immediately stretching a wide smile across his wide face when he saw Emma. "I didn't know you was in here."

Raymond and Martha had three daughters and three sons. All the daughters were thin like their *fater*. All three Glick boys were decidedly chubby, but Perry was the chubbiest. Emma always thought "chubby" was nicer than "fat," but Perry probably didn't qualify as chubby anymore. He couldn't have weighed less than 250 pounds, and he was only about five feet six inches tall. Emma was two inches taller than Perry.

Emma didn't mind "chubby." She was a little chubby herself, and she liked having curves instead of being all skin and bones. But chubby or not, she didn't especially like Perry. He was quite wrapped up in himself, unable to talk about anything that didn't directly concern him, and he ogled Emma as if he was trying to imagine what her underwear looked like. Of course, it wasn't fair to assume Perry thought about her underwear every time he looked at her. For all she knew, he might get that look on his face when he was thinking of jelly-filled doughnuts or volleyball. Still, she found him a little unpleasant and was glad he didn't work in the restaurant.

But he had appeared in the storage room at just the right time. He was heavy, but he had to be strong. Surely he could carry the flour to the kitchen for them.

"We came in to get some flour for your *mamm*," Emma said. "Will you help us? The bag's heavy."

Perry's smile faded, and he pointed to a box on the shelf. "I have to take this to Dat. He's making a green bean display. Sorry."

Green bean display? "Could you just get this flour for us? It won't take a minute."

Grunting like a hog, Perry slid the green bean box from the shelf. "Dat told me to run. He's making a tower." Perry motioned toward the space behind the open door. "There's a little cart you can use for the flour. I wish I could help, but I have a bad back."

Okay. So Perry was useless to them. It wasn't like

she'd been planning on him anyway. No wonder Martha had asked Emma to fetch the flour.

Sweating under the strain of a whole case of green beans, Perry turned and winked—actually winked!—at Emma. "You don't have to go sneaking around, Emma. Next time you want to meet me in the storage room, you just have to ask." He smiled as if he expected her to find his little joke funny. She didn't even give him a courtesy laugh as he turned and walked out the door.

"It's not Christian to speak badly of anyone," Lizzy said, "but I'm not fond of Perry Glick."

"Me either."

Lizzy slumped her shoulders. "Perry was the other one who said *hallo* to me at the gathering." She made a face. "Do you think he's interested?"

Emma stuffed her irritation back down her throat and gave Lizzy a teasing smile. "I would recommend running the other way when you see him coming."

Lizzy giggled. "I'm a fast runner."

"Then you have nothing to worry about because something tells me Perry wouldn't survive a footrace."

"That's very *gute* news."

Lizzy and Emma laughed quietly while they looked for the yeast. Just their luck, it was too high to reach. "I'll have to go find a step stool," Emma said.

"Ummm." Emma turned. Abraham Petersheim stood in the doorway as if he'd been glued there. He pushed a hand dolly loaded with boxes, and his eyes were as round as two of Martha's pancakes.

"I've . . . I've got an order of peanut butter," he mumbled, as if he was afraid someone might hear him.

"Oh," Emma said. "I don't know what to do with it."

He swallowed hard and nodded. "I know what to do with it. We bring an order every week."

"Okay." She motioned in his direction. "We'll let you to it. We're just getting some flour for Martha."

Abraham stared at Emma as if waiting for further instructions.

"Will you excuse me?" Emma said, motioning toward the door. "I need to find a stool."

Abraham stepped aside faster than Lizzy in a foot-race. "*Ach*, of course. Sorry."

"Wait," Lizzy said, the red creeping up her neck again. "Abraham, you're wonderful tall. Could you get something for us?"

Abraham nodded tentatively. "For sure and certain."

Lizzy pointed to the yeast on the top shelf. Abraham reached up and pulled it down like it was nothing. Emma always forgot how tall he was. He handed the yeast to Lizzy. "Do you need anything else?"

Lizzy glanced at Emma and pointed to the bulky bags of flour stacked in the corner. "Can you help us get the flour on the rolling thing? Martha needs another bag."

"Okay," Abraham said. "Where's the rolling thing?"

Lizzy's face glowed like a red Christmas light. "Over there."

Abraham pulled the flat dolly from behind the door and studied it for a few seconds. "It wonders me if it wouldn't be easier if I carried the bag to the kitchen for you? You might strain your back pushing this thing."

"*Jah*, okay," Lizzy said, playing with an errant strand of hair at the base of her neck.

Emma didn't know why Lizzy was so *ferhoodled*. It was only their neighbor Abraham Petersheim. But then again, most every boy in the district got Lizzy's heart going. She was sixteen after all.

Abraham went to the corner and looked at Lizzy for confirmation that those were the bags she was talking about. Lizzy nodded, and Abraham picked up one of the sacks like it was a bag of potato chips, throwing it over his shoulder and toting it all the way to the kitchen. Emma and Lizzy shuffled quickly behind him. Lizzy grabbed Emma's hand and gave her a significant look, as if every boy in the district had just asked to drive her home.

Emma wasn't as impressed.

The flour bags were heavy, but the boys in Bienenstock lifted hay bales all summer. Every one of them was as strong as Abraham Petersheim—except maybe Perry and Peter James Glick. Perry could barely lift a case of beans.

Martha showed a hint of a smile when Abraham walked into her kitchen. "That's wonderful nice," she said, pointing to the bin where she wanted the flour to go. "You always was a *gute* boy, Abraham."

"No trouble," Abraham said. "I'm delivering peanut butter."

The wrinkles around Martha's eyes deepened. "I don't know if that will last much longer."

Abraham slit open the sack and dumped the flour into the bin. "Me either."

Emma wasn't exactly sure of all the particulars, but the Petersheims and the Glicks had experienced some sort of falling-out when Abraham's brother Andrew married Mary Coblenz. Mary Coblenz had some connection to Bitsy Weaver, and the rumor was that the Glicks hated Bitsy Weaver with a passion. It all seemed a tangled mess to Emma, one that would probably make her feel sad if she knew the whole story, so she chose to ignore it.

The Glicks were the richest family in the district, and they seemed to be easily offended. Not Martha, of course. She was sweet and timid and—Emma had noticed—quite unhappy. But Raymond and his children seemed to be offended often; either that or they were picking a fight where there was no fight to pick. They didn't like the Yutzys because the Yutzys had a doughnut stand that supposedly stole business from their restaurant. They didn't like the Kanagys because the Kanagys had supposedly cheated them out of some land and Dan Kanagy had stolen Paul Glick's girlfriend. They didn't like the Kiems, the Bontragers, or the Yoders because they were related to Bitsy Weaver.

Abraham emptied the flour into Martha's bin and brushed the dust off his shirt. "Do you need anything else, Martha?"

Martha pulled a plate from the shelf. "*Nae.*" She glanced into the hall that led to the storage room. "But would you stay and eat the leftover biscuits and gravy?"

Emma drew her brows together when Abraham also glanced down the hall. "*Ach*, that sounds wonderful *gute*. But I will pay for them."

Martha tried for a smile. "I wouldn't hear of it. You helped with the flour. You can stand right here in the kitchen and finish off the biscuits. No one will notice."

Abraham cleared his throat. "Okay. *Denki*. Your biscuits and gravy are the best, but don't tell my *mamm* I said that."

"Emma made the biscuits today."

"It's Martha's recipe," Emma said, backing away from any such compliment.

Abraham took a bite and glanced at Emma. *"Appeditlich."*

Emma didn't expect the little zing of pleasure that traveled up her spine. She was glad he liked her biscuits, but it was only Abraham Petersheim. Now if the bishop's son, Adam Stoltzfus, had complimented her cooking, she might have been impressed. "I just followed Martha's directions."

Raymond Glick suddenly appeared from the back hall. "Employees only in the kitchen," he said, scowling as if Martha had let in a stray dog.

With lightning speed, Abraham set his plate on the counter and headed toward the door. "Sorry. Martha was just letting me taste her delicious cooking."

Emma quickly turned back to her dishes, and Lizzy picked up a dish towel.

Raymond was a slight man in his late fifties with a full head of dark hair and not a speck of gray in his dark horseshoe beard. He folded his arms across his chest. "We don't give away free food except to family."

"Of course not," Abraham said. Emma glanced back as Abraham pulled some money from his pocket and handed it to Martha. *"Denki* for breakfast. Next time I'll sit down in the restaurant like I should."

It was wonderful nice of Abraham to take the blame like that. In the two weeks she'd been here, Emma had discovered that Martha didn't dare stand up to Raymond. Maybe she thought she was being a *gute* wife, but Raymond was just ornery. Abraham obviously recognized it too. He didn't want Martha to get in trouble so he took the blame and paid for his half-eaten plate of biscuits and gravy. That was very sweet.

"Did you bring the peanut butter?" Raymond said.

"*Jah.* Two cases."

"Okay. Let's go count them so you can be on your way."

Raymond personally counted every order that came into the store. Maybe it was safer with some of the Englisch vendors, but did he really have to check to make sure Abraham had brought the correct number of bottles?

Did Abraham find Raymond's distrust offensive? Humiliating? Emma couldn't tell because he didn't even blink as he followed Raymond out the door. He hesitated slightly as he passed through the door. "Good-bye, Emma. Bye, Lizzy."

"Will we see you at the gathering?" Lizzy said. Emma resisted the urge to roll her eyes. That girl was so silly.

Abraham's gaze flicked in Emma's direction. "I'd like that."

What did he mean by that? He hadn't misinterpreted Lizzy's idle conversation as an invitation, had he? Surely he hadn't. You didn't invite someone to a gathering. Everybody just showed up. *Ach.* Maybe Emma wouldn't go. She didn't want Abraham to think the Wengerd girls had invited him.

"Okay, see you then," Lizzy said, as if seeing Abraham at a gathering would be the most exciting thing that happened to her all week.

Emma huffed out a breath. Lizzy's enthusiasm was going to get them both in trouble someday, but probably not with Abraham. Emma and Abraham barely knew each other. It wasn't like he'd ever expect her to be interested.

Lizzy nudged Emma with her elbow. "He's so cute."

"*Ach*, Lizzy, you think every boy is cute."

"I do not." She glanced behind her and lowered her voice. "Not Perry Glick. Or Peter James."

Emma giggled softly. "I guess I'd be very worried if you thought Perry Glick was handsome."

"Abraham is definitely handsomer than Perry."

"Who isn't?"

Lizzy rinsed off a plate and put it on the drying rack. "He carried the flour. Don't you think that was nice?"

"*Jah.* He's very nice."

Lizzy scrunched her lips together and studied Emma's face. "Why don't you like him?"

"It's not that I don't like him. He's just another boy in the district. I barely know him."

"He lives three houses away from us," Lizzy said, as if that should make them best friends.

Emma handed Lizzy another plate. "So?"

"So, I'm surprised you don't care he just did something very nice for us."

Emma shook her head and smiled. "I care, but I'm not going to fall all over myself just because he paid attention to me. He's harmless, but I don't want him to get the wrong idea."

Lizzy frowned at her plate. "What does that mean? Harmless?"

Emma shrugged. "If you're nice to a boy, he'll think you like him, and I don't want Abraham to think that. He's nice, but he's boring. And there are plenty of handsome boys to talk to at gatherings without Abraham messing things up."

Lizzy widened her eyes. "What a mean thing to say."

"It's not mean. I'm just telling the truth."

"But you said yourself you barely know him. Why do you think he's boring?"

Emma pushed a plate at Lizzy. "He hardly ever says a word."

Lizzy rinsed it off. "That doesn't mean he's boring. It means he's deep."

Lizzy had the funniest notions. At least she always kept Emma laughing.

Chapter Four

Emma and Lizzy finally made it home by 6:30 with a bag of potato peels, a small bag of carrots, and three rolls from the restaurant. The carrots were a little slimy, and the rolls were burnt on the bottom, but Emma's chickens would love them, especially the carrots.

Emma quickly cut the carrots into beak-sized pieces, gathered the carrots and potato peels in her apron, and hurried to the chain-link chicken run Dat had built her three years ago when she'd started raising her own chickens. The chain-link fence surrounding Emma's chicken coop was seven feet high and twenty feet wide by twenty feet long. Her chickens had plenty of room to roam without fear of being eaten by foxes or dogs.

Emma stepped into the chicken run and quickly closed the gate before any chickens escaped. She had three shiny Austra White hens, one Black Copper, one Buff Laced Polish, two Easter Eggers, and one beautiful Lavender Orpington. She probably shouldn't single out any of the hens and she didn't want to make the other ones feel bad, but Queenie, the Lavender Orpington hen, was definitely her favorite. Queenie was a plump hen with beautiful gray-lavender feathers and a bright red comb, and she laid the most beautiful pink-tinged eggs.

Emma didn't keep any roosters. They were aggressive and noisy and tended to be rough with the hens. When she'd first gotten chickens, she brought in one rooster, but he tried to attack Dat, and Dat had given him a swift kick to keep from getting scratched. They'd gotten rid of the rooster, and Emma had named Dat "the alpha chicken." He was much nicer than a real rooster.

Emma clucked and snapped her apron, and the hens gathered at her feet. Chickens weren't all that smart, but they were used to her bringing them a treat in her apron. She didn't really need to cluck, but it made her feel closer to her birds.

She spread the carrots and the potato peels around the little yard, and her hens pecked merrily away at their treat. It was one more reason Emma was glad she worked at the restaurant. There were always plenty of kitchen scraps to bring home. Though, if Raymond Glick ever found out Martha was letting her take the scraps, he'd probably make her pay for them.

Emma frowned. She shouldn't think such uncharitable thoughts about Raymond. He was tight with his money, which was probably why he had so much of it. There was nothing wrong with pinching pennies. And he'd probably be very happy if he knew Martha was giving away the potato peels. It was less waste to throw in the garbage. But Emma wouldn't be the one to tell him.

Emma emptied her apron and watched as her babies ate their treat. She stopped short when she saw three broken eggs up against the fence. The chickens almost always laid their eggs in their nests inside one of the four nesting coops. How had the eggs gotten out here? And how did they get broken?

She bent over and studied the eggs. Two white and one pale pink. And a single paw print right next to them.

What in the world?

She leaned in to get a closer look. It was definitely a paw print right in the dirt. A big paw print. *Inside* the chain-link fence.

Emma eyed her hens. No ruffled feathers, no nervous squawking, no aggressive behavior. If a dog had been in the run, the hens seemed surprisingly unconcerned. But that didn't make Emma feel better. The mystery dog had somehow gotten in with Emma's chickens and left three broken eggs and an incriminating footprint.

The Parkers had a dog, but she was a yappy, tiny house dog that had never come near Emma's hens. The Beilers' dog never left his fenced backyard. Besides, the Beilers were half a mile away. Why would their dog come all this way to bother Emma's chickens?

Emma took in a sharp breath. Alfie and Benji Petersheim had a dog. A new, unruly, secret dog. They'd brought it to her backyard not a week ago. She'd warned them to keep that dog away from her chickens, but since when had nine-year-old boys ever followed instructions? How could they have let this happen? She'd given them a cinnamon roll as a token of peace.

Emma hissed through her gritted teeth. That dog had broken three of her eggs and probably scared her chickens out of their wits. She wouldn't tolerate it. Not for a minute.

After making sure the run closed securely behind her, Emma marched to the house and retrieved her bonnet and shawl. Rebecca Petersheim was going to hear about this. If anyone could put those boys in their place, Rebecca could.

Emma got about halfway to Petersheims' house before she had an unfortunate recollection. Alfie had begged her to keep the dog a secret. Benji had started to cry. They didn't want their *mamm* to know about the dog because according to Benji, "Mamm will send it to the pound to get gassed." Emma didn't like dogs, but no animal deserved to be gassed—or however it was they got rid of unwanted animals. She growled and kicked a rock in her path. She didn't want to be responsible for getting Alfie and Benji's dog sent away, but he couldn't be allowed to terrorize her hens.

Did Abraham know about the dog? Probably not. And what would he do about it if he did know? Abraham didn't seem like someone who took action or made a plan or had his brothers' trust. Abraham was one of those boys who just existed. Emma doubted if anybody in his own family paid him any heed. But as she'd told Lizzy earlier today, Abraham was harmless. She'd talk to him, and maybe he could make his *bruderen* understand their dog was not to go near her chickens again.

Emma didn't hold out much hope for Abraham.

The Petersheims' home was a ten-minute walk from Emma's house, but she covered the distance in half that time. That dog had to be stopped before he did something they'd all regret, like eat one of her hens or spill the chicken feed. Well, spilling the chicken feed was forgivable. Killing a chicken was totally unacceptable.

Emma sneaked around to the backyard to try to avoid Rebecca, which was kind of silly since Rebecca was just as likely to be in the backyard as in the front. She stepped in a patch of mud, then nearly took her own head off because she didn't see the clothesline. *Ach.* The trouble she got into trying to be nice!

She ducked under the clothesline and nearly scalped herself again on another line three feet from the first one. Emma squinted into the gathering darkness. There was still one more clothesline to avoid. With five boys, Rebecca had a lot of laundry. Three clotheslines was a necessity.

She ducked under the last clothesline and wiped her mud-caked shoe on a leftover patch of snow. On this side of the house, the snow melted last in the spring. In her anger and haste, she hadn't thought this through very well. It was getting wonderful chilly out here, and all the smart people were in their warm houses, sitting around the fire eating popcorn and playing Scrabble. If she wanted to talk to Alfie, Benji, or Abraham, she'd be forced to knock on the door.

She ducked back under the three clotheslines and walked up to the front door like normal people— well, she didn't exactly walk like normal people because one foot weighed about half a pound more than the other because she hadn't been able to get much of the mud off. If she tried to stomp the mud off on the porch, she'd draw a lot more attention than she wanted. She just needed to give Benji and Alfie a stern lecture and be on her way.

Emma glanced into the Petersheims' large bay window. *Ach, du lieva.* It looked like the whole family was sitting in the living room reading. She peeked again. *Nae.* They weren't reading. They all had their eyes trained out the window looking at her.

Emma's face got warm. She gave up being sneaky and stomped her foot firmly in the porch. They'd seen her anyway. She might as well get rid of this mud.

Alfie opened the door so forcefully, it banged against the wall behind it.

"Alfie Petersheim," his *mater* said. "How do we open doors?"

Alfie's smile faded. "Aw, Mamm, can't it wait? We have a guest."

"I don't care who's at the door, young man. People will stop coming to visit us if we have holes in our walls."

Benji appeared at the door next to Alfie. "Did you come to see Abraham?" He slung his arm around Alfie's shoulder, and they both smiled as if she'd brought homemade ice cream. "We was hoping for it so bad."

"Umm," Emma said. She didn't want to give anyone the wrong impression. She hadn't come for a neighborly visit, and Abraham shouldn't get his hopes up that she wanted to be friends. She already had plenty of friends and several exotic chickens. What more could a girl want?

"Don't make her stand outside in the cold, son.

Sometimes I fear you don't have any brains in your head."

Benji took Emma's hand and pulled her into the house. Emma resisted, mostly because her shoe was still dirty. She finally gave in. It was rude to let all the cold air inside the house, but she kept herself planted on the mat by the door.

Emma cleared her throat and pressed her lips together. All eyes were pointed in her direction. Abraham's *mammi* and *dawdi* sat on the sofa with a blanket draped over their legs. Abraham's *dawdi* David had suffered a stroke almost a year ago and they lived with the Petersheims so Rebecca could help take care of him. Abraham's parents sat on the two easy chairs, and Austin was in a rocking chair. Emma liked Austin. He was as popular at the gatherings as Emma was, always laughing and talking, always looking for fun things to do. Austin liked challenging his friends to pushup contests or buggy races. He was the exact opposite of Abraham. It was funny how two very different boys could come from the same family. Abraham was obviously the scrub of the bunch.

"*Hallo*, Emma," Austin said, grinning as his gaze darted between Emma and Abraham.

Abraham stood like a post and stared at Emma. That boy never seemed to have two words to rub together.

"I'm sorry if I'm interrupting," Emma said.

Abraham's *mammi* shut the book in her hand. "We were having family reading time, but Abraham seldom gets visitors. We'll postpone it until tomorrow night."

"Yes," one of the twins whispered enthusiastically.

Rebecca practically jumped from her chair. "Abraham, you didn't tell me you were expecting a visitor. I'll get some refreshments. Emma, would you prefer Pigs-in-a-Blanket or popcorn?"

Emma stepped back. They'd gotten the wrong impression already. "Please, Rebecca, refreshments aren't necessary."

Rebecca was already in the kitchen. "It's no trouble," she called. "Pigs-in-a-Blanket don't take but twenty minutes."

"*Ach,*" Emma said. "*Denki,* but I'm not here to visit Abraham." She tried not to sound rude about it, but Abraham was one of those boys who would follow her everywhere if she paid him any attention. It was too bad because she loved Pigs-in-a-Blanket, those little hot dogs wrapped in crescent roll dough. And she hadn't eaten dinner yet.

Abraham didn't seem upset that she hadn't come to visit him. He didn't seem anything at all. That boy had the most expressionless face she'd ever seen. It was impossible to guess what he was thinking. Maybe he wasn't thinking anything. Some boys were dense that way.

"I came to talk to Alfie and Benji about some eggs." She gave the twins a significant look, hoping they'd understand her meaning.

Benji made a face. "That's as boring as family reading time."

A voice of authority came from the kitchen. "Benjamin Petersheim, apologize to your *mammi.*"

Benji shuffled his feet and looked at the floor. "Sorry, Mammi."

Benji's *mammi* clasped her hands together. "You'll

thank me someday, Benjamin. I only hope you won't wait until I'm in my grave."

Benji frowned in concentration. "How long do I have?"

Emma covered her mouth to keep from laughing.

Alfie tugged on Emma's shawl. "Do you need some money?"

"Money?"

Alfie nodded. "Do you want us to buy some eggs?"

The boys were not going to catch on to her clues. She'd have to be more blunt. "*Nae.* I want to talk to you about eggs and dogs."

Abraham snapped to attention. His gaze flicked to the kitchen before he crossed the room in three big steps. "Maybe we should go outside."

So. Abraham knew about the dog.

Gute. Emma wouldn't be on her own with two nine-year-olds, though she couldn't see how Abraham would be much help when he barely said two words at a time.

Alfie beamed like a battery-powered light bulb. "Okay. Let's go outside and talk." He sighed. "If only we had a porch swing, it would be a lot better."

"Come back for Pigs-in-a-Blanket," Rebecca called from the kitchen.

Oh, *sis yuscht.* Would Rebecca think she was rude if she didn't want to come back?

Abraham opened the door for Emma, which was nice but completely unnecessary. She knew the way. Alfie and Benji looked as if their feet were stuck to the floor.

"Come on, boys," Abraham said.

Alfie took a step backward. "You go without us. Benji and I need to get our shoes and coats on."

"I don't know where my shoes are," Benji said. "They might be under the fridge or in the cellar. We'll be out as soon as we find them."

Abraham's *mammi* clicked her tongue. "If you boys would put your shoes on the special mat, you'd never have to go looking for them."

Benji nodded. "I'm wonderful sorry for being *dumkupp*, Mammi."

Mammi's eyes widened, and she pointed to a bright blue mat next to the front door. "There's not one shoe on my special mat." She stood up with all the indignation and speed of an eighty-year-old. "Your *mater* is going to hear about this." She hobbled into the kitchen.

Abraham scrunched his lips to one side and gazed doubtfully at Emma. "Do you want to . . . ?" He motioned toward the porch.

Emma stifled a frustrated sigh and stepped outside. Abraham shut the door behind them. "I'm sorry to interrupt your family reading time."

Abraham cleared his throat. "No need to apologize. We don't mind when family reading time gets interrupted. Alfie once gave himself a bloody nose to get out of it."

Emma pulled her shawl around her shoulders. How long would she have to stand out here with Abraham? "I'd mostly like to talk to the twins," she said. She had a feeling she'd be a lot more forceful with them than Abraham ever could.

"*Ach.* Okay," Abraham said, stuffing his hands in his pockets and gluing his gaze to the right toe of his boot.

Emma always felt the need to fill uncomfortable silences, even at the risk of Abraham thinking she wanted to be friends instead of just neighbors. "I guess you know about Alfie and Benji's secret dog."

He nodded.

Emma smoothed her bonnet string between her fingers. "I'm not sure why they told me about it."

Abraham shrugged. "You're nice, and you don't gossip about people. I guess they knew you'd keep their secret."

Emma couldn't contain a smile, in spite of the broken eggs. What a very nice thing to say. She did try to stay away from gossip in the community. It was gratifying Abraham had noticed. "I will keep their secret, but I don't see how they can keep a big dog like that hidden for long. Your *mamm* is bound to find out."

"*Jah*," Abraham said. "That's what I told them. But they're already in love with that dog, and I'm not going to be the one to tell Mamm. There's nothing more heartbreaking than watching Benji cry."

Emma laughed. "*Ach*, I've seen it. He's hard to resist with tears in his eyes. I had to give him a cinnamon roll to make it stop."

Abraham cracked a smile. "I think he does it on purpose."

"No doubt. If you're that cute, you might as well use it to your advantage."

Abraham glanced behind him to the front door. He seemed as eager to get this over with as she did. "I'm not sure why the boys want to buy eggs. We bought some dog food. I don't think they should feed the dog eggs."

"*Ach*, they don't want to buy eggs, as far as I know. I came because I found a paw print and broken eggs in my coop. I think the dog has been in there, and I want to be sure they know they're not to let him near my hens."

Abraham's frown seemed to sink into his face like Emma's shoe in a patch of mud. "Those boys know better than to let Tintin near your chickens."

"Tintin?"

"That's what they named the dog. It's *dumm*." Abraham seemed even more concerned than Emma was. "We can't let Tintin hurt your chickens. Would you feel better if I took him to the pound?"

"Not really," Emma said, remembering Benji's face when he begged Emma not to tell anyone about the dog.

"I wouldn't feel better either, but I'll do what needs to be done to keep your chickens safe."

Well. That was nice. Hardly anybody particularly cared about Emma's chickens. Mamm thought they were a nuisance, although Dat liked the eggs. Lizzy was more interested in boys. And Emma never talked about her chickens at gatherings unless she wanted blank stares and glazed eyes. She was smart enough to know that no one got as excited about exotic chickens as she did.

"I appreciate that," Emma said, "but I think if I just remind them to keep the dog away from my coop, that will be enough. Most little boys have to be told several times."

"*Jah.* They still struggle with shutting doors correctly."

Benji and Alfie slid out the front door, wearing coats but no shoes. Benji had tied a piece of paper around each of his feet with a strand of yarn.

"Couldn't you find your shoes?" Abraham said.

"Mammi wouldn't let us go out unless we had

something on our feet," Benji said, shuffling his paper shoes across the wooden porch. "And she made us spray rose water on our necks."

Alfie lifted one of his feet as if Emma and Abraham hadn't noticed he was barefoot. "I sneaked out when she wasn't looking, but I still got the rose water."

Emma laughed at Alfie's disgusted expression. "Rose water?"

Benji lost one of the pieces of paper from his feet. He carefully slid it back on. "Mammi thinks we stink, so she makes us spray rose water on ourselves every time we leave the house."

"It makes us stink worse," Alfie said. "And the bees try to eat us."

Emma giggled. "I don't think a bee has ever eaten a little boy."

Alfie wiped at a trickle of rose water inching down his neck. "Well, they try. And believe me, I should know."

Benji dragged his feet forward and tugged on Emma's apron. "Abraham can count to ten thousand, and he has the biggest bird nest collection you ever saw."

Alfie nodded. "He knows fifty horse diseases, and you can talk as much as you want, and he won't interrupt."

Emma turned to Abraham. "You know fifty horse diseases?"

For some reason, Abraham's face turned a shade darker—red enough to see in the fading light. "I'm studying to help Dwayne Burkholder. He thinks he's getting too old."

Dwayne Burkholder was an Amish farmer and

local animal doctor of sorts. "You want to take care of animals?" Emma said.

Abraham lowered his eyes. "*Jah*. And farm."

Benji tugged at Emma's apron again. "He bought Tintin some food and a flea collar because he says fleas can torture a dog. I don't even know what that means, but I know it's bad."

Alfie nodded. "Abraham knows how to play basketball, and he really likes chickens."

The boys fell silent, as if letting all their news soak in. "Well," Benji said, "it's been nice talking to you, but we have to go before Mammi finds our shoes behind the fridge."

Alfie poked Benji in the arm. "You weren't supposed to tell."

"Just a minute, boys." Abraham knelt down and put a hand on each of the boys' shoulders. "Emma says Tintin got in her chicken coop and broke some eggs."

Benji pressed his lips together and glanced at Alfie. "Are you going to have him gassed?"

"Of course not," Abraham said. "I just want to make sure it doesn't happen again."

Alfie squinted in Emma's direction. "How do you know it was our dog?"

"There's no other dog it could be."

"Maybe it's the Parkers' dog," Alfie said.

"I don't think so," Emma said, even though there was no doubt about it. It could only be Alfie and Benji's dog. No other dogs in the neighborhood were so big, or so unsupervised.

Alfie and Benji looked at each other and smiled. Not exactly the reaction Emma would have expected.

Were they glad their dog had been caught? "We should go and see if it really was our dog," Alfie said.

"It was."

Alfie put his arm around Benji. "But we want to go and see."

Emma gazed into the gathering darkness. "Right now?"

Benji grabbed Abraham's hand and pulled him forward. "Abraham should come with us. He can protect us from bears."

"It's almost bedtime," Abraham said.

"Mamm won't care," Benji said. "She says it's high time you had a sweetheart."

Abraham coughed as if he'd swallowed a fly.

Emma nearly choked on her own tongue. Oh, no. First Pigs-in-a-Blanket and now this. "I didn't come over to . . . I mean . . ." What could she say? *I have no intention of dating Abraham ever, ever, ever in a million years* seemed harsh. *I've got plenty of better, more interesting boys to choose from* sounded a little unkind. *Adam Stoltzfus, the bishop's son, is more to my liking* would give Abraham the impression that she was interested in Adam Stoltzfus, which she was, but she was also interested in a dozen other boys in the *gmayna*, and Abraham was not one of them.

She forced a smile, bent closer to Benji, and tapped his nose with her finger. Hopefully, it seemed like a playful and unconcerned gesture. "I'm not interested in being anybody's sweetheart, honey."

It must have been the wrong thing to say. Alfie made a sour face, and Benji pulled back and scrubbed his nose as if he'd been licked by a goat.

"You don't tap people's noses like that," Alfie said. "It's for babies."

Benji blew a gale of air out of his nose, swiped his sleeve across his face, and smiled at Emma. "I know you didn't mean to."

She'd just offended two nine-year-olds, but she'd also managed to divert everyone's attention from any talk of sweethearts. She only hoped that topic would never be brought up again.

Benji looked up at her with those adorable brown eyes. "So do you want to be Abraham's sweetheart?"

Abraham took his big hand and shoved Benji clear out of his paper shoes. "Time for bed, you *dumkoff*."

"But we want to see the broken eggs," Alfie said.

Benji stepped on the paper that used to be his shoes. "And Mamm says it's high time that you—"

Abraham pushed his *bruderen* toward the door. "Okay. Okay. Go get your shoes on. If you're not out here in two minutes, we're not going."

The twins sprinted to the house. Abraham slid his hands into his pockets. "Sorry about that." He apparently wasn't going to say any more, not even to try to fill the awkward pause.

Emma would have to do it. She didn't like awkward pauses, and she suspected Abraham's life was one long, awkward pause. "From the day I turned sixteen, my *mamm* made note of every single boy in the *gmayna*. She was determined to find me a husband. Sometimes I think that's all my *mamm* cares about is getting her children married off."

Abraham's expression softened. "Treva Nelson came over three months ago to buy some peanut butter, and Mamm started hinting at a wedding, even though everybody knows Treva can be a pill. But Mamm can't help herself. Nothing gets her more excited than talk of courtship and weddings."

"She must have been thrilled when Andrew got married."

Abraham drew his brows together and studied her face. *Ach.* Had she said the wrong thing? Andrew had married Mary Coblenz last October. They kind of rushed it because Mary had just given birth to a baby and Andrew wasn't the father. But Emma didn't know much more than that. She didn't like to gossip.

"We love Mary," Abraham said, as if he was accusing Emma of something.

Emma frowned. "I don't know her very well, but she seems like a wonderful *gute* girl. And her baby is so cute. I love chubby cheeks."

"*Jah.* ElJay is beautiful."

"That's an unusual name."

"It's short for Elizabeth Jane, after Mary's mother and Bitsy Weaver."

"I like it."

Another awkward pause, but Emma didn't know how to fill it this time. Abraham had tensed up the minute she'd mentioned Andrew. Abraham searched Emma's face. "Some people don't care for how the baby got here."

Emma pressed her lips together. *Ach.* Now she understood his hesitation. "Because ElJay's *fater* is an Englischer and Mary wasn't married?"

Abraham nodded.

Emma straightened her shawl and pulled her shoulders back. "We all make mistakes. We wouldn't need Jesus if we weren't sinners. I think it was very brave of Mary to come back to the community. It's so sweet how she and Andrew fell in love."

Without letting his gaze stray from her face, Abraham relaxed and flashed a very handsome smile. "Me too." He wasn't bad to look at when she really looked. "Mary's parents won't even talk to her, but I should have known you wouldn't hold it against her. You've always been wonderful kind like that."

That was a very nice thing to say, even if it wasn't entirely true. She'd never been as kind to Abraham as she should have. Though, she hadn't been unkind. She'd mostly ignored him. Emma felt her face get warm. Ignoring someone was still unkind. Just ask Mary's *mamm*. "I'm sure Jane Coblenz was upset when Mary jumped the fence. She probably doesn't know how to stop hurting so she thinks she has to punish Mary and Andrew and ElJay. But there could be no better man than Andrew, and Mary is sweet. Jane's heart will soften. For sure and certain, she'll come around before Christmastime. Who doesn't want to spend Christmas with their grandchildren?"

Abraham gazed at her as if an angel had appeared on his porch. "You always try to see the best in people. I love that about you." He cleared his throat. "I mean, if we all tried to do that, there'd be a lot fewer problems in the world."

Emma shook her head. "I don't deserve such high praise. Just ask Perry Glick."

"Perry Glick?" Abraham said, suddenly on guard again.

Oh, *sis yuscht*. Sometimes trying to fill uncomfortable silences got her in trouble. "*Ach*, it is nothing. It's just that I get the feeling Perry Glick doesn't come into the storage room four times a day to count cucumbers. Sometimes I think he's spying on me."

"Spying?"

Emma laughed and waved her hand as if to swat away any concerns. "I check behind the storage room door every time I go in there now."

Abraham's eyes flashed. "Perry shouldn't bother people."

Emma didn't like to gossip, even about Perry Glick and his grumpy family. "What could be keeping the boys?"

They turned toward the window. Alfie and Benji were standing on the inside with their faces pressed against the glass watching Emma and Abraham. Abraham motioned to them, mouthed some words Emma didn't understand, and pointed to the porch, probably ordering them to "come here."

Both *buwe* withdrew from the window and were outside in a matter of seconds, looking as guilty as a cat who'd just eaten the pet hamster.

"I told you boys to hurry," Abraham said. "We've kept Emma waiting too long."

Alfie flashed a toothy smile. "We just wanted to see how it was coming along."

Benji nodded. "Mamm says nobody likes two boys getting in the way, so we try to stay out of it."

"Stay out of what?" Abraham said.

"The way," Benji said, as if it should be obvious. "Besides, Mamm told us to stall."

Alfie jabbed Benji in the ribs with his elbow. "You're not supposed to tell."

Benji stepped away from Alfie and rubbed his side. "Mamm didn't say not to tell."

Alfie stepped between Benji and Emma as if trying to pretend Benji wasn't anywhere in sight. "We're really excited to see the chickens."

Abraham looked at Emma, an apology in his gaze. "Is it still okay?"

"If it will convince the boys that it really was their dog that broke my eggs."

He shrugged. "They went to all the trouble to find their shoes. I suppose we can have a look."

Alfie grabbed Benji's hand and dragged him down the stairs. "Okay. Start walking. We'll meet you there." The boys seemed to have the wind behind them as they ran for the woods.

"Where are you going?"

"To get Tintin. He wants to come."

"You can't bring Tintin," Abraham called, but the boys were already halfway deep into the thick trees.

"They didn't hear you," Emma said.

Abraham cocked an eyebrow. "They heard me. They're just ignoring me."

"Maybe if they show Tintin what he did to my eggs, he'll feel guilty and won't bother them again."

"I don't think dogs feel guilty."

Emma giggled. "At the very least, the boys will feel guilty and might try to watch him more carefully."

"He'll probably just bark."

Emma furrowed her brow. "Will the barking upset my chickens?"

"I don't know."

"They drop their feathers when they're upset."

"They do?" Abraham said.

Emma cracked a smile. "Well, I've heard that, but

I guess I don't know for sure. My *dat* crows at them like a rooster, and they ignore him."

"Maybe he's not believable enough."

Emma laughed. "Oh, he does a pretty *gute* impression of a rooster." She glanced in the direction the twins had gone. "We'd better go. I don't want the dog to get there first."

Abraham's *mamm* hurried out onto the porch breathing heavily and carrying a heaping plate of Pigs-in-a-Blanket. "I'm so glad I didn't miss you." She handed the plate to Emma and smiled. "Nothing like warm Pigs-in-a-Blanket to make you feel welcome."

"*Ach,*" Emma said, "You didn't have to do this." Especially since she had not come to visit Abraham and they were never going to be sweethearts—Rebecca had baked on a false hope. Not to mention the fact that Abraham and Emma were both keeping a horrible secret behind Rebecca's back. Rebecca never would have made Pigs-in-a-Blanket if she knew what they knew about the dog.

"It was no trouble," Rebecca said. "They only take eleven minutes in the oven. If you wait five more minutes, the popcorn will be ready. Austin's tending to it."

"Your caramel popcorn is *appeditlich*, Mamm," Abraham said, "but we have to go. Emma wants to show me her chickens."

Unfortunately, this news seemed to please Rebecca more than a whole plate of Pigs-in-a-Blanket. "*Ach, du lieva,*" she said, smiling so hard her glasses rose up and hovered over her nose. "Well, then. You two get going and enjoy your Pigs-in-a-Blanket. Would you like ketchup? I can put some in a paper cup."

"*Nae*, Mamm. *Denki.*"

Despite the fact that Rebecca had gotten the wrong idea about Abraham and Emma, Emma was thrilled to have something to eat. Lizzy and Emma usually got off work at about 6:30, and if they were hungry, they had to pay for any food they ate. The Glick family got to eat the leftovers for free, but employees had to pay. It was cheaper to go home for a late dinner.

Emma glanced at Abraham. She didn't like to eat in front of boys. Attractive girls weren't supposed to have an appetite. But this was Abraham. She didn't really care what he thought, and she was starving. Besides, Rebecca was watching her expectantly. For sure and certain she wasn't going to go back into the house until Emma tried at least one Pig-in-a-Blanket.

Emma gingerly picked up a warm bun and took a bite. It was good, because there wasn't much you could do to ruin Pigs-in-a-Blanket. "These are *appeditlich*," she said. "*Denki*. I haven't had dinner yet."

Rebecca raised her eyebrows. "Really? In that case, *cum reu* and I'll fix you some beef stew. It'll stick to your ribs."

"I really need to get home," Emma said, not wanting to be rude but hoping to back away from any attempt to make her and Abraham a couple. There were lots of other boys she was more interested in, and she wasn't ready to settle on any of them. She was still having fun going to gatherings and flirting. Emma loved all the attention. She was pretty enough for the boys to notice her, and she enjoyed it when they gathered around her and competed for her smiles. When you got married, you cooked and did laundry all day and nobody thought you were anything special. What was wrong with wanting a few more years of fun?

And if she chose to settle down with anyone, it wouldn't be Abraham Petersheim.

"Take the whole plate with you," Rebecca said. "You can eat them on the way." She hurried to the door. "And wait right here. I'll get you some mustard and ketchup."

Emma finished off her first Pig-in-a-Blanket, grabbed another one off the plate, and polished it off in three bites. Okay, she was famished. It had been a long day. She picked up another one and held out the plate to Abraham. "Want one?"

Abraham hesitated. "Only after you get your fill."

Emma took another bite and grinned, glad she didn't care what Abraham thought of her hearty appetite. "That's very thoughtful of you and I am hungry, but I can't eat this whole plate by myself. I'm going to leave at least one."

Abraham chuckled, a low, rumbling sound that came from deep in his throat. It made Emma smile. Abraham needed more laughter in his life. He was always so reserved. He glanced at the front door. "Maybe I'll wait until we're out of sight of the house. Mamm would scold me halfway to Sunday if she caught me eating one of your Pigs-in-a-Blanket."

Rebecca popped out of the house with two paper cups. "Ketchup and mustard." She handed them to Abraham. "You'll have to carry these but have them ready when Emma wants to dip."

"Yes, Mamm."

Rebecca propped her hands on her hips and looked around the yard. "Where did those boys get to?"

"They're coming with us," Abraham said. "They want to see Emma's chickens."

Rebecca grunted. "*Ach*, for goodness' sake. I told them to stay out of the way. Those boys don't have a whole brain between them."

"They've already gone on ahead, Mamm," Abraham said. "We should catch up."

Rebecca shook her head. "No rush. Let Emma enjoy her Pigs-in-a-Blanket."

"*Denki* again," Emma said, making her way down the porch steps. "We'll see you at *gmay*."

"Don't feel like you have to wait until *gmay*," Rebecca said. "Come anytime. We're playing Scrabble on Saturday. I'm making *yummasetti*."

"I love *yummasetti*," Emma said, hoping it didn't sound like she was considering the invitation.

There was no reason. She and Abraham were never going to be sweethearts.

Chapter Five

Abraham liked absolutely everything about Emma, even the way she ate. Most girls had the silly idea they shouldn't eat in front of boys, as if boys thought eating was unattractive or something. But not Emma. She ate four plain Pigs-in-a-Blanket and then four more dipped in mustard before they got to her house. And Abraham had the privilege of holding the mustard for her. How lucky could one boy be?

She polished off her eighth Pig-in-a-Blanket as they walked into her backyard. "Well," she said, "it sounds like Alfie and Benji beat us here."

They could have found their way by the sound of Tintin's barking. He was obviously very excited to see the chickens. But did he want to eat them or just be friends? Abraham didn't hold out much hope for the "friends" option.

Emma handed Abraham the plate of leftover Pigs-in-a-Blanket and ran around to the back of the house, not even waiting for him. He couldn't blame her. She feared for her chickens.

Abraham stuffed a Pig-in-a-Blanket in his mouth and followed her to the backyard. He'd been to

Emma's house at least two dozen times—every time her family had hosted *gmay* over the years—but he'd never seen Emma's chickens.

Her *dat* had built her a grand chicken run, at least fifteen feet square surrounded by a high chain-link fence. A gate on one side was the only entrance into the run. Emma said she had found the broken eggs inside the fence. How had Tintin gotten in the first time?

Alfie and Benji stood outside the chicken run both holding Tintin's leash as Tintin jumped up and down like a mule deer, barking and carrying on. Tintin yanked the leash right out of Alfie's hands, knocking him over, and Benji held on for dear life as Tintin dragged him along the fence line looking for a way in. Tintin definitely wanted those chickens. Abraham wasn't sure how Tintin had gotten in Emma's coop, but it wasn't a stretch to think he'd been in there and broken some of the eggs.

"Tintin," Alfie growled, picking himself off the ground and grabbing the leash before Benji lost it. "They're only chickens."

A smile crept onto Abraham's face. Tintin had worked himself into a frenzy over those chickens. He was almost more than Alfie and Benji could handle. Emma was marching toward Tintin like a charging bull, but the chickens acted as if nothing unusual was happening right outside their fence. Three hens pecked at the ground near the nesting boxes, and two white hens sat right up against the fence on the side where Tintin was making such a racket, looking at Tintin as if he was a show on an Englischer's television. They blinked and bobbed their heads, their combs and waddles wiggling in time with their movements, and didn't act as if they felt threatened at all. Maybe they were smart enough to notice the fence between them and those big teeth. Maybe they were secretly taunting Tintin. *Just try to eat us, you big, hairy, slobbery monster. We're not scared.*

They were probably too *dumm* to be scared. Chickens weren't known for their smarts.

"These are beautiful hens," Abraham said.

Emma turned and flashed a smile, even though she wasn't happy about the dog. "They are, aren't they?"

Alfie and Benji together tugged hard on the leash, and Tintin stopped jumping, but he barked as if chickens were the most exciting things since garbage cans with no lids. Emma positioned herself two feet in front of Tintin and shook her finger at him. If she was afraid of the dog, she didn't show it. Abraham loved that about her. She didn't seem to be scared of anything.

He wanted to be that brave but could never find the courage.

"Now, Tintin," Emma said. "Stop barking at my chickens. Haven't you upset them enough for one day?"

Tintin swallowed his bark and gave Emma a puzzled look. She knelt down and took his face between her hands and rubbed her fingers behind his ears. He stuck out that long tongue and licked her thumb. He could probably smell the heavy scent of Pigs-in-a-Blanket on her hands. After all she'd eaten, she probably smelled like a butcher shop. She was way more interesting than a coop full of chickens.

Abraham stuffed one last Pig-in-a-Blanket in his mouth and handed one to Emma. "Feed him this, and he'll be your friend for life."

Emma gave Abraham a beautiful smile, one he definitely didn't deserve, and fed the Pig-in-a-Blanket to Tintin. Tintin finished it in one bite.

"I want one," Alfie said.

Benji jumped up and down. "Me too."

"Are you done, Emma?" Abraham asked. She'd eaten eight of them, but he had to be sure before he started doling out the rest of Emma's dinner.

Emma laughed. "You saw how I waddled over here. I'm stuffed. To the brim."

Abraham gave two Pigs-in-a-Blanket to each of the boys, and Tintin promptly snatched one out of Benji's hand. "Hey," Benji said. "That was mine."

Emma patted Tintin's head. "That was very naughty, Tintin."

"It's okay," Benji said. "I already had dinner, and Tintin has to live in the woods. He deserves a treat."

Abraham handed Benji the last Pig-in-a-Blanket. "You can have this one."

"*Denki*," Benji said, before taking a bite, then giving the rest to Tintin anyway.

Alfie pinched part of his hot dog between his fingers. "Can I give this to the chickens?"

Emma nodded. "But be careful of your fingers. To the hens, they look like juicy worms."

Alfie stuck the hot dog into one of the holes in the chain link right next to one of the white hens. She snatched the hot dog with her beak and left Alfie's fingers unscathed. Alfie's eyes lit up. "Can I feed her another one?"

After the third piece of hot dog, the other hens began to suspect they were missing out on something. They gathered near the fence and watched with their beady eyes as Alfie and Benji fed them little pieces of hot dog. Mamm wouldn't have been happy that her hard work was going to the chickens, but she didn't ever have to know.

After every last Pig-in-a-Blanket was gone, Emma stood up and pinned Tintin with a stern look. "Now, Tintin, you are a very cute dog, but I don't like dogs so you can't soften me up with those big brown eyes. You are not to break any more of my eggs or bother my chickens in any way. Do you understand?"

She was talking to Tintin, but Alfie and Benji both nodded. "Or you'll have to gas him," Benji said.

Emma cleared her throat. "Nobody is going to gas Tintin. I just want him to stay away from my hens."

Alfie seemed unimpressed. "But how do you know Tintin broke your eggs?"

Emma led them around to the other side of the chicken run where the remains of three eggs lined the fence. She pointed to the dirt inside the fence. "Do you see that paw print? Tintin has definitely been in here."

Abraham drew his brows together in puzzlement. He didn't want to question Emma's judgment, but he didn't see how Tintin could have gotten into the coop by himself. Tintin was a jumper. It seemed impossible, but maybe he'd gotten lucky and jumped over the chain-link fence. Of course, there was no way he could have gotten out of the coop once he'd gotten in. "How . . . how could he have gotten in?" he finally said. It was a fair question, even if it irritated Emma.

Emma frowned. "I don't know, but you can all see that he was in here."

"You're right," Alfie said, sounding a little too agreeable. "It looks like Tintin is guilty. We're wonderful sorry. Be sure to come over to our house and tell us if it ever happens again."

Benji stuck out his bottom lip. "We shouldn't blame Tintin. He's just a helpless dog that can't talk."

Alfie put his arm around Benji. "We talked about this already."

Benji nudged Alfie's arm off his shoulder. "You were the one who talked. I just listened and nodded my head."

Alfie folded his arms across his chest. "I'm not saying Tintin broke the eggs, but isn't it great that Emma's going to come over and talk to Abraham if it ever happens again?" He emphasized *Abraham*, as if Abraham was to blame for the dog. Well, he probably was. He'd let the boys keep Tintin and kept the secret from Mamm. They were all in this together now.

Alfie, Benji, Abraham, and Emma.

He kind of liked being in on something with Emma, even if she didn't realize they were now in a secret club.

Benji kicked at a rock on the ground. "I guess it's okay. If Emma comes over."

Emma sighed. "As long as Tintin stays away from my chickens, I won't have to come over ever again."

Abraham wasn't sure why that made him sad. It wasn't like Emma had ever come over to his house before, except for *gmay*. Her *not* coming over wasn't anything new, but she didn't have to sound so happy about it.

Maybe it wasn't happy. Maybe she sounded relieved.

Abraham tried to ignore the gaping hole in the pit of his stomach.

Who wouldn't be relieved never to have to speak to Abraham again? He wasn't anything special. Emma had lots more interesting boys to be friends with—more interesting and less *dumm.*

Abraham didn't have a talent for talking the way Emma or his *bruder* Austin had. He always ended up saying the wrong thing or not saying anything at all. When Benji had mentioned sweethearts, Abraham had been struck dumb when he should have found something clever to say like, "Aren't little *bruders* so annoying?" *Nae.* That wouldn't have been clever. Even now, twenty minutes later, he still couldn't think of anything clever to make Emma forget it had ever happened. Of course, Emma knew exactly what to say. She smoothed the whole thing over by laughing and telling a funny story about her own *mamm.* He loved that about Emma. She always knew the perfect thing to say.

Abraham never did.

Even if he couldn't always find the right words, he knew how to right a wrong. "Emma, what would you like Alfie and Benji to do to work off the price of those eggs Tintin broke?"

"It was only three eggs. As long as the boys keep Tintin away from my coop, I won't ask for anything else."

Abraham leaned in closer and tried not to let her pleasant scent distract him. "I know it's not much money," he whispered, "but the boys need to learn a lesson. Isn't there anything you could have them do to work off Tintin's debt?"

One side of Emma's mouth curled upward. "I should have thought of that." She turned to Alfie and Benji. "I'll need you to come to my house for the next three days after I get home from work to help me clean the coop."

Benji groaned and slumped his shoulders. "Do we have to? It was only three eggs, and we already paid—"

Alfie poked his elbow into Benji's ribs. "Benji! We deserve our punishment. Tintin is our dog."

Benji glared at Alfie. "But what if he didn't break the eggs?"

Alfie tugged on Abraham's hand. "Will you come with us and help with our punishment?"

There was nothing Abraham would have liked better than to help Emma clean out her chicken coop, but no matter how he felt, he refused to make a pest of himself. "We don't need to bother Emma any more than we already have."

"She doesn't mind," Alfie said. "Do you, Emma?"

Emma hesitated before propping her lips up with a smile. "Of course I don't. Less work for me."

Benji wasn't convinced. "But I hate chicken poop. It sticks to your shoes and you have to use a butter knife to get it off, and Mamm will give me the spatula if she catches me using her butter knives one more time."

Abraham made a mental note to butter his bread with a spoon from now on.

Alfie caught his breath and gave Benji a wide smile. "If we come over to clean Emma's coops, we'll miss family reading time."

A light went on in Benji's brain. "But what will we tell Mammi?"

"We'll tell her we have to work at Emma's to pay off a debt."

Benji nodded. "Okay. But maybe I'll borrow Austin's work boots."

As long as he didn't try to scrape them off afterward.

One of the chickens flapped its wings and squawked. Tintin remembered what he was really here for and started barking and jumping around again.

Alfie grabbed onto Tintin's leash—the leash Abraham had bought because no dog should be led around by a rope tied around his neck. Benji slipped his fingers around Tintin's collar and held on tight.

"The chickens are scaring Tintin," Alfie said. "We'll take him back to his house."

"His house?" Abraham said.

Benji pulled Tintin away from the fence. "We built him a house in the woods. It has two bedrooms and a bowl for his food."

"And a box to go to the bathroom," Alfie said.

Benji nodded. "But he doesn't use it because dogs don't like to go in a box like cats do."

Tintin jumped up on Abraham and tried to lick his face before Alfie and Benji, tugging with all their nine-year-old strength, pulled Tintin away into the trees. They heard Tintin barking for several more minutes after he disappeared.

Emma scrunched her lips together. "That dog is persistent."

"And bouncy." *Bouncy*? What kind of word was *bouncy*? It was a word uninteresting boys used to try to impress pretty girls and failed miserably. He should keep his mouth shut.

"Do you think Tintin will leave my chickens alone?"

"I don't know. Only if my *bruderen* remember to tie him up."

Emma walked around her chicken run studying the chain link. "I don't understand how he got in. Deer can't even clear this fence."

"I don't know how he could have done it." Maybe he shouldn't have said that. He didn't want Emma to think he didn't believe her. "Did you leave the gate open this morning when you went to work?"

She frowned. "I suppose I could have, but I can't imagine it. I'm always so careful. Maybe Dat opened the gate."

Abraham leaned his hand against the fence. "Maybe he did. But I'll make sure Tintin stays away from your chickens, if I can control my *bruderen*, which I usually can't. One time Alfie stuck a bean up his nose and couldn't get it out. We had to call the paramedics."

Emma laughed. "I don't like that dog, but I would totally adopt your *bruderen* if your *mamm* ever gets sick of them."

Abraham smiled. "I'll mention that to her." He watched one of Emma's hens scratch in the dirt. "What kind of chicken is that?"

An extra light bulb seemed to come to life behind Emma's eyes. "That's Lottie, one of my Easter Eggers. She and Hattie lay maroon-colored eggs. They're called Easter Eggers because their eggs come already colored."

"What's this one that looks like she's wearing a hat?" Abraham said, pointing to a tan hen with a bouquet of beige feathers on her head.

"*Ach*, that's Tabitha, my Buff Laced Polish hen.

Isn't she something?" Emma pulled her shawl higher on her shoulders.

"You're probably wishing I'd go away so you can get in the house and get warm."

Emma raised her eyebrows and smiled. "I don't mind. Unless you need to go."

Abraham didn't have anyplace he needed to be, and he'd rather be here than anywhere else in the world. "Will you tell me about your hens?"

For the first time in probably his whole life, it seemed he'd said the right thing. Emma's expression bloomed with excitement. "You really want to know about my hens?"

"Of course. I've never seen anything like them."

"Well then," she said. "Soon it will be too dark. I'll go get my flashlight." She ran inside and was back before Abraham could count to sixty.

He followed her around the run, and she opened the gate and led him inside. He tried not to read too much into it, but Abraham got the impression that not everyone was allowed into Emma's chicken coop. His heart had no business flipping over like a pancake, but it did anyway.

Emma shined her light on a large red and black hen. "This is a Black Copper Maran. I call her Red. My *aendi* Berta got her for me for my birthday. Red lays chocolate-brown eggs. They're supposed to be quite expensive, but I just sell them for the regular price." After about twenty minutes of lively and interesting discussion about chickens, Emma smiled and wrapped her shawl tighter around her shoulders. "Am I boring you? Lizzy starts yawning when I talk about my chickens."

"It's fascinating," Abraham said, and he meant it.

No wonder Emma loved her chickens. Two looked like white pillows; another one could have been an Englischer with a feathered hat.

Emma handed Abraham the flashlight, then cornered a fat gray hen and gathered it in her arms like a baby. "This is Queenie. She's a Lavender Orpington." Emma made his pulse race when she leaned closer and whispered, "Queenie is my favorite, but don't tell the others. I don't want them to get their feelings hurt."

Abraham smiled even as his tongue felt like a thick slab of bacon. "Why is she your favorite?"

"If you see her in better light, her feathers are purple, and she lays beautiful pinkish-orange eggs. And she's not quite as uppity as my other chickens, even though she's the most beautiful." She smoothed Queenie's feathers and set her on the ground. "You should come back tomorrow. I don't have to work until noon, and Queenie is stunning in full sun." Her smile faded. "Unless you don't want to. Most people aren't as excited about chickens as I am."

"I wouldn't miss it," Abraham said. "I'd really like to see the purple feathers and those colorful eggs. Do they taste the same as normal eggs?"

"Dat thinks each chicken's eggs taste a little bit different, but I wouldn't know. I hate eggs. I'll only eat them if they're scrambled with about a pound of cheese."

"You hate eggs?"

"I know," Emma said. "A chicken keeper who hates the taste of eggs. I'm strange."

"I think you're *wunderbarr*." *Ach, du lieva.* Had he just said that out loud? He thought he might be sick at his own stupidity. While his head spun like a tornado, he pretended to examine the carpentry work on the coop. It wasn't very *gute*. He cleared his throat. "What I mean is, I think eggs are *wunderbarr*."

If she noticed his horrible mistake, she was too polite to mention it. That was something he really liked about her. "Everybody in my family likes eggs, and I sell them to neighbors and some to the Yutzys for their doughnut stand."

"It wonders me if Raymond Glick would want to sell them at his market."

She shook her head. "Raymond won't sell anything but white eggs. He says the colored ones scare his customers."

"Who's scared of an egg?"

Emma giggled. "I know! Are people going to run out of the store screaming?" They strolled out of the chicken run, and Emma made sure the gate was latched behind them. "It doesn't matter if the Glicks won't buy them. There are plenty of people who want my eggs, including your *bruderen*. They bought a dozen two days ago."

Abraham raised his eyebrows. "Why would they buy eggs? Did my *mamm* ask them to?"

Emma shook her head. "She bought a dozen yesterday. Maybe they want to feed them to Tintin."

"I never know what my *bruderen* are up to, and I've learned it's better not to ask. I hate tattling on them, but there are only so many secrets I can keep from Mamm. Three weeks ago they set the garbage on fire because they were trying to burn a secret note. At least that's what they told me. I dowsed the fire with a hose, and we scrubbed out the garbage can. There was only a slight hint of smoke in the air when Mamm got home."

Emma laughed, and Abraham thought he might have a heart attack. Was there anything better than making Emma laugh? "I'd love to know what was in that secret note. It must have been very important."

"I didn't want to know. After all that, they ended up burning everything except the note because it floated out of the garbage can when they started the fire. Alfie stomped on it then tore it into little pieces and buried it. I wasn't curious enough to sneak out and dig it up."

"I would have."

Abraham chuckled and leaned against the chain-link fence. He should go home, but he couldn't bring himself to leave, not when Emma was smiling at him and acting as if he was one of her friends instead of just some boy from the *gmayna*. It couldn't last. He'd savor the feeling for as long as possible. "It was wonderful nice of you to keep the dog a secret from my *mamm*, even though he broke your eggs. You're always so kind like that."

Emma lowered her eyes. "That is very nice of you to say, but I can't let you keep thinking it's true. Lizzy and I fuss at each other all the time."

"That's what siblings do. That doesn't count. You were always nice to the younger girls at school, and you always try to make sure everyone has a *gute* time at gatherings. I remember when Gary Yoder moved here from Ohio. You invited him to play volleyball, then introduced him to some of the other boys. And gave him a cookie yet."

She might have been blushing. He couldn't tell in the gathering darkness. "That wasn't anything."

"It was to Gary. He'd just lost his *dat*."

Doubt overtook her face. "I don't want you to get

the wrong idea about me. I'm not as nice as you think I am."

Abraham wanted to kick himself. Yet again, he'd said the wrong thing. He'd meant every word, but a girl like Emma would think he was flattering her, tempting her to be proud. No wonder she looked concerned. But he didn't know what to say. He never did, so he fell silent and hoped she'd forgive him.

She straightened her shawl. "I should go now. Mamm will wonder what happened to me."

"*Jah.* Okay." He barely dared ask the next question. "Is it still *gute* if I come tomorrow to visit your chickens?"

She cracked a smile. Abraham breathed a sigh of relief. "I don't think my chickens have ever had anything so fancy as a visitor before. They'd love it, for sure and certain."

Abraham nodded. "Okay. I will bring them a present."

Her smile got wider. "A present? They'll be beside themselves."

"How is ten o'clock?"

"Wonderful *gute*."

He really had to go now, or she'd think he was a bother. "Emma, I didn't say what I said to flatter you or tempt your pride. I would never do that. I think you're just the right amount of nice."

She got that look on her face again, but he sensed she didn't bear him any ill will. "*Denki*, Abraham. I'm going to try to live up to your opinion of me."

She turned, strolled to her back door, and disappeared into her house.

He shouldn't have said that. Had he made her feel bad? Or put extra pressure on her?

It was time to go back to staying silent. He didn't usually get himself into trouble when he kept his mouth shut.

Mammi always said, "You can't stick your foot in your mouth if it's shut."

Chapter Six

"You seem in a wonderful big hurry today," Lizzy said, as they walked home after their shift from the restaurant.

Emma immediately slowed her pace. Nobody, not even Lizzy, should think for even a minute that she was eager to get home, because she wasn't. Abraham and his *bruderen* would just have to wait for her. It wasn't like she was excited to see Abraham. He'd come to her house two days this week already. She could take or leave another visit, even though she really liked how interested he was in her chickens.

Abraham had come over by himself on Tuesday while his *bruderen* were at school so he could see the chickens in the daylight. Queenie was especially beautiful on Tuesday. The chicken run and coop were in a nice shady spot under two big maple trees, so Emma had taken Queenie out of the fenced area and let her run around the yard so Abraham could see her in full sun.

Except for herself, Emma had never seen anyone so excited about exotic chickens, and Emma could tell Abraham hadn't been faking his enthusiasm. He truly thrilled at the sight of Queenie's purple feathers and Tabitha's feathered hat. Emma didn't much approve of pretenders. Annie Shirk pretended to like dogs so Matt Gingerich would ask to drive her home. Tyler Kauffmann pretended to like Scilla Lambright's cookies because he wanted to kiss her behind the barn. Sarah King laughed at all Mervin Schrock's jokes because Mervin's *dat* was the minister and Sarah wanted to marry somebody important in the district.

Abraham wasn't sneaky or devious like that. He was just Abraham, sweet and harmless.

He'd brought the chickens a treat, just as he said he would—a whole tub of cottage cheese. He'd done his research. Either that or he simply knew a lot about chickens to begin with. Benji had said Abraham wanted to be an Amish veterinarian. He probably knew plenty about animals already.

Last night, Abraham and his little *bruderen* had come over and helped Emma clean out the coop and put fresh straw in the nesting boxes. The boys had brought Tintin and tied him to one of the maples in the yard with a long leash—long enough that he could get close to the coop and bark at the chickens. Emma's hens hadn't seemed to care that a big dog with sharp teeth stood just inches outside the fence barking at them, so Emma hadn't worried about them either. Tintin made a lot of noise, but he was mostly harmless. Like Abraham—except Abraham didn't make a lot of noise and he was pleasant to have around.

Tonight Abraham and the twins were coming over to finish cleaning out the coop. Emma had been impressed at what *gute* workers those little boys were. They were probably just happy to be getting out of family reading time.

But Emma wasn't especially eager to see any of them. Walking fast was just a habit.

Mamm had left some cold pizza on the table for Emma and Lizzy. It didn't take Emma long to finish, mostly because she'd always been a fast eater. She cleared and washed her plate before Lizzy had finished half her slice.

"Where are you going?" Lizzy said.

"I need to check on the chickens," she said, pulling on her coat and black bonnet.

"Abraham must be coming over," Lizzy said, smiling as if she was in on a great secret.

Emma didn't like that look one bit. "What are you smiling about?"

"He's cute," Lizzy said. "Don't you think he's cute?"

"I suppose he's handsome in his own way."

Lizzy giggled. "You suppose? Of course you think he's handsome. You practically ran home from the bus stop and swallowed your pizza whole. You're excited to see him."

Emma shook her head. Sixteen-year-olds had some strange notions. "If I don't get out there right quick, the twins will barge in and scare my chickens or let their dog chew on Queenie's neck. I'm only thinking of my chickens."

Lizzy arched her brows. "Are you sure? You're in an awful hurry."

Lizzy thought she was so clever. "I'm sure, Lizzy. I'm not interested in Abraham Petersheim."

"You should be. I like him. He doesn't ignore me when you walk in the room."

Emma frowned at her sister. "What is that supposed to mean?"

"You're a thousand times prettier than I am. Boys barely notice me when you're around."

Emma rolled her eyes. "That's not true. I'm of marriageable age, and you're not. The boys are looking for a *fraa*."

Lizzy popped a piece of pepperoni into her mouth. "Well, last night when Abraham came over with his *bruderen*, he came to the door and talked to only me for five minutes even while you were standing there, like he cared just as much about me as he does about you. He was being nice to be nice, not just to get your attention."

"Lizzy, boys aren't nice to you just to get my attention. That's silly."

"*Nae* it isn't. I've seen it. Tyler Kauffmann helped me up when I fell in volleyball, but only after he checked to make sure you were watching. Moses Zook said hi to me so he could get closer to you."

"He did not," Emma said, even though she knew what Lizzy was talking about. The boys liked her. She couldn't help that. But they should be nice to Lizzy no matter what.

"Abraham is different," Lizzy said. "He doesn't say much, but he's nice to everybody."

Emma couldn't argue with that. Everyone seemed to like Abraham, even if he didn't have many close friends, and he was exceptionally patient with his little *bruderen*. "I'm glad he's nice to you. Everybody should be nice to you."

"*Denki*," Lizzy said with a wry smile. "I agree."

"Do you want to come out and help us clean the nesting boxes? You could say hello to Abraham."

"Ha, ha," Lizzy said, wrinkling her nose. "I wouldn't deprive those boys of working off their full debt."

Emma finished tying her bonnet strings. "Okay. You know where I'll be if you change your mind."

She strolled out the door as if she had no place in particular she had to be. She wasn't going to give Lizzy the wrong impression, especially after Lizzy had made such a fuss about Abraham. Abraham liked her chickens, and he was pleasant company. He was harmless, and Emma liked it that way.

Abraham and the twins were squatting outside the chicken run intently studying something in the grass. Tintin stood next to Alfie with his head cocked to one side and his tail wagging like a flag in the wind. He didn't seem interested in barking at the chickens. Benji saw Emma first, ran to her, and threw his arms around her waist. "We found three ladybugs, and we're trying to get them to turn around and go back the other way. If they crawl into the chicken coop, Queenie will eat them. We don't want them to get eaten because ladybugs are a helpful insect." Benji took Emma's hand and pulled her toward the coop.

Abraham scooped up the ladybugs into his hand and let them crawl around his palm. He gave Emma a tentative smile, as if he didn't want to impose on her if she'd rather not be smiled at.

Benji made sure Emma got a good look at the ladybugs. "Can we take them to our house? We don't want the chickens to eat them."

"Abraham says you can tell how old they are by

how many spots they have," Alfie said. "Did you know that? I didn't know that. Abraham is so smart. Don't you think Abraham is smart?"

Emma didn't really have an opinion on whether Abraham was smart or not. Until about a week ago, she hadn't had a full conversation with him. Lizzy said he was deep, and Emma had to admit that Abraham wasn't like those boys who talked and talked just to hear the sound of their own voices. They'd spent a good half hour on Tuesday talking about eggs and chickens and the best food to feed them and how to get them to lay more eggs. She didn't know if Abraham was smart, but he knew a lot about chickens and that impressed Emma more than just about anything.

"You are welcome to take the ladybugs home," Emma said.

Benji nodded. "Put them in your pocket, Abraham."

Alfie nudged Benji with his elbow. "They'll die for sure and certain in Abraham's pocket."

Benji frowned. "Could they sit on Tintin's back until we're ready to go home?"

Abraham stood up. "I'll let them crawl on the trunk of this tree."

"But what if they crawl away?"

"If they crawl away, it means they have children they need to take care of." Abraham certainly was patient with his *bruderen*. Most boys would have squished those ladybugs so they wouldn't have to be bothered.

Tintin was tied to the tree where Abraham left the ladybugs. Like before, they had attached a rope to Tintin's leash and tied the rope around the tree.

The rope had to be at least twenty feet long. Tintin wouldn't be able to run into the woods, but he could roam freely about Emma's backyard and get right up to the chain-link fence and harass Emma's chickens.

Tintin jogged around the tree as Abraham and the little boys deposited their ladybugs on the trunk, then he sniffed the ground from the base of the tree all the way to the chicken run. Four of Emma's hens sat right up against the fence, almost as if they had known Tintin was coming and wanted to be ready to greet him. Instead of barking, Tintin started sniffing at the chickens as if he was trying to pick the juiciest one.

Benji scratched Tintin behind the ears. "Good boy. Good dog." He looked at Emma. "Tintin wants to be friends with your chickens. Abraham says dogs remember things by smelling. Dogs have to smell other dogs' bottoms so they'll remember who their friends are."

Emma giggled. "I've never heard that before."

Benji hooked his thumbs under his suspenders. "*Ach*, haven't you ever seen a dog smell another dog's bottom? It's their way of shaking hands."

Abraham turned his attention from the tree. "Benji, don't say things like that to a girl."

"It's okay," Emma said, unable to contain a wide smile. "I learn a lot from your *bruderen*."

Abraham scrunched his lips to one side of his face. "Half of it's nonsense."

Emma couldn't resist. She gave Abraham an innocent look. "But if it's nonsense, why *do* dogs smell other dogs' bottoms?" The laughter exploded from between her lips.

Abraham grinned and shook his head. "You're as bad as the boys."

"You're the animal expert. I want to know."

"I'll go to the library first thing in the morning."

"I'm sure you will. I know you're as curious as I am."

Abraham chuckled. "I brought you something."

Emma raised her eyebrows. "Me?"

He went to the tree and picked up a pile of what looked like big black sheets of cardboard. "My *bruder* Andrew just finished reroofing his house and had these shingles left over. I thought we could put them on the roof of your chicken coop. We don't want it to leak in the rain."

Emma was truly astounded. No one had ever been so thoughtful about her chickens before. Well, she hadn't expected anyone but her to think about her chickens. Who cared about chickens? "The coop leaked last fall. I kept a tarp over the roof all winter."

Abraham pointed to a toolbox also sitting by the tree. "I can get them on in less than two hours."

"That's very nice of you."

"Chickens don't like to be wet."

She nodded. "You know the expression 'Mad as a wet hen.' It's the truth."

Abraham went back to the tree and picked up the toolbox. "That's what I like about you. You know stuff like why hens get mad and how many eggs they lay every week. You're so smart."

Emma felt herself blush. He didn't need to say that. She knew a lot about chickens, but that didn't make her smart. Besides, boys didn't like smart girls. Well, most boys. Her chicken knowledge didn't seem to bother Abraham.

Abraham looked at his boots. "I shouldn't have said that. I didn't mean to make you uncomfortable."

She studied his face. "You didn't make me uncomfortable. I just think you're wrong. I'm not that smart."

"You can talk to anybody. Old people, little kids, boys at gatherings. Of course you're smart. I say something *dumm* every time I open my mouth."

Emma couldn't remember hearing anything *dumm* from Abraham. "You're not *dumm*. You're deep. There's a difference." Well, Lizzy thought Abraham was deep. Emma hadn't decided yet. But it was nice to see that frown disappear.

"I'll start on the shingles."

"Alfie and Benji and I will clean out the nesting boxes."

Benji groaned. "I hate cleaning out the nesting boxes. They stink."

Abraham draped the shingles over his shoulder. "Lord willing, the smell will remind you to keep Tintin away from Emma's chickens."

Alfie shook his head. "It probably won't. Us little kids have a hard time remembering stuff."

When the twins finished cleaning out the nesting boxes, Emma let them pet the chickens. Benji sat down and clucked softly. Lottie, one of Emma's Easter Eggers, walked right into Benji's arms and laid her beak on Benji's shoulder as if she was giving him a hug. Benji wrapped his arms around Lottie and patted her on the back like a newborn *buplie*. It was the cutest thing Emma had seen all day. Alfie was less comfortable with the hens. He patted a few of them on the back, then stood against the fence twirling one of Queenie's feathers in his fingers. Alfie always seemed to be thinking deep thoughts or planning grand adventures in his head.

While the boys played with the hens, Emma held Queenie in her arms and watched Abraham staple shingles to the roof with his special staple gun. There was something almost athletic about the way he picked up a shingle, set it in place on the roof, then stapled it down in one fluid motion. The muscles in his back and arms strained against his shirt as he worked, and Emma couldn't look away.

But maybe she should look away. Should she? Was there anything wrong with watching a boy and his muscles put shingles on her chicken coop? Should she ask the bishop? Who would dare ask the bishop such a thing? Maybe Mamm would have an opinion. Well, Mamm would surely have an opinion, but the question might bring on one of her headaches.

Maybe Emma could just mention it to Lizzy. Lizzy wouldn't know the answer, but she'd be on Emma's side—the side that said not to look away.

Abraham glanced in her direction. "If you need to go inside, I don't mind. I can send the boys home and finish on my own."

"Do you . . . want me to go inside?"

He paused. "*Nae*, unless you want to."

Maybe it was a sin, but she didn't want to. It was a shame the roof wasn't bigger. He'd be done in a matter of minutes. "I don't have to work until noon tomorrow. I don't have to get up until six."

"Do you like working at the restaurant?"

"*Jah*. I get to meet some interesting people. Sol Kiem comes in every Friday and orders three pancakes, three slices of bacon, and a piece of pie. Last week an Englischer with tattoos all over his arms came in. Lizzy didn't dare talk to him, but he was very nice and gave me a big tip. Another woman told me she was a doctor who operated on brand-new babies."

"What were the babies' names?" Benji asked.

Emma smiled. "She didn't say."

"Martha Glick is a wonderful *gute* cook," Abraham said.

"Her rolls are famous," Benji said, "but we don't eat there because Raymond Glick is mad at Andrew."

Abraham's staple gun went silent. "Don't talk about things you don't know, Benji."

Alfie picked up a kernel of corn and fed it to Lottie. "Benji knows. He listens, and people think he's just a little kid."

"*Jah*," said Benji. "Mamm says Raymond Glick is mad at Andrew because Andrew married Mary, and Bitsy took Mary in when she was going to have a baby, and Raymond hates Bitsy because Dan Kanagy stole Paul Glick's girlfriend."

It was just as well none of that made sense to Emma. She didn't like to think ill of anyone, even Raymond Glick, who wasn't very likable.

"That's gossip," Abraham said. "And you shouldn't spread gossip."

Alfie leaned against the fence. "It's not gossip if it's true."

Abraham picked up another shingle. "It's gossip no matter what."

Alfie's gaze traveled from Abraham to Emma and back again. "How much longer do you have, Abraham?"

"Three more shingles."

Alfie stretched his arms over his head and let out the biggest yawn Emma had ever heard. "It's past my bedtime. Benji and I are going to take Tintin home and go to bed. In the cellar."

"It's not past your bedtime," Abraham said.

Alfie yawned again as if he couldn't help it. "We like to be in bed before it gets dark in the cellar. That's when the spiders and the rats come out, and we don't want to get eaten."

Abraham shrugged. "Okay. Go home. I'll follow in a few minutes."

"You don't have to hurry. Your bedtime isn't for hours."

Emma reluctantly pulled her gaze from Abraham and set Queenie on the ground. "*Denki* for helping me clean the coop, boys. You did a good job and your punishment is over."

Benji stood and nudged the dirt with his toe. "Well, maybe we won't be back and maybe we will."

"Just keep Tintin out of trouble, and you won't have to come back."

Alfie nudged Benji's arm. "Did you hear that?"

Benji grimaced. "I heard. I just don't like it."

Alfie sort of growled between his teeth. "It's part of our plan. Don't forget the plan."

"Okay," Benji snapped. "I won't forget the stupid plan."

The boys opened the gate and ambled out of the coop. Benji held on to Tintin's leash while Alfie untied the rope from the tree. Benji tapped on the chain link and motioned for Emma to come closer. Tintin licked her hand through the fence. "Emma,"

Benji whispered, "Abraham is too shy, but he wants to drive you home from the gathering tomorrow night."

Emma's heart plummeted to her toes and thudded on the ground at her feet. Abraham was nice and had muscles, but he was just Abraham Petersheim. She shouldn't have eaten Pigs-in-a-Blanket with him or let him put shingles on her roof or let him see Queenie in full sun. Boys thought you were interested when you were nice to them. But it wasn't like she could be rude.

A wonderful *gute* evening had been ruined, and now she was going to have to walk over there and break Abraham's heart. And after he'd done something so nice for her. *Ach.* She shouldn't have gone to his house in the first place to complain about the dog. She was in a pickle, and it was her own fault.

Alfie and Benji skipped into the woods with Tintin leading the way as if there was a big bowl of dog food waiting for him at home. Maybe there was.

Emma sighed, set Queenie down, and took the five short steps toward Abraham. He had finished the shingles and climbed down from the roof and was arranging his tools in the toolbox. "*Denki* for putting shingles on my roof," she said, with as much enthusiasm as she could muster.

His lips curled upward. "It was no trouble and didn't cost either of us a penny."

Ach. This was going to be harder than she thought. He had really white teeth and looked at her as if he thought she was the nicest girl in the world. She cleared her throat. "Abraham, you are such a nice boy, but I'm going to have to say *nae*. I'm not interested. I'm sorry."

His smile sputtered, then went out, and a look of

deep confusion traveled across his face. "Say *nae* to what?"

"To what Benji said."

Deeper confusion. "What did Benji say?"

He wasn't making this easy, and she was sort of losing her patience. "Benji said you were too shy to ask if you could drive me home from the gathering tomorrow. I don't want to hurt your feelings, but there are other boys I'm more interested in." Abraham stared at her doubtfully. She needed to make herself perfectly clear, even if she felt horrible for doing it. "I'm not interested in you. You understand, don't you?"

He was silent for so long, she thought maybe he'd lost the power of speech. "*Ach.* I didn't say that."

"Say what?"

"Say that to Benji."

"Say what to Benji?" Oh, *sis yuscht.* It was getting worse and worse.

Even though it was nearly dark, she could still see the crimson heat creep up his neck. "I don't know what Benji's up to, but I never asked him to ask you if I could drive you home." It was obvious he was deeply embarrassed, and she could see he measured his words carefully. "I'm not *dumm* enough to think you would ever be interested in someone like me."

Of course he wasn't *dumm.* "I thought since I was nice to you . . ." she said, trailing off.

"You're nice to everybody, and I'm not that stupid."

Stupid was a bitter word, and Emma felt it down to her bones. "I'm sorry. I didn't mean to offend you."

"You didn't offend me." He looked up and attempted a smile. "I'm irritated that Benji made you uncomfortable and that you were forced to tell me what I already know."

Emma's stomach twisted into a knot. He was upset, but he was trying his best to make her feel better about it. "Don't be too hard on Benji. Little boys are wired to be annoying and make mischief. Next time I'll know not to believe a word that comes out of his mouth."

"That would be wise," Abraham said, without even pretending to smile anymore. He gathered up the shingles scraps and stuffed them in his toolbox, then draped the few leftover shingles over his shoulder. "Let me know if the roof has problems, and if you need any other repairs, I'd be happy to help."

"I'm relieved about the roof, but I don't think there's anything else you can do for me."

He nodded as if expecting that answer. "Okay."

She followed him as he tromped out of the chicken coop and made sure the gate was latched tightly. "I can't thank you enough. Tell the boys *denki* again. They worked hard."

"Okay," he said, turning away from her and walking slowly in the direction of his house. "It looks like rain," he called. "Keep an eye on that roof."

She should have been happy at how well that conversation had gone. She should have been relieved to know Abraham had never expected anything from her. She should have been excited for the gathering tomorrow night.

All she felt was rotten.

Chapter Seven

Abraham swept extra slowly after dinner, and Mammi wasn't even hovering to make sure he did it right. Maybe he'd mop as soon as the dishes were done. Mamm shouldn't have to be the one to mop the floor every week. She had four capable sons who could ease her burden by taking on more chores around the house.

Mamm rinsed the last plate and handed it to Alfie to dry. "Abraham, will you take out the garbage before you leave? There's something stinky in there."

"Okay," Abraham said, making himself extra busy with the sweeping. He wasn't going anywhere tonight, but Mamm didn't need to know that until it was too late to do anything about it.

Austin finished wiping the table while the boys dried dishes. "Junior's *dat* got a new mare. He's bringing it to the gathering. She used to be a race-horse, and Junior says she can beat anybody in a dead run."

Mamm dried her hands and propped them on her hips. "You are not going to race horses tonight, young man. You'll fall off and break your skull."

"I won't break anything, Mamm," Austin said.

"*Jah*, you will, and I refuse to visit anyone who's in the hospital for being foolish. You can tell Junior I won't visit him either."

Alfie set his dry plate on the counter. "Willie had to go to the hospital last week. He cut himself with a pocketknife. Five stitches."

Mamm grunted. "I won't visit anyone in the hospital who's too *dumm* to not know how to use a pocketknife."

Austin hung the dishrag on the hook and grabbed the dustpan from the closet. "Let's go, Abraham. I want to get there before all the eats are gone."

Abraham meticulously swept every last crumb into a neat little pile and passed the broom under the fridge one more time because dirt had a habit of hiding there.

Austin waved the dustpan in front of Abraham's face. "Come on, Abe. Let's go."

"Go without me," Abraham said, without looking up. "I want to mop."

All movement from Mamm's side of the room stopped. "That is the biggest lie anyone has ever told in this room, young man."

"It's not a lie. I really want to mop, Mamm." Way more than he wanted to go to the gathering. He made his pile smaller and smaller with his broom. "You mop the floor every week, and we boys should ease your burdens by—"

Mamm waved dismissively in Abraham's direction. "Who cares about my burdens? I don't have more than my share of burdens, and since when do you think mopping is more exciting than going to a gathering?"

"Since forever," Abraham said. That was probably true. He played a lot of basketball at gatherings, but he was too embarrassed to talk to girls and he always came home feeling like an idiot—especially since he'd started taking interest in a girl who would never in a million years be interested back.

Mamm studied his face. "Emma's going to be there," she said, shifting into her "nice" voice. Abraham hated Mamm's "nice" voice. She only used it on Abraham because she thought Abraham was fragile or stupid or too sensitive to be scolded.

He wished she wouldn't. Abraham didn't have a lot of friends because he didn't say much, but the friends he had were good, close friends he could always depend on. Girls weren't interested because he was too tall or too quiet or maybe just too ugly, but Abraham had very recently made peace with the fact that he'd be a bachelor the rest of his life.

In fact, he'd made peace with that fact at about three o'clock this morning. He was never again going to even skirt the humiliation he'd been put through last night. And he wasn't going to show his face at that gathering. He didn't need Emma's pity. He wasn't going to do that to himself.

Benji took the dustpan from Austin and held it on the floor so Abraham could sweep his crumbs into it. "Did you hear what Mamm said? Emma's going to be there."

Abraham nearly lost his temper—even though he'd never had much of one. It was Benji's fault that Emma saw Abraham as an object of pity instead of just one of the boys in the *gmayna*. But he couldn't be mad at Benji because he *had* been considering maybe possibly saying hello to Emma at the gathering. Benji had probably saved him from worse embarrassment in the long run.

"Lots of people are going to be there, Mamm. There's a gathering every week. I want to mop. You cook dinner for us every night and wash the clothes and clean the toilets."

"I clean the toilets," Austin said.

Mamm's "nice" voice again. "But you've been to Emma's house four times this week. And she loved the Pigs-in-a-Blanket."

How did Mamm know it had been four visits? He hadn't told anyone where he'd gone Tuesday morning. It was spooky how Mamm knew so much. Abraham probably couldn't sneeze without her finding out about it. But if he was going to salvage his wounded pride, he had to hide any feelings he had for Emma. Or used to have. He was fine dying a bachelor. "Andrew had some extra shingles. Emma's chicken coop leaked. I was just helping her out."

"That was nice of you," Mamm said.

"I finished the shingles last night."

Mamm smiled. "Well, now you have to go to the gathering to give her a chance to thank you."

"She thanked me already. There's really nothing more to say."

Abraham didn't know what he said—maybe it was something in his voice he couldn't hide—but Austin quit smiling and eyed Abraham as if he only had three months to live. But he didn't say anything in front of Mamm. Abraham was grateful for that.

Mamm's voice got "nicer," if that was even possible. "I won't hear of you missing a gathering to mop the floor for me. What kind of a *mater* would

I be if I deprived my son of the chance to be with his friends?"

"I'm not going, Mamm."

Mamm took the broom from his hands and actually shoved him in the direction of the front door. "I won't hear any more such talk. Of course you're going."

"I don't want to go."

"Nice" Mamm disappeared and no-nonsense Mamm came back. It was almost a relief that she didn't think he was completely hopeless. "I dirtied three pans making Pigs-in-a-Blanket, young man. You're going to that gathering, and you're going to have a *gute* time. And if Emma wants to play volleyball, it won't kill you to join the game. It's a free country. Emma can play volleyball. You can play volleyball. Maybe she'll want to stop by later for some popcorn or my peanut butter chocolate pie. And if she does"—Mamm shook her finger in Abraham's face—"if she does, you will not tell her *nae*. Do you understand?"

"*Jah*, Mamm."

"*Gute*. Now go with your *bruder*. Alfie and Benji can mop."

The twins groaned in unison. "Ah, Mamm," Alfie said. "We already dried all the dishes and the pots."

"And you can mop the floor as your reward."

Benji looked as if he'd been stricken with a dread disease. "But we don't even know how to mop."

"It's high time you learned," Mamm said.

Alfie folded his arms across his chest. "Willie says it's child labor, and it's illegal."

Mamm gave Alfie the stink eye. "Maybe I should

give you the child labor spatula and see how you like that."

Alfie slumped his shoulders. "I was just joking, Mamm."

"Don't joke with me unless you want three weeks of mucking out the barn."

"Okay, Mamm."

Mamm glanced at Austin. "Why are you two still here?"

Austin hitched up the buggy while Abraham sulked just outside the barn. He had retrieved two basketballs from his room, because the gathering was at the park where there was a basketball court. He wouldn't have to talk to anyone tonight. He'd rather shoot hoops anyway.

Austin was a *gute bruder*. He worked hard, told funny jokes, and didn't stick his nose in Abraham's business. How could Abraham have known that was about to change? "So," Austin said, as he guided the horse down the gravel driveway, "it wonders me if Emma didn't put you down good yesterday."

Abraham really didn't want to have this conversation. "Why do you say that?"

"Because you look about as low as a tipped-over outhouse. Even Mamm noticed."

"*Even* Mamm? She notices everything."

"Okay then. Even I noticed."

That was probably the more honest answer. Austin was a *gute bruder*, but he could be a little self-centered. Abraham didn't mind. Austin was handsome and talkative and fun to be around. He had plenty of girls to talk to. He didn't really care how Abraham spent his time at gatherings. That didn't mean he didn't care about Abraham. He just had places to go and people to see and didn't have time to make sure Abraham had a good time. Abraham had never wanted him to. He didn't need his little *bruder* to babysit him.

He needed to say just enough to satisfy Austin's curiosity without actually telling him anything. The pain was too fresh, and even though Austin meant well, he'd forget his promise and tease Abraham mercilessly. That's what little *bruderen* did. "Benji and Alfie are up to something, and Emma isn't too happy about it. She doesn't want anyone bothering her chickens."

Austin smiled. "Is that all? Emma will get over it, and who can be mad at Alfie and Benji? Well, Mamm can, but she's the only one. Girls think the twins are cute. I'm tempted to bring them to a gathering and show them off." His smile got wider. "I think Scilla Lambright is going to be here tonight. Should I ask to drive her home?"

Austin worked hard, told funny jokes, and didn't stick his nose in Abraham's business. And he was a little self-centered and easily distracted. He was a very *gute bruder*.

There were about a dozen buggies in the parking lot at the city park and that many more scooters and bicycles. Abraham kept his gaze squarely on the three-foot patch of grass in front of him. If Emma was there, he didn't want her to look up and catch him looking at her, because he wasn't there to see her and he didn't want to make her feel uncomfortable.

With one basketball pressed against each hip,

Abraham made a beeline for the court on the other side of the park. Mark Hoover met him halfway across the lawn and relieved him of one of his balls. Mark tried to walk and twirl the basketball on his middle finger at the same time. He wasn't very good at it, but he kept trying. He grinned at Abraham every time he dropped the ball. Abraham just shook his head and smiled back.

"*Hallo*, Abraham. Can we play?" Tyler Kaufmann and Mahlon Zook jogged across the grass to join Abraham and Mark.

"For sure and certain," Abraham said. Maybe he'd have a *gute* time at the park after all. Tyler was almost as tall as Abraham, and he had a *gute* vertical leap, and Mahlon was a *gute* defender.

By the time Abraham reached the basketball court, he had accumulated seven friends who all wanted to play. While they chose teams, Abraham made the mistake of glancing over at a group of girls and boys huddled around a park bench. Emma stood right in the middle of the pack, laughing and talking. He loved that she was so happy and always seemed to have fun, no matter where she was. And she was as nice as she was pretty. Even the way she'd told him she wasn't interested had been kind.

His breath caught in his throat just thinking about how humiliated he'd been, even though Emma had been wonderful nice about it. Abraham loved that about her. He didn't even deserve her notice, but she had been kind all the same.

He let his gaze linger for a second too long, and Emma glanced in his direction. Oh, *sis yuscht*. Her smile faltered on her lips, but she raised her hand to wave at him. Abraham quickly averted his eyes. She was just trying to be nice, but for her sake, Abraham didn't want anyone to catch her waving at him. He turned his back and shot a basket. No one would guess she'd been waving at him.

Lord willing, nothing like that would happen again tonight. She knew where he was and what she had to do to avoid him. He got his own rebound and shot the ball again. He wasn't there to make trouble for Emma. He was only there to play some basketball and avoid the girls. How hard could that be?

Abraham knocked on the door and heard the pitter-patter of bare feet against a wood floor. Mary opened the door with her daughter, ElJay, propped on her hip and a smudge of flour on her cheek. She lit up like a sparkler when she saw Abraham. "How wonderful." She grabbed his sleeve and pulled him into the house. "*Cum reu* and see the new trick ElJay can do."

She led him into the great room and set ElJay in the middle of the wood floor. "She's determined to follow me around the house." Mary squatted about four feet from ElJay and held out her hands. "Come on," she coaxed. "Come on, *heartzley.*"

ElJay smiled and giggled and looked at Abraham as if she was fully aware she was performing for her *onkel.* She stuck her fingers in her mouth, pulled them out again, and squealed as if this was the most fun in the whole world.

"Come on, *heartzley,*" Mary said. "Come get Onkel Abraham."

ElJay giggled uncontrollably as she drew in her feet and pushed them away from her body. Rocking herself back and forth with her legs, she was able to scoot across the floor on her bottom. Mary squealed in delight as ElJay made the four-feet trip across the floor into her *mater*'s arms.

Abraham clapped. "Wonderful *gute*, ElJay. But it looks so much harder than crawling."

"For sure and certain," Mary said. "I've gotten down on my hands and knees to show her how to crawl, but she just laughs at me. She thinks I'm pretending to be Alfie and Benji's dog."

The laughter exploded from Abraham's lips. "You know about the dog?"

Mary giggled. "They tried to convince us to let them hide him here, but I've got enough to take care of with a baby and a cow. I don't need a dog. But I do let them keep him in the barn most nights. It still gets cold, and I don't want a frozen dog on my conscience."

"I can't believe they told you about the dog. The more people who are in on the secret, the more likely Mamm will find out about it."

Mary nodded and gave him a wry smile. "Oh, she is for sure and certain going to find out. We're all just holding our breath waiting to see if Tintin will get gassed this month or next."

Abraham winced. "Don't let Benji hear you say that."

"I'm joking. I'm sure Tintin will find a *gute* home when the time comes."

"That time might come soon. Mamm is bound to notice the big piles of poop in the woods."

Mary laughed and shook her head. "Poor Alfie and Benji. Every little boy needs a dog."

"*Jah.*"

"I'm guessing you didn't come to see ElJay do her trick. Andrew's in his shop. Do you want to go out?"

"I'm just returning the leftover shingles," Abraham said.

Mary scooped ElJay from the floor. "*Cum.* We'll go with you. Andrew's making a rocking chair for an Englischer in Green Bay. Maple. It's going to be beautiful."

Mary grabbed a blanket that was slung over a kitchen chair, wrapped up ElJay, and handed her to Abraham. "You carry the baby. I'll grab Andrew's lunch."

Abraham knew how to hold babies, even if he wasn't especially comfortable with them. He'd helped Mamm with the twins when they were little, but that had been a long time ago and he was sort of rusty. Mary never seemed to be concerned about leaving her baby in Abraham's care. It was always a nice feeling when somebody trusted you to hold her baby. He wouldn't let her down.

Mary and Andrew lived in Mammi and Dawdi Petersheim's old house, about a fifteen-minute walk from the family home. When Dawdi had suffered a stroke, Mammi and Dawdi had moved in with Abraham's family and rented the house to some cousins. When Andrew got married, he and Mary moved into Mammi and Dawdi's house. Andrew had reinforced the old shed and set up his woodshop out there where Mary wouldn't be bothered with the noise or the dust.

Mary and Andrew were wildly happy, even though their relationship had a rocky start. Maybe that was why they were so happy. Love becomes deeper and stronger when you have to fight for it. A year ago, Mary had returned to their Amish community without any money, without any friends, and without a place to stay. Her parents wouldn't let her back into the house because she was going to have a baby so Bitsy Weaver took Mary in. Honeybee Farm was where Mary and Andrew had fallen in love.

Mary's parents still weren't speaking to her, and the Glicks had practically banned Mary from their store because they were mad at Bitsy Weaver. And since Mary was married to a Petersheim, the Glicks didn't much like Abraham's family either. Everything got messy when you held on to a grudge. It was kind of surprising that Raymond Glick still bought Petersheim Brothers' Peanut Butter. Maybe he was biding his time until he could find somewhere else to buy peanut butter. He might be waiting a long time. Petersheim Brothers' Peanut Butter was the best peanut butter in Wisconsin.

Mary and Abraham walked out the back door, and Abraham tucked ElJay's blanket tighter around her little legs. Abraham envied the happiness Andrew had found with Mary. But coveting Andrew's happiness was what had gotten Abraham in trouble with Emma. He should be content with the things Gotte had given him.

The gas-powered generator clattered noisily on its perch outside the shed. Generators were kept outside because they were so loud, but Andrew also wore a pair of earplugs and kept the shed door open during the day because his woodworking tools made a lot of noise too. Andrew looked up and grinned as

Mary and Abraham came into his shop. Mary's smile grew even more beautiful.

Abraham's heart ached but only a little. He was going to be perfectly happy as a bachelor.

Andrew turned off his saw and pulled the earplugs from his ears. "There's my little sweetheart," he said, holding out his arms to ElJay. ElJay reached for her *dat* and settled comfortably in his arms. "Isn't she the chubbiest baby you've ever seen?" Andrew said.

Abraham nodded. "The chubbiest."

"I brought you some lunch," Mary said, showing Andrew the sandwich wrapped in plastic.

It didn't look like much of a lunch to Abraham, but Andrew acted like she'd brought him Thanksgiving dinner. He gave her a kiss on the cheek. "You are so *gute* to me." Andrew sat down on the workbench, and Mary sidled next to him.

ElJay might as well have been Andrew's biological daughter for how much Andrew doted on that little girl. ElJay's real father had threatened to sue for custody, but Mary and Andrew hadn't heard a peep from him since ElJay had been born. Rumor was he had another girlfriend and had given up trying to get Mary back using ElJay as ammunition.

"Here," Abraham said, pulling up a three-legged stool and sitting down. "Let me hold the baby so you can eat."

ElJay came right to him and started playing with the buttons on his shirt. Abraham patted her on the head. "I brought back the extra shingles."

Andrew took a bite of what looked like a very soggy tuna fish sandwich. "How did they work out?"

Abraham didn't know what to say about that. "*Gute.*"

Andrew got a mischievous glint in his eye. "Emma

is a wonderful *gute* girl. Mamm says she came over to our house."

"One time," Abraham said. But never again, for sure and certain.

"And she ate Pigs-in-a-Blanket," Andrew said, as if he found Pigs-in-a-Blanket very amusing.

Mary covered ElJay's wiggly foot with the blanket. "Was Emma pleased with the shingles?"

Was Emma pleased? *Nae.* She was mortified. *I'm really relieved about the roof, but I don't think there's anything else you can do for me.* She might as well have said, *Please go away and never come back. You're scaring the other boys away.*

Abraham kissed ElJay's forehead and gazed out the open door. "The shingles will keep her hens dry."

"That was thoughtful of you," Mary said. "Emma loves her chickens."

"*Jah.*"

Mary's smile faded. "Didn't she like the shingles?"

"*Jah.*"

Mary glanced at Andrew. "Isn't Emma . . . is everything okay with Emma?"

"There's nothing to be okay with. I fixed her roof. We don't really know each other very well."

"You could change that," Andrew said, a tease twitching on his lips. "Her *dat* has a whole barn, and I've got more shingles. Or you could take up knitting and make sweaters for the chickens." He laughed. "For sure and certain, she'd fall in love with you if you did sweaters."

Abraham usually laughed at Andrew's jokes, but not today. He couldn't laugh at anything, not when he had sixty years of bachelorhood ahead of him.

Mary patted Andrew on the leg. It was some sort

of secret signal because Andrew shut his mouth. Mary studied Abraham's face. "Did Emma say something to upset you?"

Abraham didn't really want to compound his humiliation by sharing it, but Mary always sensed when something wasn't right, and she wasn't one to let it go if she thought she could fix it. Abraham folded his arms. "Benji did something stupid that embarrassed me." He was embarrassed even saying the words. It sounded so childish.

Andrew obviously thought so too. "You've got to get a thicker skin, Abe. Benji and Alfie do something embarrassing every day. They used to climb trees and spy on me and Mary." Andrew glanced at Mary, who was giving him another secret signal with her eyes. It wasn't hard to tell what she was thinking. "Okay. I'm sorry. I'll shut up."

"I know," Abraham said. "It's *dumm*. I shouldn't let two nine-year-olds get to me."

Mary reached out and patted Abraham's leg. If it was a secret signal, he didn't know what it meant. "If it makes you this upset, it isn't *dumm*. Alfie almost got himself killed a couple of times. No doubt, two nine-year-olds can get to you."

Abraham smoothed ElJay's wispy hair. "The boys came with me when I shingled Emma's coop. Benji told Emma that I was too scared to ask but that I wanted to drive her home from the gathering. She told me she wasn't interested."

Andrew winced as if he'd been poked with a pin. "But you *are* interested, aren't you?"

"I'm not interested in the way you think I'm interested. Emma is *wunderbarr*, but I'd be a *dummkoff* to think she'd ever give me a second look. I never would have ever asked to drive her home."

Mary drew her brows together. "*Ach.* I'm sorry."

"But why did it upset you so much if you were never planning on asking in the first place?" Andrew said.

Mary looked at Andrew as if he'd just tried to hammer a nail with a spatula. "She said it out loud. If she hadn't said it out loud, Abraham could have held out a little bit of hope that maybe she liked him too. Now all hope is gone."

It sounded so serious when Mary said it like that. Well, maybe it was. The ache in Abraham's chest was proof of that. "It's my own fault for even letting the thought enter my mind, but it's hard to think straight when I'm around her."

Mary gave him a sympathetic smile. "Emma is pretty, and everybody likes her."

"She was afraid I'd gotten the idea that she was interested when she just wanted to be nice."

"That's how it is with Emma," Mary said. "There are boys who think she likes them just because she's nice to everybody."

"Like Perry Glick," Abraham said. "But I told her I wasn't that stupid to believe a girl like her would ever be interested in a boy like me. I think I hurt her feelings."

"There's entirely too much thinking going on between the two of you," Andrew said. He was trying to be funny, but it didn't help. Mary patted him on the leg again. He cleared his throat. "Look, Abraham, Mary is wrong."

Mary cuffed him playfully on the shoulder. "You think I'm wrong?"

He laughed as he tried to deflect the blow. "All hope is not gone. I'm not just saying this because I'm your *bruder*. It isn't stupid to think Emma would be interested in you. Any girl would be lucky to catch you."

"That's not true."

Mary scrunched her lips together. "It's true, even if you can't see it. Maybe I am wrong. All hope is not lost."

"I love it when you admit you're wrong," Andrew said.

"I'm sure you do, *heartzley*," Mary said. She turned her attention to Abraham. "I go to quilting frolics, and I hear lots of talk. Girls in the district think you're not interested in any of them because you don't even try. When you go to gatherings, you head right for the basketball court, and if there isn't basketball, you play volleyball. But you won't talk to anybody except to say things like, 'Nice shot,' or 'Good hit.' The girls have kind of stopped trying because they don't want to be rejected and they don't want anyone to think they're flirting. So, they've moved on to other boys. Like Austin. He talks to all of them."

Abraham cracked a smile. "Yes, he does. But it's not because they've moved on from me. Austin's like Emma. He can talk to anybody. The girls like it when he talks to them, and I don't talk. I don't know what to say, and I mess up when I try to be clever."

Mary shook her head. "You don't have to pretend to be anybody you're not. Just be yourself."

Abraham sighed. "I do try to be myself. That's why Emma's not interested." There was a pain in his heart that he had no right to feel. Emma didn't owe him anything.

Andrew finished off the last bite of his sandwich. "Emma has no idea what she's missing. She's too busy being the center of the universe."

"I appreciate you trying to make me feel better," Abraham said, "but Emma's not like that. It's just that everybody likes her and wants to be around her."

"And she likes the attention," Mary said. "It's not a bad thing, but all that attention can go to your head. Don't think for one minute that you're not worthy of Emma or any other girl."

Andrew tried to be helpful. "Girls like tall boys."

Mary smiled at Andrew. "Being tall isn't Abraham's only *gute* quality. He helped you put in that windmill last fall, and he helped you plant corn this spring. He never loses his temper, and he loves animals. What girl wouldn't like that? And he has a way with ElJay. She loves him to death."

As if to prove her *mater*'s point, ElJay reached up, grabbed onto Abraham's ear, and gave him a slobbery kiss on the cheek. Abraham smiled and wiped the moisture off with her blanket. At least somebody liked him.

"If Emma isn't interested, there's lots of girls out there who are," Mary said. "You just have to make some effort. Put down that basketball and go socialize."

Abraham sprouted a weak smile. "But my team needs me."

"Yes, well, they should all be flirting with the girls at gatherings instead of shooting baskets. And you can tell them I said so. It's time to kill the basketball game."

Andrew's mouth fell open in mock horror. "Kill

basketball? What are you thinking? Thousands of players everywhere are turning over in their graves."

Mary laughed. "Sometimes a man just has to be a man."

Abraham patted ElJay's back while she played with his ear. "Flirting with girls is how I'm supposed to prove my manhood?"

"*Jah*," Mary said. "You don't want to end up a bachelor."

"*Ach*, I'm going to end up a bachelor no matter what. Might as well face the truth."

"You are not," Mary protested. "Andrew is right. There's still hope."

Andrew gave Mary a wide smile. "I love it when you admit I'm right."

She tilted her head to the side. "You're right most of the time, *heartzley*."

Maybe Abraham would have to go home and rethink the bachelor idea. He'd willingly give up basketball if someone would look at him the way Mary looked at Andrew.

"And if Perry Glick is your only competition, there is still hope," Andrew said.

Mary pressed her lips together. "Don't even joke about that, Andrew." She turned to Abraham. "Does Perry like Emma?"

Abraham's gut tightened. "I think so. She says he hides in the storage room at work and spies on her."

Mary narrowed her eyes. "Perry is a snake. Last year when I came back to town, he tried to kiss me in the harness shop."

Andrew sucked in a breath. "He did? Why didn't you tell me?"

"As I remember, you didn't like me all that much at the time."

"I loved you from the day I met you," Andrew said. It was true. Though he had resisted the thought of loving a girl who'd jumped the fence and gotten pregnant, Andrew had been smitten with Mary from the very beginning. Abraham had noticed it, even though he hadn't told anybody. Andrew took Mary's hand. "I'm going to talk to the bishop. Perry shouldn't get away with that."

"Don't worry," Mary said. "I smacked him across the face, and he ran away. He had a bruise for a week. I got real satisfaction out of that bruise."

"I'm glad you hit him," Abraham said. Perry Glick thought he could get away with bad behavior because his family was rich.

Mary sighed. "He's despicable, but he's not vicious. It's like Emma said. When any girl is nice to him, he thinks she likes him. I think he'd fooled himself into believing that since I was pregnant, I was willing. I showed him otherwise. You should warn Emma."

Abraham nodded. He'd promised himself he'd never speak to Emma again, but this was worth breaking his silence.

Abraham stood up. "I should get back. We're making peanut butter this afternoon."

Mary took ElJay and fixed her blanket around her legs. "Don't give up hope, Abraham. If Emma's not the girl for you, you'll find someone else. You just have to open your mouth."

"My foot tends to end up there when I open it."

Mary grinned. "Shoe leather doesn't taste very good."

Chapter Eight

Lizzy and Emma cleared the table together and found two dollars under one of the plates. A two-dollar tip for six people? Englischers could be so rude. And so cheap. She smiled in resignation and handed one of the dollars to Lizzy. "Go buy yourself something nice," she said.

Lizzy giggled. "A pen at the dollar store. Or a statue that says 'World's Best Teacher.' I can't believe it. I refilled their water glasses about six times."

The breakfast rush was over, but there were still four tables to bus and napkin dispensers to fill. Once the tables were clean, Emma would take her lunch break. Raymond let her eat breakfast leftovers for half price. She usually ended up bringing a sandwich from home. Even at half price, she couldn't afford to eat at Glick's Family Restaurant, especially if she kept getting two-dollar tips.

Somebody had left half a biscuit on his plate, and Emma put it in the special bag she used to collect treats for her chickens. Martha said it was okay, but they both kept it a secret from Raymond just in case he thought Emma should be paying for the table scraps too.

Her chickens loved bread. They had gobbled up some leftover French toast Abraham had brought over one day. Abraham was so smart with animals.

Emma pressed her lips together. She hadn't seen Abraham for over a week, not since the night of the gathering when he had played basketball until it was too dark to see the ball. He hadn't said hello to her, hadn't tried to join in any of her conversations, hadn't even made eye contact except that one time when she glanced at him and he quickly looked away. She had told herself she was relieved that he had left her alone, but by the end of the night she was kind of disappointed that he'd ignored her completely. Most of the boys, including Adam Stoltzfus, wanted to either play basketball or watch it, so there weren't that many boys to talk to. Some of the girls wandered over to watch the game, mostly because so many boys were over there, but Emma didn't dare join them. She didn't want Abraham to think she'd changed her mind about him. She couldn't let him ruin her chances with other boys.

But that was silly, and she knew it. Abraham had been offended when she even suggested he might be interested in her. He'd said he wasn't that stupid, which made her feel bad for the way she'd treated him in the past.

Instead, she played volleyball, ate cookies, and watched the basketball game out of the corner of her eye. Abraham was truly a wonder on the court. He could jump high enough to dunk the ball, and he was quick. Tyler Kaufmann could barely guard him.

She couldn't figure out why she was so disappointed after the gathering. Probably because

Abraham had drawn away all the fun boys to watch his game and there was no one left to talk to but Anna Schrock and Sadie Herschberger.

Why was she even thinking about Abraham Petersheim? He had brought her chickens cottage cheese and French toast and given them a dry place to roost, but he was just Abraham. He was tall and had muscles and nice teeth, but he wasn't any more special than two dozen other boys in the *gmayna*. Abraham was really nice, pleasant to be around, and he liked her chickens. He was completely harmless.

Emma groaned. They were out of napkins, and she'd have to get more from the storage room. She avoided the storage room whenever possible because Perry Glick, it seemed, had taken to living there. She'd go in, and he'd appear from behind one of the shelves and attempt to be charming and witty and funny, and he just ended up being pathetic and desperate. She was going to have to have a talk with him, like the one she'd had with Abraham. *I'm not interested, Perry. I will never, ever, ever be interested in you. Will you please quit lurking in the storage room and go back to your regular job, whatever it is?*

She glanced at Lizzy. There were still two tables to clean. She couldn't justify taking her into the storage room just for company.

The storage room door was open and the light was on, a sure sign that Perry was propped against one of the walls playing games on his phone. Would it be better to tiptoe or run as fast as she could? She opted for running. She knew exactly where the napkins were, and she could be in and out before Perry had a chance to turn off his game and slip his phone into his pocket.

Emma raced down the second aisle, and her heart sank. Oh, *sis yuscht*. It was a new box of napkins sealed tight with tape. She pulled a pen from her apron pocket, stabbed into the tape, and drew her pen down the seam. She'd almost finished when Perry came slinking around the corner. "*Hallo*, Emma."

Although she'd been expecting it, the anticipation had made her tense and she nearly jumped out of her skin. Her hand jerked upward, and the pen flew apart. The spring, ink cartridge, and cap clattered to the floor, and she was left trying to cut the tape with the empty pen barrel. She stood up straight and hid the remnants of her pen behind her back almost as if Perry had caught her doing something wrong.

"Is everything okay in here?" Abraham Peter-sheim, with his two cases of peanut butter, stood at the end of the aisle, eyeing Emma with concern.

Perry, who'd just gotten there himself, swiped his palms down the sides of his pants and shuffled past Abraham and his dolly without another word.

Emma clapped her hand over her mouth.

Abraham abandoned that dolly and was by her side in three brisk strides. "Did he hurt you? Are you all right?"

She couldn't hold it back any longer. Laughter burst from her lips like watermelon seeds in a spitting contest.

The look of sheer confusion on Abraham's face was priceless. He raised one eyebrow. "Are you okay?"

It was hard to talk between giggles, but Emma

couldn't stop laughing. She held up what was left of her pen. "My pen. My poor, innocent pen."

Abraham bent over and picked up the scattered parts. "It says 'Shawano Community Bank.'"

Emma tried to catch her breath. "They give them out free. And suckers too. They're cheap because they're free. Of course they're going to break. Time to start carrying a box cutter in my pocket." She was sure she wasn't making any sense, and Abraham must have thought she was terribly scatterbrained. He looked as if he might be ready to call an ambulance.

"But are you okay?"

Another fit of giggles. "Perry startled me, and I broke my pen, then you showed up and . . . and *ach*, the look on Perry's face. I think you surprised him even worse than he startled me."

"Did he hurt you?"

Why was he so concerned that she was hurt? She wasn't bleeding, she was on her feet, and she was laughing hysterically. "I'm fine, but I feel bad for my pen. I was only trying to open this box."

Abraham pulled out a pocketknife and made short work of the tape. He reached his hand into the box. "How many do you need?"

"Umm, two will be fine."

He pulled two packages of napkins from the box and handed them to her. "I'm *froh* you're safe."

She appreciated his concern, even if she had no idea why he was so concerned.

He pointed to the dolly full of peanut butter. "I have to take this invoice to Raymond, but then would you have a minute to talk?"

"Okay," she said, hoping he wouldn't hear the hesitation in her voice. She didn't think she'd have to tell him again that she wasn't interested, but she had no idea what he wanted, and she didn't like the thought of hurting his feelings again. "I was just about to eat my lunch. I'll meet you behind the restaurant as soon as the tables are clean."

Abraham nodded. Whatever he wanted to talk to her about, he was serious.

Lizzy had everything wiped down when Emma got back with the napkins. "I'm going to take lunch. Is that okay?"

"*Jah,*" Lizzy said. "I'll start the dishes."

Emma grabbed two empty plastic ten-gallon buckets and went outside. She beat Abraham because Raymond had to count every jar of peanut butter before he signed Abraham's invoice. Benji was right. For some roundabout reason, Raymond Glick did not like the Petersheims.

Abraham ambled out the back door, stuffing a piece of paper into his pocket. "Sorry to keep you waiting."

Emma overturned the buckets and motioned for Abraham to sit. "I thought we could sit here," she said. "It's not comfortable, especially for someone tall like you, but I didn't think Martha would appreciate if I dragged chairs from the restaurant."

She was joking, but he didn't seem to think it was funny. "I don't want anyone to get in trouble." He sort of folded himself onto the bucket. Maybe he'd be more comfortable standing after all. "I don't want you to worry. I won't take but three minutes." His gaze flicked around the back lot. It was bordered by a chain-link fence with an empty field on the other side. "I don't think anyone will see us together here, and if anyone walks by, I'll duck into the store."

Emma felt her face get warm. That was very nice of him to think of her feelings. And she was ashamed that he thought he had to sneak out back to have a conversation with her.

He drew his brows together. "Don't be mad, but I have to ask the question. It's none of my business, but you said you are interested in other boys. Are you interested in Perry Glick?"

That question probably should have offended her, but because she was already in a flighty mood, Emma giggled softly. "You think I'm interested in Perry Glick? He is the highest on my list of boys I'm not interested in."

"You have a list?"

Abraham was so earnest, she couldn't help but laugh again. "Of course I don't have a list. I'm not interested in Perry in the least. He thinks he's clever, and he . . . well, I'm not going to list all his qualities. You know what they are."

Abraham nodded. Everybody knew. "I hope that didn't embarrass you, but I didn't want to speak ill of him if you like him."

She should probably have been a little offended. How could Abraham think someone like her would ever be attracted to Perry Glick? But it was also sweet that he didn't want to say anything bad about a person she might like. "Okay?"

"My sister-in-law Mary wanted me to warn you."

"Mary?"

"*Jah.* I would have kept far away if Mary hadn't

asked me to talk to you, but once I've delivered my message, you don't have to worry. I won't bother you again."

Emma swallowed the lump in her throat. *Ach.* She had made a mess of things. Abraham had gotten the notion that he wasn't allowed to talk to her. "You're . . . you're not bothering me."

"Mary asked me to tell you, so I'm not breaking any confidences or telling something she doesn't want you to know. And I hope you don't think it's gossip. I heard it right from Mary." He shifted on his small, uncomfortable bucket. "Last summer, Perry Glick tried to kiss Mary in the harness shop. She slapped him, and he ran away."

Emma pressed her lips together. "That doesn't surprise me. It makes me mad, but I'm not surprised."

Abraham nodded. "*Jah.* Perry has a reputation. Since you're working here, Mary just wanted you to be careful, and when you told me he spies on you sometimes, I had to warn you."

Emma curled one side of her mouth. "Perry thinks very highly of himself, but he's mostly harmless."

"Probably."

"But *denki.* I will be careful." She grinned at Abraham. "Maybe I should bring my *dat*'s cattle prod to work."

He cracked a smile. "I'd feel better if you would."

She tapped on her chin with her finger and looked up into the sky. "If only a cattle prod would inspire people to give better tips."

Abraham laughed. "It couldn't hurt." He seemed to think better of laughing and closed his mouth.

"That's all I wanted to tell you." He stood up. "I will let you eat your lunch in peace now."

"Wait." Emma didn't know what she should say, but she wasn't going to let Abraham think he had to grovel in her presence. She pulled her slightly flat sandwich from her apron pocket. "It's peanut butter and honey. Do you want to share?"

Confusion flashed in his eyes. "*Nae, denki.* That's not even enough for you."

"I have a small appetite," she said, even though he knew differently. He'd seen her eat eight Pigs-in-a-Blanket the other night.

"I should get home."

She held up her bag and waved it back and forth like a clock pendulum. "It's Petersheim Brothers' Peanut Butter."

His confusion got deeper. "But. I don't want to bother you."

She blew a puff of air from between her lips. "Please sit, Abraham."

He did as he was told, probably because he was completely puzzled by her behavior. She pulled her sorry excuse for a sandwich out of the bag and gave him half. He nibbled on a corner and eyed her doubtfully. "Abraham, what do you want from me?"

He coughed on his bird-sized bite of sandwich. "Nothing."

"You don't even want to be my friend?"

He swallowed hard. "Why do you ask?"

"You know what I like about you?"

He frowned. "I can't think of anything you'd like about me."

Ach. She really had made a mess of things. "Well,

for one thing, you're wonderful *gute* at laying shingles." So good that she could watch him do it for hours.

Abraham squinted in her direction. "You don't owe me anything for that. I was happy to do it."

Emma sighed. "Abraham, when Benji told me you wanted to drive me home—"

"I didn't say that."

"I know. But when Benji said it, I sort of panicked because usually if I'm nice to a boy, he thinks I'm interested. Like Perry Glick."

"I'm nothing like Perry Glick."

"I know that too." She fingered the hair at the nape of her neck. At one time, she'd considered both Perry and Abraham "harmless." Abraham might be harmless, but he wasn't harmless in the irritating way Perry was harmless. Perry thought of himself as charming and clever and attractive. He wasn't any of those things, and nobody took him seriously. Truth be told, nobody liked him, because he thought so highly of himself.

Abraham was harmless in that he didn't try to force himself where he wasn't wanted. He didn't like to be the center of attention, and he didn't ever steal the attention from anyone else. He played basketball or volleyball at gatherings, but he didn't have to win and he didn't hog the ball, even though he was probably the best player in the whole county. When they had a gathering at the park, Abraham would often spend the whole time playing basketball—and if no one wanted to play with him, he played by himself. It seemed he found happiness in doing what he liked without having to impress anyone else.

Maybe Abraham wasn't harmless. Maybe he was meek.

There was a lot to like about someone who was as meek as Abraham.

She took a bite of her sandwich. Petersheim Brothers' Peanut Butter was truly delicious. "Can we be friends?"

Abraham finished off his half of the sandwich and folded his arms. His folded arms accentuated his nice biceps. "I don't understand."

"Now that I know you don't expect anything from me, I thought maybe we could just be friends."

"Okay," he said. It was definitely a question.

"Which means you don't have to worry you're bothering me if you want to say hello."

"Okay." Still a question.

"Do you *want* to be my friend?"

To her surprise, he hesitated. "I don't know."

Not what she expected. She was a nice girl. Didn't everybody want to be her friend? She caught her bottom lip between her teeth. She hadn't treated Abraham very well. She hadn't been mean to him, but she certainly hadn't gone out of her way to be nice. Why would Abraham want to be friends with her? "*Ach*," she said. "Okay." Should she give him a day or two to think about it?

He leaned forward and propped his elbows on his knees. "I guess I could be your friend, but I don't want to embarrass you in front of your other friends. I'm not clever, and I never say the right thing."

The knot in Emma's stomach untied itself. "Is that all? You don't have to hang out with me and my friends at the park or anything like that."

His expression relaxed a little. "I'd embarrass you."

"You wouldn't."

He nodded. "Okay. I guess we can be friends."

"But when you come to gatherings, you at least need to say hello to me."

"Is it okay if I just wave?"

"*Jah.* But don't ignore me," she said.

"It's okay if you ignore me. I know you're interested in other boys."

"That's wonderful nice of you, Abraham, but what kind of friend would I be if I ignored you?"

He got a funny look on his face, then stood up and shook out his feet. That bucket wasn't comfortable for long legs. "I should go now. *Denki* for the sandwich."

"*Denki* for the warning." She gave him her most grateful smile. He nodded and smiled back, but the smile didn't quite reach his eyes. What was he unhappy about? Was he worried about Perry or about being her friend?

Was he just being nice when he had agreed to be her friend?

That thought troubled her for the rest of the day.

After the lunch rush, Emma wiped down tables while Lizzy refilled the ketchup and mustard, and the salt and pepper. The bell over the door rang, and Alfie and Benji Petersheim walked into the restaurant and looked around as if they'd never been out in public before. Alfie caught sight of Emma and nudged Benji, who was carrying a paper bag dotted with grease.

"*Hallo*, Emma," Alfie said.

Emma set her rag on the table. "Did you boys come for supper?"

Benji handed Emma the paper bag. "Abraham made these and asked us to bring them over. He said he ate half your lunch."

Emma peeked in the bag. There were at least half a dozen Pigs-in-a-Blanket in there. Her heart did a little skip. "*Ach.* He didn't have to do that."

"He likes doing stuff for you," Alfie said.

Benji pulled three napkins from the nearest dispenser. "Here you go."

Emma couldn't help but smile. "*Denki.* I will eat them as soon as I clean up. I get off work in ten minutes."

"If you come over tonight, Mamm will make popcorn," Benji said.

Alfie beamed. "And Mammi will cancel family reading time."

"I'm afraid I can't come over tonight," Emma said, hoping the boys wouldn't need any more of an explanation than that.

Of course she was wrong. "Why not?" Alfie said.

"I just can't. But will you tell Abraham *denki* for me?"

Alfie scrunched his lips together and slid his hands in his pockets. "You could tell him yourself if you came over tonight."

"You tell him for me."

Alfie and Benji glanced at each other. Benji shrugged. "Okay. See you later."

The boys strolled out the door, and Emma went to the window to see where they went. Had they walked all the way here?

A buggy was parked a hundred feet down the street, and Abraham sat in the front with his hat pulled over his face like he didn't want to be recognized. Like he didn't want any of the other boys to know he and Emma were friends.

She truly didn't know how she felt about that.

Chapter Nine

"Is she here yet? Over."

Benji's voice crackled over the walkie-talkie. "*Nae.* But a bus just stopped at the end of the road. I think it's hers. Spatula."

Alfie rolled his eyes, even though there was no one up in the tree with him to see it. "Benji, you're supposed to say 'over' when you're done talking on the walkie-talkie, not 'spatula.' Over." Benji used to say "pancake" instead of "spatula" but the word lost its excitement after Mammi made zucchini pancakes for breakfast one morning. Alfie shifted his position in the tree. The leaves rustled on the end of the branch.

"Spatula is my favorite word," Benji said. "It sounds like I'm speaking a different language. Spatula."

"Okay, okay, just watch for Emma and keep quiet. Over."

Benji, of course, did not follow directions. "I still don't like this."

Alfie paused, but Benji didn't say anything else. "Benji, you're supposed to say 'spatula' so I know you're done. Over."

"I thought you wanted me to say 'over.' And Tintin is just a poor, innocent dog. Spatula."

Alfie tried not to growl. "Can we talk about this later? Over."

"We never talk about it later. Spatula."

"Is she coming yet? Over."

A long pause. Benji was probably watching ants crawl along the road. "*Jah.* Lizzy and her are walking down the road. Spatula."

Alfie's heart jumped like a skater bug. "Go to radio silence." "Radio silence" was something he'd learned from Willie Glick. It meant you don't talk or someone might catch you spying on them. Alfie stuffed his walkie-talkie into his pocket and wrapped his fingers around the binoculars hanging from his neck. Dawdi had let them borrow his hunting binoculars for their important spy work, and he hadn't told anyone. Dawdi mostly couldn't talk, so he was good at keeping secrets. Alfie pressed the binoculars to his eyes and focused on Emma's chicken coop. He could see okay except when his eyelashes got in the way. There were Emma's chickens, scratching in the dirt. There was the big pile of dog poop right in the middle of the chicken run where Emma would see it.

His walkie-talkie crackled. Oh, *sis yuscht.* He should have turned it off. Benji could not be trusted with radio silence. "She just went in the house. Spatula."

Alfie let the binoculars dangle from his neck long enough to turn off his walkie-talkie. If Benji tried to contact him again, the walkie-talkie would give away Alfie's position. Benji was a *gute* partner, but he didn't know anything about spying.

Alfie put the binoculars up to his eyes again and

held his breath as Emma walked out her back door and strolled to the chicken coop. She had a little bowl of something orange in her hand, but Alfie couldn't tell what it was. She opened the gate, stepped into the chicken run, and stopped. Her back was to him, but Alfie could tell she was looking right at the pile of poop. She turned her face to the sky and stomped her foot. "Abraham Petersheim!" she yelled.

Alfie lowered his binoculars and grinned. It was a job well done.

Dawdi was getting a little better every day. He still needed to use a walker, but he could walk from the bedroom to the kitchen table without any help. It took him about five minutes, but at least he could support his own weight and put one foot in front of the other.

Abraham helped Dawdi with his exercises every morning, and even though progress was slow, they could all see it. Everybody wanted Dawdi to get better, and Mamm probably secretly wanted Mammi out of her house.

Mammi was slicing a loaf of her famous home-made bread in the kitchen while Mamm stirred spaghetti sauce on the stove. Poor Mamm! She liked having her kitchen to herself, especially when she prepared dinner, but Mammi wanted to be helpful. When she and Dawdi had moved in, she had tried to take control of the kitchen. For a few months, the kitchen had felt like a war zone, Mamm and Mammi each trying to gain the advantage, each wanting to run the kitchen her own way. Mamm had never lost her temper with Mammi, but Abraham was sure he had seen steam puffing out of Mamm's ears every day around five o'clock. Mamm ended up winning the kitchen battle in the end because Mammi was too busy with Dawdi to take over the kitchen completely. But she still made her presence felt around dinnertime.

"Rebecca," Mammi said, "why aren't you using that new Italian spice blend I bought? They had samples at the store, and your spaghetti would taste a hundred times better if you used it."

Mamm kept stirring her spaghetti sauce with no attempt to explain herself. "Truer words were never spoken," she said, which was what she said to Mammi every time she didn't want to give her an answer but couldn't just say nothing.

Abraham looked at the clock. Five minutes before dinnertime, and Alfie and Benji had disappeared. If they didn't hurry, Mamm would venture into the woods to find them and surely find the dog. Mamm usually sent Austin or Abraham to summon the twins to dinner, but when she needed a break from Mammi, she went herself. Of course, if she wasn't here to guard her spaghetti sauce, Mammi might take dinner into her own hands.

Alfie and Benji burst into the kitchen like two tornadoes, threw open the basement door, and clomped down the stairs without saying a word. It looked as if Alfie was hiding something bulky under his shirt, and Benji's pockets were bulging.

"Benji! Alfie!" Mamm yelled. "You get back here and give your family a proper greeting."

Alfie yelled something back, but no one understood what he said.

By the time Abraham got Dawdi settled in his chair, Alfie and Benji were back with flat pockets and nothing under their shirts.

Mamm turned around and propped a hand on her hip. "You boys need to apologize to your *mammi* and *dawdi* for the rude way you entered the house."

Mammi folded her hands over her stomach and looked at the boys with a scold in her expression. "Well-behaved little boys walk quietly into the house and beg pardon being late." She glanced at Mamm as if to scold her for raising such rowdy boys.

"We're not late," Alfie said, pointing to the clock. "Two minutes to spare."

Mammi gasped and looked at Mamm.

Mamm huffed out a breath, which came out more like a sigh. "Don't argue with your *mammi*, young man."

Mammi reached underneath the sink and pulled out the spray bottle of rose water. "Come here, Alfie, Benji. You stink like pond slime and wet dog. What have you been doing out there?"

The twins knew better than to complain about Mammi's rose water. She sprayed it on their necks twice a day because she said they smelled bad. Sometimes Abraham got sprayed too, but he showered every day, sometimes with Mammi's special soap, and that was usually good enough for her.

Alfie and Benji slouched over to Mammi and valiantly took their sprays of rose water. With Mammi, it was better to surrender, because if you didn't, you might get something even smellier the next time.

Dat came in even later than Benji and Alfie, but Mammi never scolded him. He was her favorite person in the house, probably including Dawdi. Dat smiled at Mammi, patted Dawdi's shoulder, and gave Mamm a peck on the cheek. "It smells *appeditlich*, Rebecca," he said. He washed his hands and sat down at the table next to Dawdi with Mammi on his other side. Together, they helped Dawdi eat.

Benji washed his hands while Alfie opened up the fridge and gazed inside.

"Shut the fridge," Mamm said. "You don't need to cool the whole kitchen."

"There's nothing to eat in this house," Alfie said.

Mamm raised a sharp eyebrow. "Nothing to eat? If you'll walk three feet to the north, you'll find spaghetti on the table."

Mammi huffed out a breath. "If you used my spices, the boys would eat better."

"Truer words were never spoken," Mamm said.

"I mean treats," Alfie said. "Emma's coming over tonight, and we need treats."

The serving bowl of spaghetti clattered to the table. "Emma's coming over?" Mamm smoothed her hands down her apron. "Why didn't you say so? Somebody should have told me." She eyed Abraham as if to accuse him, but he just shrugged his shoulders and tried to look uninterested, even though his heart jumped into his throat and nearly choked him.

"She's probably coming," Benji said, nodding vigorously at Alfie. "And we need treats."

Mamm folded her arms across her chest. She wasn't going to get worked up about a visit from Emma until she was sure it was going to happen. The twins weren't the most reliable messengers. *"Probably?"*

Alfie glared at Benji, then smiled at Mamm. "She's coming. You need to make something delicious."

Austin beamed in Abraham's direction. "I guess she got over being mad about her chickens."

Alfie tried to look sufficiently dejected. "And we'll have to cancel family reading time."

Mammi pressed her lips together. "We've canceled too many family reading times. It is wonderful important to your religious education, and sometimes I feel like I'm the only one who takes it seriously."

"Truer words were never spoken," Mamm said.

"I take it seriously," Dat said, which was one of the reasons he was Mammi's favorite. "*Martyrs Mirror* inspires me every time I read it."

"But don't you think if Emma comes over, we should play games or tell stories?"

Tell stories? Mamm was grasping at straws. There was only one reason Emma would come to their house, and it had nothing to do with wanting to spend time with the Petersheim family. Tintin had made trouble in Emma's coop again. And the boys knew about it.

"Playing games will not make your sons better men, Rebecca."

For some strange reason, Mamm switched into her "nice" voice. "For Abraham's sake, I think we should play games and have treats. Don't you, Martha?"

Mammi opened her mouth—probably to protest—then glanced at Abraham and smiled as if she was in on some secret he wasn't. "Scrabble is a *gute* game. It teaches spelling."

Abraham groaned inwardly. Even at the risk of bringing back family reading time, he'd have to set Mamm and Mammi straight or they'd never give him any peace. "Mamm, Emma is a wonderful *gute* girl, but she's not interested in me."

Still the "nice" voice. "I love that you're so humble, but why would she come over if she's not interested? I saw her looking at you in *gmay* last week."

Abraham didn't know whether to laugh or growl. If Emma had been caught looking in his direction, it was only because he had sat between Matt Gingerich and Tyler Kaufmann during services. Abraham tried to let Mamm down as gently as possible. Mamm was so eager to get Abraham married off, and he felt bad for dashing her hopes. Just one more sign he didn't deserve Emma. He couldn't even make his *mater* happy. "Emma told me she's not interested," he said, a little more forcefully than he'd intended. "She just wants to be friends."

A frown settled into Mamm's face. "Friends? Are you sure?"

Abraham nodded, too embarrassed to actually speak. How could Mamm put him through this?

Mamm got that determined look on her face, like she wasn't going to take no for an answer. "Well, we'll just have to change her mind. I'll make caramel popcorn."

"I have a wonderful *gute* apple cake recipe," Mammi said.

Mamm sat down at the table. "I don't have any apples."

Mammi tucked Dawdi's napkin into his collar. "What about oatmeal cake?"

"*Ach,* I love oatmeal cake," Mamm said. "Your recipe is delicious."

It seemed nothing could bring two women together like the thought of getting Abraham married off. Mamm lost that slightly annoyed look she usually wore when Mammi was around, and as soon as silent prayer was over, Mamm and Mammi started talking over their favorite dessert recipes. If someone didn't stop them, they'd bake a dozen desserts and Emma wouldn't even come over.

Abraham wasn't going to say any more about it. He was already embarrassed enough that Emma wasn't interested in him. It would be complete humiliation to try to explain to Mamm why her son was such a failure.

Abraham wanted to crawl under the table and pretend he couldn't hear Mamm and Mammi talking about scones with honey butter. Emma didn't really want to be friends. That was just something girls told boys to make them feel better about themselves, but it wasn't ever true. Emma felt sorry for him. Her pity was written all over her face. Abraham felt it clear down to his bones. He needed to work on being less pathetic.

After dinner, Mammi and Mamm decided to make caramel popcorn and snickerdoodles—snacks you could eat while you played games. Alfie and Benji were going to be in big trouble if Emma didn't show up. They were also going to be in big trouble if Emma did show up. What had happened with her chickens, and how was Abraham going to fix it?

A few minutes after six, a knock at the door sent everybody but Dawdi and Abraham scrambling. Mammi was just pulling the last of the cookies from the oven, and Mamm gave a little squeak as she picked up the bowl of caramel popcorn and hugged it. Even Austin seemed excited, as if all the girls in the *gmayna* were on the porch. Benji and Alfie raced to the door and momentarily fought over who would get to open it. Alfie finally won out because Benji decided it was more important to be the first to greet whoever was at the door than to actually open it.

Abraham was in the kitchen polishing the table legs with Orange Glo, because he'd been meaning to get to that for months. He tried his best not to be interested in who was at the door. It might be Emma, but she just wanted to be his friend, and he wasn't about to be that pathetic.

"Abraham," Mamm hissed. "Get up off that floor. You're going to get your pants dirty."

Abraham knew for a fact he wasn't going to get his pants dirty, because he'd carefully swept the floor only minutes earlier.

Mammi shook her head at Mamm. "*Nae*," she whispered. "Girls like it when boys do chores. Let Emma see him working."

Abraham stood up so fast, he bumped his head on the table. He didn't care what Emma thought and wouldn't do anything that might be interpreted as trying to impress her.

Benji strolled into the kitchen as if he had nothing better to do, as if somebody wasn't waiting at the front door. "Abraham, Emma wants to talk to you. Out on the porch."

Mamm seemed to think this was a good thing. She burst into a smile. "Go, Abraham, and be sure to invite her in for cookies and popcorn."

Abraham wasn't planning on doing any such thing, though Mamm would have killed him if she'd known. Inviting Emma in would seem pathetic. He was done being pathetic.

To his surprise, Emma and her sister Lizzy were both

standing on the porch. Lizzy was a cute, energetic girl, who seemed to like everybody and have fun just being herself. She was a lot like Emma. Abraham's heart twisted. It didn't matter what Emma was like.

Emma draped her arm around Lizzy's shoulder. "I hope you don't mind. I brought Lizzy. She wanted to know where I was going so I told her about the dog."

Lizzy nodded earnestly. "I hope it's okay. I won't tell anyone."

At this point, Abraham didn't care who knew about Tintin. Alfie and Benji were careless. They were going to learn a hard lesson. "What did Tintin do?"

Emma did not look happy. "I'm sorry to have to say the word, but there was a big pile of dog poop in the chicken run when I got home from work today."

Abraham couldn't blame her for being upset. "I'm wonderful sorry, Emma. It would be a shame if anything happened to your hens. What do you want me to do? I hate to send Tintin to the pound, but we have to keep your chickens safe."

"*Ach*, don't send him to the pound," Lizzy said. "That would be cruel."

Emma's look sent warmth pulsing through his veins all the way down to his toes. "*Denki* for caring about my chickens, but Lizzy is right. We can't send Tintin to the pound. He's cute, and we can't blame him for behaving like a dog. Alfie and Benji need to watch him more carefully. That's all I'm asking for."

Abraham slid his hands into his pockets. "We need to come up with a harsher punishment so they're more careful with Tintin."

"Like what?" Emma said.

"Coming over in the evenings to clean the chicken

coop got them out of family reading time. We can't do that again."

An idea lit up Lizzy's face. "What if they came over on Saturdays and worked in our garden? Mamm would love it."

"They'd have to do their own chores here first," Abraham said.

Emma grinned. "All the better. We'll wear them out, and they'll think twice about being careless with Tintin."

It was a *gute* plan. "Okay. I'll send them over Saturday after their chores are done."

"You could come too," Emma said, looking down at her hands.

Abraham's heart skipped a beat until he remembered Emma thought he was pathetic. She only wanted him to come so he could keep an eye on the boys. "I guess it would be best so I can supervise them."

Lizzy's eyes sparkled. "*Ach*, we can supervise them ourselves."

"Of course we can," Emma said, giving her sister a look Abraham couldn't begin to understand. "I just thought it would be nice if you wanted to come over. And maybe talk about chickens and peanut butter and other stuff."

Did she feel sorry for him? Obligated to invite him? "Umm, I don't know."

"You said we could be friends," Emma prodded.

Abraham didn't know what to say. *I didn't think you really meant it* didn't seem very nice and maybe would sound a little pouty.

If he wanted to be less pathetic, not being pouty was a *gute* first step. "Okay. I will come."

He didn't expect the wide smile Emma gave him. "*Gute.* We'll get those twins whipped into shape." Emma seemed at a loss for words, which wasn't like her at all. She cleared her throat. "*Denki* for the Pigs-in-a-Blanket. I was starving after lunch."

"I thought you would be."

Alfie and Benji came storming out of the house. Alfie grabbed Emma's arm, and Benji pulled on Lizzy's apron. "Can you come in and play games?" Benji said. "Mammi made snickerdoodles, and Mamm made caramel popcorn and lemonade."

Lemonade? Mamm must be desperate.

Lizzy glanced at Emma. "What games?"

Alfie pulled on Emma's arm. "Anything Emma wants to play. That's what Mamm said."

"Alfie, quit hanging on Emma."

Alfie let go of Emma and grabbed onto Abraham's arm. "We really want Emma to come in."

Benji looked up at Lizzy with those big, wide eyes of his. He was cute, but it was all an act. "If you say yes, we get to skip family reading time."

Lizzy melted at Benji's pitiful expression. "What is family reading time?"

Alfie swiped the back of his hand across his nose. "It's when Mammi makes us read boring books like *Martyrs Mirror* and the Holy Bible."

"Oh," Lizzy said, obviously not quite sure how to respond to Alfie calling the Bible boring. She looked at Emma. "It's up to you, but I think it would be cruel to make the boys do family reading time when they could be playing Life on the Farm."

Alfie nodded enthusiastically. "I love Life on the Farm."

"I like it too," Emma said.

Benji shook his head. "Abraham hates that game."

Alfie lightly shoved Benji away from Lizzy, like he hoped if he did it gently enough no one would notice. "Benji, if Emma wants to play Life on the Farm, then we're going to play Life on the Farm."

Abraham seriously disliked Life on the Farm, but Benji should keep his mouth shut. He'd play anything if Emma agreed to stay.

Emma hesitated, probably thinking up a reason they couldn't stay. Abraham tried not to let it upset him. She wanted to be friends, but not close friends or *gute* friends. Emma glanced at Lizzy, then smiled so brightly, Abraham could have read by the light of it. "We would love to stay, if it's not too much trouble."

"No trouble at all," Alfie said, as if he was in charge of game night.

Alfie and Benji led the way into the house. Mamm popped out of the kitchen with her bowl of popcorn still cradled in her arms. She'd been waiting for them. "Emma and Lizzy, how nice of you to come."

Dawdi was comfortably settled on the sofa with a blanket around his legs. Mammi sat next to him with a plate of snickerdoodles in her lap. She probably felt the need to guard them from Alfie and Benji before games started. Austin leaned against the wall between the kitchen and the living room, grinning like a mischievous cat. Great. Everybody was in on the joke. Abraham wouldn't have minded it so much if the joke hadn't been on him.

Mamm set the bowl of popcorn on the coffee table in the living room. "I was just telling Martha that I can't remember the last time we had a game night. You inspired us."

Mamm was a sensible kind of person who said what she thought and couldn't abide nonsense from anyone. Abraham had always liked that about her. But right now she was using her "nice" voice. She was wonderful eager to get Abraham married. He should have been offended that she didn't think he could do it himself, but he mostly felt sad that her efforts were wasted on Emma. Emma wasn't interested, and that was that.

It wasn't like any girl was ever going to be interested in Abraham. And being a bachelor sounded a lot better than getting his heart broken.

"*Denki* for inviting us," Emma said. "Mamm and Dat are at my *bruder* Peter's tonight with the grandchildren."

"*Cum*," Mamm said. "Sit, and we'll decide on a game. What do you like to play?"

Dawdi and Mammi and the boys sat on the sofa. Mamm had pulled four chairs from the kitchen, and she motioned for Emma and Lizzy to sit in the comfortable chairs. Dat, Austin, and Mamm took the hard chairs. The only chair left for Abraham was the kitchen chair next to Emma. Had his family planned that? Of course they'd planned it, but Abraham wasn't going to make a fuss about it. Let Mamm and Mammi and everybody else scheme all they wanted. It wouldn't get them anywhere.

But Abraham had to admit it was nice to sit next to Emma.

Ach. It was really going to hurt when Emma got tired of being his friend. Or got married. Really going to hurt a lot.

Benji took Dawdi's hand. "Emma likes Life on the Farm," he said.

Mamm's face lit up. "You do?" Life on the Farm was a boring game, but it could also last for hours. Mamm was hoping for a long game night.

Emma smiled. "I do like Life on the Farm, but Benji said Abraham doesn't like it. Let's play something else."

Well. That was nice.

"I don't know why Abraham doesn't like that game," Mamm said, losing the nice voice and sounding more like herself. "He almost always wins."

"I like Pictionary," Lizzy said.

Emma eyed Abraham. "Do you like Pictionary?"

Abraham loved Pictionary, but he'd rather nibble on his toenails than put any pressure on Emma to play it. "What do you want to play?"

Emma grinned. "It's very nice of you to ask. My *bruder* doesn't ask. We always have to play what he wants."

Abraham tried not to smile too wide. He'd actually said the right thing for once. Could that moment be repeated?

"What are your favorite games?" Emma said. "I'll tell you what mine are and then we all can pick. I like Sorry, Clue, Rook, and Pictionary and Scrabble."

"Scrabble is good for Alfie's growing brain," Mammi said. Apparently, Benji didn't need any help in that area.

"And I like Settlers of Catan," Emma said.

"Let's play that," Mamm said. Another long one. Emma and Lizzy might be here until nine, way past the twins' bedtime. When Mamm got an idea in her head, there was no talking her out of it.

"Let's play Pictionary," Austin said. "Settlers is too long. We don't want Emma and Lizzy to fall asleep."

Emma looked at Abraham and smiled. She was going to have to stop doing that or he wouldn't be able to think straight for the game. "Do you like Pictionary?"

"I love it. But I don't want you to feel like you have to play it just because I like it."

"I love it too," Emma said, "even though I'm a terrible artist. My team usually loses."

Austin laughed. "Abraham is the best artist in the family. You two can be on the same team and cancel each other out."

Mamm was probably the happiest person in the whole world at that moment. "What a *gute* idea."

She was going to be very disappointed when Emma married someone else. *Ach, vell.* There was nothing Abraham could do about that. Might as well have fun while Emma was here. There would be plenty of time to wallow in what might have been.

Lizzy and Austin were on the same team with Mamm, Dat, and Alfie. Benji was on Abraham's team, and he liked to explain what he was drawing while he drew it. More than once, Alfie called him out for cheating, but nobody really minded that Benji had to narrate his pictures. He was wonderful cute, and nobody could guess his words anyway.

It turned out that Emma was a terrible artist but a very *gute* guesser, which came in handy when Mammi was up to draw for their team. Mammi started every one of her drawings with a circle, and Emma was very persistent at guessing.

When it was Mammi's turn for the third time, she drew her circle, and Emma started calling out guesses. "Egg? Waffle? Breakfast cereal?"

"*Jah!*" Mammi said, clapping her hands in delight. "I knew you'd get that one."

"You draw very well," Emma said.

Abraham wiped his hand across his mouth to keep from laughing. Mammi didn't draw well at all, but Emma was kind and patient and didn't care who won, just as long as everyone had a *gute* time, even Mammi.

Mammi put down her pencil. "I feel like we have a connection. You're young, but you understand me."

When it was Abraham's turn to draw, he got *banana boat*. He drew a crescent for the banana and a crescent for the boat. Before he could draw sails, Emma had guessed it.

"Banana boat!"

How did she do that?

Maybe they had a connection too. Abraham's heart swelled like a river in a flood.

He swallowed hard and came back to reality. If it was a connection, it was one-sided.

The Pictionary game ended in a tie. The cookies and the popcorn were gone except for the kernels in the bottom of the bowl. Alfie scooped up a handful, sucked off the leftover caramel, and spit them back into the bowl.

"Alfie Petersheim," Mamm said. "That is terribly rude. Take that bowl into the kitchen and dump the rest of the popcorn into the garbage."

"But, Mamm."

"It has your spit all over it."

Alfie stood and dragged his feet across the floor. "I didn't want to waste any. You always say to finish our dinner."

"You know better, young man."

Alfie came back to the living room carrying a stack of napkins. "Does anyone want a napkin? That popcorn was sticky."

Mamm raised her eyebrows. "I just don't understand what goes on in that head of yours. One minute you're spitting in the popcorn bowl. The next you're doing something thoughtful."

Benji nodded. "Alfie's wonderful nice to kids at school and animals. Tintin loves him."

Abraham held his breath. Emma's gaze flicked in his direction.

Alfie turned on his heels and pinned Benji with the stinkiest stink eye ever seen. "Benji!" he snapped. *Ach, vell.* He was nine years old and couldn't be expected to be discreet.

Mamm pursed her lips and drew her brows together. "Alfie, come here." Alfie clamped his mouth shut and took the long four steps to Mamm's side. Mamm took his chin in her hand and turned his face one way and then the other. "What have you done to your eyelashes?"

Alfie looked momentarily confused, then utter relief traveled across his face. Mamm hadn't noticed Benji's little mention of Tintin, or if she had, she hadn't thought anything of it. She obviously had something else on her mind. "My eyelashes?"

"*Jah.* What happened to them?"

"I cut them." Alfie touched his eyelid, as if to make sure they were still gone.

Abraham looked closer. He hadn't noticed until now, but Alfie's beautiful long eyelashes were now stubs.

Mamm raise an eyebrow. "You cut them?"

"They were getting in the way."

Mamm raised the other eyebrow. "Getting in the way of what?"

Alfie put both hands behind his back as if to hide something. "Things."

Benji had an explanation for everything. Sort of. "He can't tell you because it's a secret, but it's for a really important plan."

It wasn't like Mamm, but she seemed to accept Benji's answer and didn't press for more. "And when did you cut your eyelashes?"

"Right after dinner. I didn't want to forget."

"You didn't want to forget?" Mamm pushed her glasses up her nose, which was usually a sign she was preparing to explode. She didn't disappoint. "You could have poked your eye out. Did you think of that?"

"I didn't use scissors."

Mamm narrowed her eyes. "You didn't use scissors?"

"I used the fingernail clippers."

This was probably the wrong thing to say. "The fingernail clippers? You could have blinded yourself. You could have poked a hole right through your sinuses. Did you even think of that?"

"What are sinuses?" Alfie said.

"Don't change the subject, young man. Do you know what this means? You won't be able to sit around a campfire for weeks. Things will drop from the sky and fall in your eyes, and you won't be able to do a thing about it."

"I don't think that's a real thing," Alfie said, because he couldn't just keep his mouth shut.

A blood vessel bulged in Mamm's neck. "For sure

and certain, it's a thing. Did you trim your eyelashes in the bathroom?"

"I suppose," Alfie said, not wanting to commit until he heard what Mamm had to say.

"You go up there and clean all that hair out of the sink right now, young man. And if I so much as find one eyelash on the counter, you will clean the toilet every day for two weeks."

Benji frowned. "But what if it's not Alfie's eyelash? Sometimes my eyelashes fall in the bathroom. And sometimes Austin's do too. I find his eyelashes in there all the time."

Emma hid a smile behind her hand. Abraham bit the side of his cheek to keep from laughing. Just how many eyelashes did Benji notice on a regular basis? It sounded like Austin was pretty untidy with his eyelashes.

Mamm wasn't impressed with Benji's questions. "Go up and clean that bathroom and think on your sins, young man. And never cut your eyelashes again without my permission. Do you understand?"

She probably didn't have to add "without my permission." It went without saying that Alfie should never cut his eyelashes again under any circumstances.

Emma looked like she was having a hard time containing a smile. She finally gave up. "Lizzy and I should get going. *Denki* for inviting us over."

Mamm's indignation came to rest right there on the sofa. "*Ach.* You girls are welcome anytime."

"I'll walk you home," Abraham said.

Emma tied her bonnet under her chin. "We'll be okay."

Abraham shook his head. "I'm still walking you home. It's dark."

"Of course Abraham will walk you home. I taught him better than to let you walk alone." Mamm followed them out to the porch. "What do you girls like to eat, and I'll be sure to make it next time."

Lizzy giggled. "We like everything, except I don't like mustard, peas, rice, cherries, or broccoli."

Mamm seemed to take Lizzy's list very seriously. "I'll remember. What about you, Emma?"

"*Ach.* I like everything. I just like to eat."

Emma liked food. Abraham loved that about her.

It was really going to hurt when she didn't want to be his friend anymore.

Chapter Ten

"Mamm," Alfie called up the stairs. "Can we go outside with Dawdi?"

"Put a blanket around his legs," Mamm called back.

Yesss! Now all they needed to do was get away from the house unseen, and if they got in trouble, they could honestly say Mamm had given them permission.

Mammi and Dat had gone to Walmart in Shawano, and Austin and Abraham were off doing whatever it was older boys did in their spare time. There would never be a better time to carry out their plan.

Dawdi was already in his wheelchair, because it was easier for Mamm to take him to the bathroom, even though he was pretty *gute* at walking two or three steps by himself. Alfie moved the rug by the front door so the wheels wouldn't get caught on it, then grabbed one of Dawdi's handlebars. Benji took the other one and together they pushed Dawdi's wheelchair out the front door and onto the porch. Benji tucked the blanket around Dawdi's legs. "Are you ready, Dawdi?"

Dawdi smiled and nodded his head, which meant "Let's go!" At least that's what Benji said it meant, and Benji understood Dawdi's signals better than anyone else in the family.

Alfie had borrowed a big sheet of plywood from the barn. As fast as they could, they laid the wood over the top of the steps and wheeled Dawdi down the homemade ramp. He nearly fell out of the wheelchair when they hit a big bump at the bottom, but Benji grabbed Dawdi's shoulder and pulled him back. "You okay, Dawdi?"

A low gurgle came from deep in Dawdi's throat. Alfie glanced at Benji. Benji smiled. "He's laughing. He likes it."

Alfie didn't know if that was really true, but now was not a good time to question Benji's decoding skills. They'd gotten Dawdi down the steps. The hard part was over. Now all they had to do was push his wheelchair into the woods to Tintin's hideout. Easy.

Alfie glanced back at the house as they pushed Dawdi around the side yard and across the lawn. Mamm probably wouldn't come out to check on them anytime soon. When she got sewing, it was like she didn't notice anything, not even the spider bite Alfie got from sleeping in the cellar last night. Abraham had to marry Emma soon or Alfie would probably be dead by July.

They got to the end of the grass, pushed past the hard dirt at the edge of the garden, and then nudged the wheelchair into the woods on the little path that led to Tintin's house. Alfie pushed with all his might. Benji's face was red. They'd made it about five feet into the trees when they had to stop to rest.

"It's too hard," Benji said, panting as if he'd just

run all the way from Bienenstock. "I don't think the wheelchair was built for going on a trip to the woods."

Alfie would not accept defeat. Dawdi wanted to meet Tintin. They couldn't disappoint him. "Go get the wagon, Benji. We can put Dawdi in the wagon and take him to the hideout."

"*Nae.* The wagon is smaller than the wheelchair, and Dawdi can't hold on."

Alfie took Dawdi's hand. "Could you walk? Benji can get your walker."

Dawdi smiled and looked down the trail. "*Nae*, Allie."

That's what Dawdi called Alfie. *Allie.* It sounded like a girl's name, but Dawdi was still learning to talk. Alfie tried to be patient when Dawdi called him a girl.

"Here," Benji said. "If we push him behind this tree, Mamm can't see us and we can bring Tintin to Dawdi."

Alfie frowned. "I don't know. We've never brought Tintin so close to the house before."

"But Dawdi wants to meet him. He loves dogs."

Dawdi never lost that smile. "Dog."

Alfie's mouth fell open. "Hey. He said 'dog.'"

"I know," Benji said. "And he said 'cat' once when we were sitting on the sofa reading the Bible together. He knows lots of words."

They pushed Dawdi's wheelchair behind a big tree in between two bushes. Mamm wouldn't be able to see them even if she looked out the window at this very spot. They straightened Dawdi in his chair and fixed his blanket. "Okay, Benji. Go get Tintin. And don't let him bark. Mamm will hear."

Benji took off like a shot down the little trail. Benji was a *gute* partner most of the time. He followed directions and didn't lollygag. Now was no time for lollygagging.

"We used your binoculars to spy on Emma," Alfie said. "They don't work very well with long eyelashes, but Mamm won't let me cut mine again."

"Emma," Dawdi said.

"Hey! You said 'Emma.'"

Dawdi nodded.

Benji came down the trail holding tightly to Tintin's leash, but he wasn't running, because Tintin barked if you ran with him. Benji was smart that way. "Dawdi, this is Tintin," Benji said. "He is a wonderful *gute* dog. He likes oatmeal."

Dawdi held out his hand, and Tintin licked Dawdi's fingers. "He likes you, Dawdi."

"*Jah,*" Dawdi said.

Benji ran his hand all the way down Tintin's back. "He is a real nice dog."

Dawdi nodded.

Benji pressed his lips together and frowned at Alfie. "I don't want to do the plan anymore."

Alfie frowned right back. "Do you want to sleep in the cellar for the rest of your life?"

Benji rubbed Tintin's ears. "It won't be for the rest of my life. I'll move out when I get married."

"We have to stick to the plan."

"Plan?" Dawdi said.

He talked a lot better than Alfie thought. "Emma comes over every time she thinks Tintin has been in her chicken coop."

Benji looked at Dawdi. "But he doesn't go in her

chicken coop. It's too high and it has a gate. We shouldn't keep blaming Tintin."

"It's not blaming. It's called 'framing.'" Benji was a *gute* partner, but he didn't know the right spy words. "We bought some eggs from Emma and broke them in her coop and made a big paw print in the dirt." It had been a wonderful *gute* paw print. Benji had done it with his toes. "Emma thought Tintin broke her eggs so she came over to visit Abraham. They had a romantic talk on the porch. Then last night we scooped some of Tintin's poop from the woods and put it in the coop."

Benji wrinkled his nose. "It was disgusting."

"The poop worked even better than the broken eggs. Emma came over and played games."

"But it wasn't Tintin's fault. He's just an innocent dog, and Emma hates him. And Abraham will send him to the pound." Benji got tears in his eyes. He always got tears in his eyes when he talked about the pound.

"Abraham won't send Tintin to the pound. But if Emma doesn't come over, she and Abraham won't fall in love."

Benji folded his arms tightly across his chest. "What if Emma tells Mamm about Tintin? Then she'll send him to the pound."

Alfie hesitated. Abraham would never send Tintin to the pound. He was too nice, but Mamm would definitely send Tintin to the pound. But he couldn't worry about Mamm. If they ever wanted to be out of that cellar, they had to stick to the plan. "Mamm isn't going to find out. Tintin has a hideout in the woods."

Benji didn't like that answer. "What do you think, Dawdi?"

"Nice," Dawdi said. He reached out and patted Benji's arm. "Abe Emma."

Benji leaned closer to Dawdi. "Abraham needs Emma?"

Dawdi smiled.

Benji glanced at Alfie. "But we need Tintin."

Dawdi nodded. "Abe health."

"Do you mean 'Abe help'?" Alfie said. He looked at Benji. "Abraham helped us buy food for Tintin. He won't let Mamm send him to the pound."

Benji stuck out his lower lip. "But I don't like framing Tintin. He's innocent."

"When Abraham and Emma get married, we can tell them everything," Alfie said. "They'll thank us for getting them together."

Dawdi nodded.

Benji drew a line in the dirt with his big toe. "Okay. I guess I don't mind." He knelt down and took Tintin by the collar. "I'm sorry, Tintin. You're wonderful nice to let us blame you for all the bad stuff. We love you so much, and if Alfie didn't want to get out of the cellar so bad, you could just live in peace in your hideout. But we need you, boy. I hope you understand."

Tintin licked Benji's cheek. That was all the answer they needed. Tintin was in on the plan.

Alfie looked toward the house, though he couldn't actually see the house because they were deep in the bushes. "We need to get Dawdi home before Mamm finds out."

Benji led Tintin back down the trail.

Alfie fixed Dawdi's blanket. "You're almost cured, Dawdi. We should go fishing when you get better. Benji and I found a secret spot to fish that no one has ever been to before. We'll show you sometime, but you can't tell anybody. Benji sometimes accidentally tells our secrets, but he doesn't mean to. He's just not as smart as I am. I'm the smartest, Abraham is the nicest, and Benji is the best at falling asleep."

Benji came racing down the path. "I gave Tintin a dog treat for being so good."

"Benji, we don't have any dog treats to spare. We need them for our next plan."

Benji scrunched his lips together. "He deserves a dog treat. He didn't bark once."

"Okay, okay," Alfie said. "You should have told me first. We're partners. We need to agree on things before we do them."

They each grabbed a handlebar, counted to three, and heaved the wheelchair forward. Dawdi almost slipped out again, but he was holding on tight to his armrests and pulled himself upright. He was almost cured.

It took them ten minutes to push Dawdi out of the woods and onto the grass. The hard part was over. Going across the lawn would be easier. Dawdi would be back on the porch in no time.

"Oh, *sis yuscht*," Dawdi said, or at least that's what it sounded like, but Alfie couldn't be sure. Dawdi was still pretty hard to understand.

Alfie's heart jumped into his throat. Mamm was running, running across the lawn toward them. Mamm never ran. Her face was a wonderful dark purple color, and her glasses were sort of crooked on her face.

Couldn't she have sewed for ten more minutes? Would that have been so hard for Gotte to arrange?

They were in trouble. Big, big trouble.

He had forgotten one thing. Mamm always found out.

It was Saturday morning, and Emma had never hurried through her chores so fast. Abraham was bringing Alfie and Benji over as soon as they were done with their own chores, and they were going to help Mamm in the garden. Emma didn't care about the garden as much as she cared about seeing Abraham. And the twins, of course.

Emma liked being with Abraham. She didn't have to be clever or funny or interesting when she was with him because she didn't feel any need to impress him. They were just friends, and she liked that she could be herself around him—like she could with Lizzy or her *bruder* Peter. She loved gatherings and *singeons*, but it was exhausting trying to be the most exciting girl at every party. Being with Abraham was relaxing. She didn't have to impress him because he already liked her and he didn't expect anything from her. She could eat too much, and he didn't care. She laughed until she snorted, and he thought it was funny. She scribbled the worst pictures in Pictionary, and he told her they were good. She spent hours just being with her chickens, and he didn't think that was strange at all.

He was truly, genuinely interested in her chickens.

Last week he'd taken out an old, moldy nesting box from her coop and installed a new one while she was at work. He did stuff like that without caring if she thanked him or even noticed.

And he made delicious Pigs-in-a-Blanket.

Emma gathered the eggs and took them into the house to wash and put in cartons. Tabitha laid the most beautiful chocolate-brown eggs. A specialty grocer in Shawano bought every one she could get.

Lizzy was cleaning out the fridge. "Is Abraham here yet?"

"*Nae,* but it should be soon. He said when the twins finish their chores at home."

Lizzy grinned. "He's so handsome."

"I'm not interested," Emma said.

"But you think he's cute, don't you?"

Emma scrunched her lips to one side of her face. "He's handsome, but we're just friends."

Lizzy shrugged. "If you're not interested, you're not interested. I wish I was four years older."

Emma laughed. "Don't wish your life away for a boy."

Lizzy looked at her sort of sideways. "It doesn't matter. Even if I was four years older, I'm not pretty enough for Abraham."

"Don't say that. You're pretty enough for any boy—too pretty for most of them."

Lizzy cracked a smile. "It doesn't matter. There are three or four girls in the *gmayna* who have their eye on Abraham. But he doesn't talk very much, and they don't want to be forward."

Emma hadn't heard any such thing. "What girls?"

"*Ach.* Linda Eicher, Ruth Schlabach. And Anna Schrock. And probably Sarah King."

"Sarah likes all the boys. I wouldn't take her seriously."

Lizzy raised her eyebrows. "*You* like all the boys."

Emma hesitated. "But I'm not a flirt. You . . . you don't think I'm a flirt, do you?"

"Of course not. You like to have fun at gatherings, that's all. About twenty boys want to ask to drive you home, but they're afraid you'll say no."

Maybe she would say no. Who wanted to settle down with a boy unless he was very handsome and wonderful nice? Like the bishop's son or Matt Gingerich. Emma didn't feel like smiling anymore. Finding a husband was so much pressure. Couldn't she put it off for a while?

Lizzy turned back to the fridge. "You should tell Abraham when he comes. Since you're such *gute* friends."

"Tell him what?"

"Tell him about Sarah and the others. If he wants to find a wife, he needs to talk to the girls."

Emma didn't know what had put her teeth on edge, but she suddenly felt snippy. "I'm not going to ask Abraham to do something he's not comfortable with."

Lizzy eyed her curiously. "You don't have to do that. Just mention there are some girls interested. I think he'd want to know."

A knock on the door saved Emma from having to reply. Abraham stood on her porch with a bag of carrot peelings. His navy blue shirt accented his sky blue eyes and the reddish tint to his chestnut brown hair. When he grew a beard, for sure and certain it would come in red. But Emma didn't want to think about Abraham growing a beard. Amish men only grew beards when they got married or when they got old enough to be called a bachelor. Abraham could grow a beard when he was a bachelor. It would be red.

"*Hallo*, Abraham," Lizzy called from the kitchen.

"*Hallo*," he said, showing off those very white teeth.

"Where are the boys?" Emma said.

Abraham handed her the bag of carrot peels. They were for her chickens, of course. "Alfie and Benji are in trouble with Mamm so they won't be coming for the next three Saturdays."

"*Ach.* What happened?"

"They sneaked Dawdi out of the house in his wheelchair and pushed him into the woods."

Emma gasped. "Oh, dear."

"Mamm was upstairs sewing. It took her a few minutes to notice they were gone. I've never heard her yell that loud before. Austin and I heard her from the barn. She got dizzy from screaming and had to sit on the porch to catch her breath. She probably had a mild heart attack."

"Is your *dawdi* okay?"

"He's fine. I think he enjoyed the ride. He needs to get out more. They wanted him to meet Tintin."

Emma nibbled on her bottom lip. "Did your *mamm* catch Tintin?"

"By some miracle, *nae.*"

"That's a relief. I'm afraid those boys are going to be heartbroken over that dog one day."

"Me too," Abraham said. "But for now, Tintin is safe. And so is Dawdi."

Emma giggled. "I would have liked to see the look

on your *mamm*'s face when she caught the boys with your *dawdi*." She sucked in her breath. "Is it wrong to say that? I'm sure she was surprised."

Abraham chuckled. "She was surprised. So surprised that the boys have to wash walls and baseboards every day until the whole house is done. I think they'll learn their lesson."

Emma smiled sympathetically. "Those poor little boys. It's hard being nine. There are so many mistakes to make." She almost told Abraham not to worry about bringing the boys over to her house to work in the garden. They'd been punished enough. But if the boys didn't come over, neither would Abraham. She'd have to think on that another time. "*Denki* for bringing the carrots anyway."

He smiled. "It wonders me if you'd be up for a little trip."

"A trip?"

"We will be gone about two hours, so if you have to work in the garden, I understand."

Emma wanted to go on a little trip so badly, she thought maybe she could taste it on her tongue. Two hours with a boy who was just a friend sounded so refreshing. "Well . . . Mamm needs help in the garden."

Lizzy slammed the fridge door so hard, the bottles on the door rattled. "I'll finish the garden. It's just tying up the raspberries."

Tying up the raspberries was not a simple or quick job. Emma turned her back on Abraham and mouthed the words "Are you sure?" to Lizzy.

Lizzy glanced past Emma at Abraham and smiled. "What little trip?"

"It's sort of a surprise, unless Emma doesn't like surprises then I can tell you."

Emma turned around. "*Ach.* I like surprises, unless you want to take me to the cattle auction. I hate cattle auctions. They smell."

"Aren't you the girl who has eight chickens in the backyard?" Abraham said. "They don't smell like flowers."

"Cows are worse than chickens. And there is nothing more boring than a cattle auction. Are you taking me to an auction?"

"*Nae,*" Abraham said, more eager than Emma had ever seen him.

How could she say *nae* to such enthusiasm? "Do I need special clothes like a swimsuit? What about mosquito repellant? Sunscreen? Should I pack a lunch? I don't like being hungry."

"Already packed and in the car," Abraham said.

"The car? You hired a driver?"

Abraham nodded.

"What if I'd said *nae*?"

Abraham shrugged. "I would have gone myself. It's a fun place to go on a little adventure."

Emma couldn't keep a wide smile from her face. Abraham had hired a driver? No wonder he was excited. "Okay then. Let me get my bonnet."

Emma decided then and there she wouldn't mention anything about other girls who might be interested in Abraham. She knew Abraham well enough to know it would make him extremely uncomfortable.

Why ruin a perfectly *gute* adventure?

Abraham sat in the back with Emma, and Clark Newman sat in the front with his wife, Penny, who was driving. Penny and Clark lived in Shawano and sometimes drove the Amish to get groceries.

After Emma and Abraham had settled in the car and introductions had been made, Emma thanked Penny for the ride. "We need to go to Green Bay to take something to our son," Penny said. "So it worked out perfect yet."

Clark craned his neck to look at Emma. "Our son likes the big city, but it's too crowded for us. Shawano is just the right size, but sometimes it gets overrun by tourists."

Emma turned to Abraham. "We're going to Green Bay?"

"Not quite," he said.

The drive took forty minutes, and Emma spent a very pleasant time visiting with Abraham, Clark, and Penny. Clark was a talker, but Emma didn't mind. He told stories about the war, though Emma never learned which one, and he acted as if he was thrilled to have Emma and Abraham in his car.

They exited the interstate and followed a road called County Truck Highway C. There was lots of *gute* farmland plus a few subdivisions. They were getting closer to the big city, as Clark called it. Clark navigated from his phone, and before long, Penny pulled off the road onto a dirt driveway that ran alongside a little blue house. "Is this the right place?" Penny said.

Clark looked at his phone. "Siri says it is."

"I think so," Abraham said. "They told me the house was blue yet."

Penny glanced at Clark's phone. "Well then, this has to be it. Blue houses aren't real common."

Abraham opened the door and stepped out of the

car to get a better look at the house. "This has to be the one, if your phone is right."

"I don't know," Penny said. "Sometimes it can't even find the Walmart in Shawano."

Emma slid out on Abraham's side. "Let's go ask."

Abraham smiled at her as if she'd just cured cancer. "You're so brave."

Abraham walked with her up to the front door, which was cherry red with white trim. Abraham winked at her. "They like bright colors."

Emma knocked, and they waited. They heard shuffling behind the door, so someone was obviously home. Either the residents were scrambling to find a *gute* hiding place or they just took a long time to answer the door.

The wrinkliest man Emma had ever seen opened the door, holding a cane and a can of spray paint. "Can I help you?" he said, squinting as if he had a hard time seeing them. He probably did, if he was as old as he looked.

"Are you Mr. Steuben?" Abraham asked.

"Yes I am, but it says so on the mailbox so it's not hard to guess."

Mailbox? Emma hadn't seen a mailbox.

"I'm Abraham Petersheim. I called you last week."

The man's skin pulled tight across his face when he smiled. "The Amish fellow."

"Yes."

The old man motioned with his cane. "Come in. I'll put on some coffee."

Abraham smiled at Emma and waved to Penny and Clark.

"We'll be back in an hour," Penny called as she backed down the driveway.

Abraham motioned for Emma to go ahead of him, and Emma kind of wished he wasn't so polite. She'd rather he go first. At least he knew why they were here.

The room was dimly lit and stuffy, as if Mr. Steuben hadn't opened his windows in twenty years. Two heavy brass lamps with lacy lampshades sat on either side of an old brown sofa that had a large doily draped over the back. There were photos and paintings and calendars on the walls, and there wasn't an inch of space to hang anything else.

Mr. Steuben set the can of spray paint on the coffee table next to a stack of books and two piles of coasters. The table also held three angel statuettes, seven small frames with pictures of smiling children, two elephants carved out of wood, and an unfinished game of checkers.

Emma wondered if Mr. Steuben ever had anyone to play with.

"Have you been painting?" Abraham said, motioning to the can of spray paint.

"I always answer the door with a can of spray paint. Anyone who tries to rob me will get a mouthful of acetone." Mr. Steuben took three steps toward a doorway at the other end of the room. "Helen," he called. "We've got visitors."

A woman with snowy white hair and purple-rimmed glasses bounded into the room like a jackrabbit. Wrinkles lined her face like plowed furrows, but she had lively eyes that made her look years younger than Mr. Steuben. "How nice. Amish people. We don't get Amish around here often, but we're always happy to welcome fellow chicken lovers." She held out her hand. Emma shook it. "I'm

Helen Steuben. This is my husband, Leonard. We're going on sixty-five years of marriage."

"I'm Emma Wengerd, and this is Abraham Peter-sheim."

Helen raised an eyebrow, and her eyes twinkled mischievously. "Not married. Are you sweethearts?"

Abraham laughed uncomfortably. Emma smiled. "*Nae.* Just friends."

Helen pursed her lips. "Hmm. Well. There's plenty of time to fix that. I hear you like exotic chickens."

"We do," Abraham said.

A ribbon of warmth traveled up Emma's back. She didn't broadcast to the world that she liked chickens. The boys thought it was strange. But Abraham didn't think it was strange at all. She liked that she didn't have to pretend when she was with him.

"Well, come on out," Helen said, motioning for them to follow. Helen moved like someone much younger than a woman who had been married for sixty-five years. They walked out the back door and left Leonard to catch up.

Emma gasped. Behind Leonard and Helen's house were seven chicken runs, all about twice the size of Emma's. Each run was surrounded by chain-link fencing and covered over the top with mesh netting. Chicken coops sat inside each fence and at least twenty chickens pranced around inside each chicken run. But they weren't everyday, run-of-the-mill chickens. Each chicken run contained a different kind of exotic chicken. There were at least a dozen Lavender Orpingtons in one run, fourteen Laken-velders in another. There were also two dozen or so Rhode Island Reds running free outside the fences and a couple of White Leghorns for good measure.

"What do you think?" Abraham said, anticipation written all over his face.

"I've never seen anything so *wunderbarr* in my life."

His expression relaxed into a smile. "My *onkel* told me about this place. I wanted to show you, but I was afraid it wouldn't be as grand as he said. Sometimes Onkel Menno exaggerates."

Emma walked between the fences until she came to a run with chickens that looked like they had fur instead of feathers. She'd never seen that kind before. "What are these?"

Helen opened up the gate. "Come in and hold one." She scooped one from the ground and handed it to Emma. It was so soft, it could have been a bunny rabbit. "These are Silkies. We've got white and blue ones, but they come in all sorts of colors yet. They're gentle and friendly so you shouldn't keep them with the more aggressive breeds or they'll get picked on. And even though it looks like fur, you have to keep them warm in the winter. We have a little solar-powered space heater. I know the Amish can use solar power, so that might work. They are more like pets than chickens yet. The grandkids love 'em, but they're not especially good layers."

Emma buried her face into the soft feathers of the white Silkie. Wouldn't one of these be fun to add to her collection?

Helen gave them a tour of all seven chicken runs. Each fenced-in area had a different kind of chicken in it. Some held at least two varieties. Emma kept smiling at Abraham. It was as if they'd discovered a hidden cave of treasure. It was amazing more people didn't know about this place.

Ach, vell, maybe they did. Being Amish, Emma

wasn't on the Internet or chatting with other chicken lovers on her phone. Maybe everybody but her knew about the Steubens and their amazing collection of chickens.

"This is the most wonderful place," Emma said. "When did you start collecting chickens?"

Helen laughed. "We've been raising chickens for a good sixty years yet. I kept buying chickens, and Leonard kept building fences. It was a good hobby for the kids. They won a couple two three blue ribbons in 4-H." She pulled a handful of grapes out of her pocket and fed them to the Rhode Island Red that had been following them around for the whole tour. "The Silkie chicks are twenty dollars, which is way overpriced, but Leonard says people will pay it so I'm not going to argue about it. The others are fifteen or ten. Which one would you like? Or would you like more than one? Sometimes it's hard to choose a favorite."

"Oh," Emma said. "What . . . what do you mean?"

Abraham leaned his hand against the fence and curled his fingers around the chain links. "I want to buy you some chickens," he said. "Maybe a rooster and a hen so you can breed more if you want."

Emma's mouth fell open. "You want to buy me some chickens."

"*Jah,* but only if you want more chickens." He acted as if he was offering her a stick of gum instead of a whole new chicken adventure.

"Abraham, I don't know what to say."

He drew his brows together. "I wasn't sure if you even want more chickens. It's okay if you don't. I thought it would be fun to come out here and see all the different breeds, even if we don't buy anything."

"For sure and certain." Emma was truly speechless. No one had ever done anything so thoughtful or so crazy for her before. Abraham was more unpredictable and engaging than she'd ever realized. Why didn't more people know this about Abraham?

Ach, vell, maybe everybody but Emma knew. Emma was too busy having fun and trying to impress the boys to have noticed. She should start noticing things.

Helen fed the last of the grapes to her Rhode Island Red. "There are seven new Silkie spring chickens this year, plus lots of chicks in the other coops. You can take your pick. Some of them haven't been sexed, but we know at least one of the Silkie chicks is a rooster."

Emma turned to Abraham and studied his face. It was obvious he wasn't trying to impress her or make her feel obligated to be his friend. He was just being nice, and he liked chickens almost as much as she did. "This is just too much, Abraham."

One side of his mouth curled upward. "It's not that much."

"Not that much? You paid a driver to bring us all the way out here, and now you're offering to buy me a chicken."

He silently searched her face, a hesitant smile on his lips.

There was nothing to do but wholeheartedly accept such amazing kindness. She smiled. "I would love a Silkie."

Abraham had been holding out on her. He exploded into a dazzling smile that made Emma almost dizzy. "Helen, can we get a rooster and a hen?"

"You betcha," Helen said, squinting into the sky.

"Looks like it's close to noon yet. Why don't you stay for lunch, and I'll box them up for you."

"*Ach,*" Abraham said. "I left our lunches in the car."

Helen blew a puff of air between her lips. "No need for that. I made potato rolls this morning, and we've got some good hard cheese and ham. You're allowed to eat ham, aren't you?"

"Yes. That's very kind of you."

Helen started toward the house, then stopped short. "On second thought, there's a little pond just across the field north. It's got a bench and everything, and it's a real nice place for young people to sit together and eat. My son Todd proposed to Connie there." She nodded as if she had all the world's problems figured out. "That's where you should eat. I'll get your food together in two shakes."

"I'll help," Emma said.

"Of course not," Helen said. "Youse two pick the Silkies you want. I'll come out and show you the rooster and the hens we know of."

Abraham and Emma went to the chicken run with the Silkies. Some were white like bunnies. Others were bluish gray with beaks and faces the color of blueberry syrup. Absolutely beautiful. It didn't take long for them to pick out the young rooster. He crowed as if he was ushering the sun across the sky.

Helen emerged from the house with a large paper grocery bag and handed it to Abraham. "There's meat and cheese and rolls in there and two Capri Suns. The grandkids love them. And I put a couple three oatmeal cookies in there too. They aren't homemade, but I made rolls so I'm not apologizing."

"It sounds wonderful," Emma said. "*Denki.*"

"Take your time at the pond. I won't box up the chickens until you get back."

Helen pointed the way to the pond, and Abraham and Emma set off. Emma wasn't quite sure why they had to eat their lunch at the pond, but if Helen recommended it, it must be nice. Maybe it would be another adventure in a day of adventures.

They followed the path Helen told them to take and soon came to the pond, right where Helen had said it would be, except it wasn't a pond. It was a puddle of water about twelve feet across surrounded by juneberry bushes and bog birch. Abraham probably could have walked across it without getting his knees wet.

Abraham glanced at Emma, raised both eyebrows, and chuckled. "I hope Todd and Connie are still married. It doesn't seem like a very *gute* beginning to a relationship."

Emma giggled. "*Ach, vell,* there is a bench." Such as it was—a log planed on one side sitting crosswise atop two other logs.

"Will we get splinters?"

Emma took the paper bag from Abraham and walked around the mud puddle. "If it's good enough for Todd and Connie, it's good enough for us."

They gingerly sat down on the log, and Emma pulled their lunch from the bag. She flattened the paper bag and spread it between them on the log like a tablecloth. Then she laid the Ziploc bags of rolls, ham, and cheese on top of it. "You can make your own sandwich or just eat everything à la carte."

"What does à la carte mean?"

"I read it in a menu once. I think it means to eat everything separately."

"I like separately," Abraham said, taking a huge bite of potato roll.

Emma scrunched her lips to one side of her face in an attempt not to smile. Abraham wasn't shy about eating in front of her. She wasn't going to be shy eating in front of him, especially since he'd already seen what she could do to a plate of Pigs-in-a-Blanket. "I think we should pray," she said.

The look on his face was comical. He quit chewing and bowed his head. Emma bowed her head too and thanked Gotte for the food and for Helen and Leonard's chicken farm. She opened her eyes and picked up a piece of ham. "I guess we eat with our fingers."

"*Jah*," Abraham said. "We're sitting on a log next to a puddle, and a squirrel is eyeing our lunch from that branch over there. This is not the place for forks."

Emma finished off her piece of ham in three bites and licked her fingers. "*Appeditlich*. And the rolls melt in your mouth like butter. As *gute* as Martha Glick's, but don't tell her I said that. I wouldn't want to hurt her feelings."

She felt him tense beside her. "Martha is a wonderful *gute* cook."

Emma broke a piece of Swiss cheese in half. "Last week, Raymond Glick caught Perry in the storage room playing on his phone when he should have been working. He's assigned Perry to sweep the floor and dust the shelves in the store every day. And when he finishes, Raymond makes him do it all over again. I haven't seen much of Perry since then."

His expression relaxed. "Don't tell anyone, but I don't like Perry."

Emma laughed. "That makes just about all of us. Raymond is a minister and the Glicks are rich, but I don't know if Perry will be able to talk anybody into marrying him."

Abraham shook his head. "I hope not."

"I can't believe you once wondered if I was interested in Perry."

He leaned back and propped his hand on the log. It was a dangerous move. He was likely to come away with several splinters. "I didn't think you were, but I had to be sure. I didn't want to speak badly of your boyfriend."

"I've never heard you speak badly of anyone."

"If you tell me who your boyfriend is, I will make sure never to say a bad word about him, even if he has bad breath."

Emma rolled her eyes. "I don't have a boyfriend, and you know it. I don't want a boyfriend."

Abraham eyed her curiously. "Don't you want to get married?"

Emma didn't know what to say to that. Everybody assumed that every Amish girl her age was eagerly looking for a husband. "I guess I do. But not yet."

Abraham didn't even bat an eye. He certainly didn't appear shocked by such an admission. "You have fun at gatherings. Do you think marriage will ruin your fun?"

It wasn't an accusation, which is how her *mamm* or her *bruder* would have asked the question. "I have to get married eventually because I don't want to be an old maid. Old maids end up being the nanny for the nieces and nephews or the caretaker for the old folks. But I'm having so much fun right now, going to gatherings, being with *die youngie*. Once you get a boyfriend, none of the other boys pay you any attention. They don't try to make you laugh or look at you like you're somebody special." She felt her face get warm. She'd probably said too much, but Abraham was so easy to talk to and he already knew about her chickens and her appetite. "I like the attention I get from the boys. Is that bad?"

"Of course not. I like to play basketball. There's nothing wrong with that. But I don't think you like the attention from Perry."

Emma groaned. "I would be happy if he ignored me for the rest of my life."

Abraham took another roll from the bag. "Perry makes me angry, even though we're not supposed to be angry with anyone."

"You don't seem like the type to get angry. It wonders me if you take after your *fater*."

"I suppose I do," Abraham said. "I've only seen Dat angry one time. It was years ago when Austin went to play with friends and left Mamm to carry boxes of peanut butter to the buggy. Mamm has a temper, but that temper has kept five sons in line. She yells and carries on, but we know she loves us, even if she doesn't always show it. Alfie and Benji probably would have died in some horrible accident by now if the fear of Mamm's temper didn't keep them in check. It's better this way."

Emma laughed. "*Ach*. Those boys know how to find trouble. I wonder what your *dawdi* was thinking when they pushed him into the woods."

"He probably loved it."

Emma stabbed the straw into her juice pouch. "You don't seem like a boy who ever loses his temper."

"I guess I don't. Most things aren't worth getting worked up about. I only remember one time getting so mad I hit someone. Okay, I hit two people. But that was the only time."

Emma almost choked on her drink. "You hit someone?" Getting angry was one thing, but the Amish tried to live a strictly nonviolent existence.

"I was fourteen."

"What happened?"

"There was a family that used to lived near Bitsy Weaver's farm. I passed by there one day and these two boys had tied their dog to a tree and were throwing rocks at him. The poor dog was crying and whining. I told them to stop, and they started taunting me and kept throwing rocks. I smacked both of them in the mouth, then took my pocketknife and untied their dog. They didn't try to stop me. I was taller than both of them."

"You've always been the tallest boy in the *gmayna*."

"I did something else that I'm not ashamed of, even though I broke one of the Ten Commandments."

Emma held tight to her juice box and held her breath. She didn't want to choke if he told her something shocking. "What did you do?"

"I only told one person."

"You don't have to tell if you don't want to."

Abraham fingered the last bit of roll in his hand. "I stole their dog."

"You stole the dog?"

"They weren't ever going to be good to that dog,

so I sneaked out of the house one night and stole their dog right out of their backyard."

Emma completely abandoned her juice box. Abraham was full of pleasant surprises. "Weren't you afraid you'd get caught?"

He nodded. "Every day for six months."

"But what did you do with the dog? I know you didn't keep it, or Alfie and Benji would never have needed a dog of their own."

Abraham popped the rest of the roll into his mouth. "I walked all night and gave the dog to my *onkel* Menno, who lives on the other side of the lake. I figured they wouldn't go that far to look for their dog. Onkel Menno drove me home in his buggy. I got home in time for breakfast. Mamm was mad, but I never told her what happened."

"Did she make you scrub walls and baseboards?"

"*Nae.* She yelled for a few minutes, but that was it. Mamm was never hard on me. She always seemed to feel sorry for me."

"It's because you're so hard on yourself," Emma said. "But maybe she secretly knew what you had done. It's about the bravest thing I've ever heard anyone do."

"I don't know about that. I couldn't hardly sneak into their yard my knees were shaking so bad."

Emma finished off her juice pouch. "But you still did it. You risked a lot to steal that dog."

"I couldn't stand the thought of them beating up on him. Nobody should do that to an animal."

"I agree." There was one last roll in the bag. Emma glanced at Abraham.

"You'd better eat it," he said. "I don't want you blowing away when the wind whips up."

She looked up at the sky as if she was thinking about it. "I can do that."

He handed her the roll. "How do you think Connie felt about being proposed to at a puddle?"

Emma laughed. "She might have thought it was romantic, unless there were mosquitoes. When you propose to a girl, Abraham, make sure it's at least as big as a lake. The girl deserves a lake."

Abraham sprouted a crooked grin. "There won't be any lake or any girl. I'm going to be a bachelor."

Emma wanted to protest, to tell him that a lot of girls were interested in him, but then he might start asking questions and want to know names. She didn't want to put that kind of pressure on him. "You're only twenty-two years old and already planning on being a bachelor?"

"If you haven't noticed, I have trouble talking to girls."

Emma looked at him sideways. "You don't seem to have any trouble talking to me."

"That's because you've already heard me say a hundred stupid things," he said. "There aren't that many more stupid things to say. And I'm trying to be less pathetic."

"What do you mean by that?"

"Nothing. But I'm hopeless around other girls. I guess I try too hard."

She thought about giving him some advice but reconsidered. He just didn't need the pressure. If he got better at flirting, the girls would swarm him like bees on honeycomb.

Abraham pulled his watch out of his pocket. "I don't want to cut our pond time short, but we should get back. Clark and Penny will be here soon."

Emma didn't anticipate the disappointment that washed over her. She'd been having such a *gute* time, and there were still three more pieces of cheese and two cookies. "What about the cookies?"

Abraham pulled the cookies out of the bag. They were those flat, hard, tasteless store-bought things that were as delicious as cardboard. "Helen said she wasn't going to feel guilty about the cookies. She made potato rolls."

"Will we hurt Helen's feelings if we don't eat them?"

Abraham handed Emma the bag, stretched his arm behind his head, and pitched one of the cookies into the puddle. It skipped four times and landed at the edge of the puddle on the other side. He grinned. "I was always good at skipping stones."

"Let me try." He gave her the second cookie, and she wound up and threw with all her might. The cookie splashed loudly into the water and sank to the bottom. Not one hop, skip, or jump.

Abraham shook his head in mock dejection. "A waste of a perfectly *gute* cookie."

Emma giggled. "Not that *gute*."

They strolled back to the house where Helen was waiting to box up their chickens. "I put a little straw and some seed in the bottom of the box. Keep the lid on unless you want chicken poop in the car."

Penny and Clark were already there, visiting with Leonard in the living room and admiring the souvenir spoon collection on the wall. Penny looked up and smiled. "Ready to go?"

"We have some chickens," Emma said, pointing to the box Abraham was holding. "Is that okay?"

Penny stood up and pulled Clark with her. "Abraham warned us there might be livestock on the trip home. I brought some old towels to put on the seat yet."

The drive home was lovely. Emma stuck her hand in the little hole on the side of the box and petted her chickens. She got nipped occasionally, but the pain was worth it. She had two new Silkies in her collection. Abraham didn't say much, but he smiled at her a lot, especially when she mentioned how happy she was to have her chickens.

It was after three o'clock when Penny turned down Emma's road. She hadn't thought about home once the whole trip. Lord willing, it hadn't taken Lizzy too long to finish the garden.

Abraham glanced out the front windshield and sat bolt upright. "Penny, could you pull over right here?"

Penny pulled to the side of the road about a hundred yards from Emma's house. "Is something wrong?"

Abraham nudged Emma's shoulder and pointed out the window. "Look who's at your house."

Emma pressed her lips together. Matt Gingerich, Sam Beiler, and Adam Stoltzfus were standing on the front lawn talking to Dat. What would they think when she pulled up to the house with Abraham Petersheim and a box of chickens? Her face got warm and her hands turned cold.

"It will ruin all future gatherings if they see you with me," Abraham said. "Especially like this." He ducked behind Penny's seat as best he could. Being so tall, he was a little bit cramped. "Penny, can you back up around the corner?"

"I can, but it might draw more attention than not."

Abraham frowned. "Emma, if you get out right here, you can walk the rest of the way, and they will never know I was here. Then Penny can drive me to my house, and I'll sneak around the back and put your chickens in the coop without being seen."

A big, selfish lump lodged in Emma's throat.

How could she just get out of the car and pretend Abraham didn't exist? He was thoughtful and loyal and kind, and he'd bought her two chickens. Was she his friend or not?

She should have opened her mouth and told Penny to drive all the way to her house. She wasn't ashamed of Abraham or her chickens. But she found herself grateful that Abraham had suggested she get out of the car and walk home by herself. She still wanted to be the center of attention at gatherings, didn't she? She still wanted boys to be interested in her and, yes, flirt with her, didn't she? She wasn't ready to get married, and if anyone thought she and Abraham were dating, that would be the end of all her fun. The boys would give up on her, and she'd be stuck hanging out with Lizzy and her friends at gatherings. Not that there was anything wrong with Lizzy and her friends, except they were teenagers and spent gatherings huddled in a little group giggling about cute boys.

Before the lump in her throat choked her, Emma hopped out of the car and started walking toward her house. Penny drove away while Abraham hunkered down in the back seat. No one would have been able to guess there was someone in the back of Penny's car.

No one ever had to know that Emma had spent a glorious afternoon with Abraham, skipping cookies in a puddle, petting furry chickens, and eating potato rolls from a Ziploc bag.

Her secret was safe.

Chapter Eleven

Emma sighed as she refilled ketchup bottles and salt shakers. The breakfast rush had been especially busy this morning, and she'd barely had time to think, which was probably a *gute* thing. She didn't like where her thoughts took her these days. She knew she was behaving badly. But Abraham made it so easy to be selfish and small-minded that she'd talked herself into thinking that he didn't mind how she treated him.

She was wrong and she knew it, and she just couldn't bring herself to make it right. There were still so many boys to flirt with and so many gatherings to go to. Adam Stoltzfus was starting to take more of an interest. She couldn't change things. Not just yet.

And it was true that Abraham seemed perfectly happy to be her secret friend. She liked that about him. He didn't expect anything from her. It took the pressure off her to find a way to include him in her circle of friends at fellowship suppers and gatherings. But it was also true that she should be a better friend to Abraham. Then again, he said he didn't want to be included in her group of friends. It made him nervous to have to try to talk to people. So maybe she was doing him a favor.

And maybe she knew better.

At the next table over, Lizzy growled and made a face at Emma. "Look at this."

Whoever had sat there had put Lizzy's tip in the water pitcher in dimes and nickels. Lizzy stuck her hand in the water and gathered up the coins. She set the dripping coins on the table and counted them. "Three dollars and ten cents. At least it's a fair tip. And the son was cute."

"He was an *Englischer*."

"That doesn't mean he can't be cute."

Emma giggled. "I guess not, but you think everybody is cute."

Lizzy got a mischievous glint in her eye. "Abraham is cute."

Emma wasn't going to take the bait. "Abraham is a wonderful *gute* friend. I'm very grateful to him for helping me with my chickens."

"Have you told him that Linda Eicher and Ruth Schlabach are interested in him yet?"

"Of course not. I don't want to spread rumors that might not be true."

"*Ach*, they're true. Ruth told me herself."

Emma finished wiping the table. "I'm not going to be Ruth's matchmaker. If she's interested, she should talk to Abraham herself." Or maybe Ruth should look for someone else. She and Abraham would never suit. Ruth talked too much.

"You don't have to get huffy about it. Abraham isn't your own private friend."

"I never said he was. He's been very kind to me, and I care about his feelings."

Lizzy puckered her lips and lifted an eyebrow. "How much do you care?"

Emma threw a napkin in Lizzy's direction, and it landed in the water pitcher. They both laughed. "I care very much that you finish your tables. I want to go eat lunch."

Some questions were easier not to answer.

Abraham had been over almost every day last week to help Emma with her Silkies. Helen had said it was better to keep them separate from the more aggressive breeds, and Emma's Maran hen could be pretty mean when she wanted to. Abraham had taken the Silkies to his house that first day and had rounded up a little portable two-feet-by-three-feet chicken coop that could be moved anywhere around a yard or field. He had left the Silkies in the little coop a few feet from her big chicken run with a note that he'd be back later to build them a better place to live.

On Monday, Abraham had come over with plans for building a smaller coop and chicken run for the Silkies, complete with a solar-powered heater for the winter months. On Tuesday, he'd started building it. Emma had spent some of her egg money to buy the materials, and since they didn't use chain-link fencing, the construction wasn't all that expensive.

The coop was done by Friday, and they had a little ceremony to move the Silkies into their new home. Alfie and Benji somehow managed to get permission to come see the new coop, and they had brought Tintin with them. Abraham opened the coop door made of chicken wire and wood, and Alfie and Benji had sung all five verses of "The Puppy Parable" while Emma carried the Silkies to their new home. Tintin yawned and scratched behind his ear, but other than that seemed uninterested in the new chickens.

Abraham had made Pigs-in-a-Blanket, and Emma had baked a pineapple coconut cake. Alfie and Benji, along with Abraham, Lizzy, Emma, and Mamm and Dat, ate cake and played Clue until Alfie and Benji had to get home for bed. Emma and Abraham sat out on the porch that night and talked until almost eleven. It had been way too late, but Abraham was so easy to talk to, and even though he didn't think he was very clever, he had made her laugh more than a few times.

Abraham was humble and meek, but that didn't mean he was weak-minded or shallow. Lizzy had once insisted that Abraham was deep instead of boring, and she was right. Abraham thought very seriously in many subjects, and Emma loved hearing his opinion on Gotte and the church and *Gelassenheit*, the Amish belief of yielding to Gotte and the Ordnung. She liked disagreeing with him too because he was never disagreeable and didn't have to be right, even if he usually was.

He hadn't come to the gathering last week, and Emma had been both disappointed and relieved. She had played volleyball, and Matt Gingerich and Tyler Kaufmann was on her team. She and Adam Stoltzfus had engaged in a nice conversation about cookies and last week's sermon, and Moses and Mahlon Zook smiled and waved at her. It had been wonderful nice, and when she'd gotten home, Abraham had been waiting to give her an update on her chickens and how the coop was coming along. She should have told him how much they'd all missed him at the gathering, but he had been so pre-occupied talking to her about eggs and solar heaters that the topic of the gathering hadn't come up.

Emma wiped her last table, helped Lizzy finish the dishes, and took her lunch outside, along with a bucket to sit on. It was a beautiful June day, and Emma intended to enjoy it by not thinking about Silkies or coops or Abraham Petersheim. Of course, her sandwich was made from Petersheim Brothers' Peanut Butter, so every bite made her think of him. She should have made tuna fish this morning.

"You planned this, didn't you?"

Emma turned around. Perry stood in the back doorway holding a plate of biscuits and gravy, for sure and certain left over from breakfast in the restaurant, and a white bucket like the one Emma sat on. She groaned inwardly. She had been too pre-dictable, sitting outside to eat her lunch every day for three weeks. She had thought she was safe from Perry because his *dat* kept him busy in the store, but either his *dat* wasn't there today or Perry had man-aged to sneak out.

"I'm just finishing my lunch," Emma said. She took a big bite of her sandwich and shoved her chips and cookies back into her lunchbox. She'd eat them later, maybe standing in the bathroom with the door locked.

"I'm taking my lunch break too," Perry said, setting his bucket next to hers and sitting down. Emma wasn't so sure the bucket could hold up under Perry's significant weight. Of course, it had held up for Abraham just fine, and he probably weighed close to what Perry did. Abraham's weight was in height and muscle. Perry's was in compacted fat.

Two bites left. Emma was tempted to throw the rest into the field on the other side of the fence, but she was going to be wonderful hungry later if she did.

Perry shoved a forkful of biscuits with gravy into his mouth. "My *dat* gave me some land on the farm to build a house."

"That's nice."

"It's more than nice. Once it's done, I'll be able to get married, and my *fraa* will get two whole bathrooms out of it." Perry didn't have a lot to recommend him as a husband, but two bathrooms might be a significant temptation to the right girl.

Emma stuffed her crinkled napkin into her lunchbox. "No house should be without a bathroom."

Realizing she was leaving him, Perry jumped as if someone had scared him. He set his plate and fork on the pavement and snatched Emma's hand as if he was trying to catch mosquitoes. He laid his other hand on top of hers.

Emma gasped, more out of surprise than anything else. Perry was harmless, but he was also as thick as a slab of raw meat. "Perry, let go," she said. She tried to pull away, but his hands were surprisingly strong. Probably from all those games he played on his phone. Those could really build up your finger muscles.

"Don't be shy. I know how you feel. I caught you staring at me the other day."

Emma could not for the life of her remember ever staring at Perry, but he could believe whatever he wanted. "I have to get back to the restaurant."

He held fast to her hand. She was going to have to sit here and listen to whatever he had to say until he relaxed his grip and she could escape. "You come in the storage room just because you know I'll be there. You like me." Emma felt slightly nauseated. *Ach.* He got down on one knee. "I'm going to have a big house with two bathrooms, and my family is rich. Will you let me drive you home from the next gathering so we can start courting?"

Emma tugged with all her might, but he had a hundred pounds on her and his hands were like quilting clamps. "I'm sorry if I've given you the wrong impression, Perry, but I'm not interested in you. Please let go of my hand." He still wouldn't give up. "Let go," she said, in her loudest scolding voice. She had only used that voice when her *bruder* Peter had picked on her as a little girl.

She pulled again but couldn't extricate herself from his grasp. *Ach!* Perry was really starting to annoy her.

His bucket scraped against the ground as he leaned closer and puckered his lips. Was he trying to kiss her? Because if that was the case, it was time to use her foot. She stood up. He stood up with her and somehow got his arm around her back. He smelled of garlic and window cleaner. She shuddered and struggled as he pressed his moist lips to hers. It was disgusting, and it was time to use her teeth.

From out of nowhere, Abraham appeared with fire in his eyes. He grabbed Perry by the collar and pulled him away from Emma, then laid a swift and solid punch on Perry's mouth. Not surprisingly, Perry immediately let go of Emma's hand as shock popped all over his face. The punch sent him backward, and he tripped over his bucket and landed on his backside. He raised his hands to protect his face. "Stop. Don't hurt me," he whined.

"Leave Emma alone," Abraham said, standing over Perry with a long finger in his face.

Stunned and more than a little irritated, Emma wiped Perry's saliva from her face, grabbed a handful of Abraham's shirt, and pulled him backward. "Abraham, stop it. What do you think you're doing?"

Abraham's eyes flashed like lightning. "He kissed you."

Perry jumped to his feet, moving faster than Emma would have thought possible. He stepped in his biscuits and gravy and cracked the plate with his shoe. "You gave me a bloody lip," he said, rubbing his face with those sausage-like fingers. "I'm telling Dat." Perry opened the back door, ran into the store, and slammed the door behind him, no doubt leaving a trail of gravy footprints down the back hall.

Emma gulped air into her lungs and smoothed her hand down her apron. Her heart was racing about a thousand beats per minutes. *Ach!* How she detested Perry Glick. How she wished she had eaten lunch in the kitchen. "Abraham, you can't hit people."

Abraham's anger seemed to run out as if he were a sieve. He slumped his shoulders. "He wouldn't let go of you. I got mad. I'm sorry."

She pressed her fingers to her forehead. "I sound

like I'm ungrateful. I'm not, but I'm not helpless. I would have used my teeth. And my knee."

He cracked a reluctant smile even though his breathing was labored and heavy. "I don't think I would have wanted to see that."

"I wanted to see it. But I'll have to settle for the look on Perry's face when you hit him."

"I thought of Mary and Erna Bieler and you, and my blood just started boiling. Mary lived with the Englisch once. There's no one tougher than she is, but Perry still scared her. You're not helpless, but he shouldn't have done that to you."

"*Nae*, he shouldn't have. What about Erna Beiler?"

"Didn't you know? She used to work here, but Perry wouldn't leave her alone. That's why she quit."

Emma folded her arms and let out a long breath. "And why I got the job."

"I didn't hit him wonderful hard, just hard enough that he'll think twice before doing it again. I'm not ashamed I did it, but I'm sorry if I embarrassed you."

Emma felt sick to her stomach. It had been a sweet gesture, but so unlike Abraham. He had such a gentle spirit. "You don't have to apologize, Abraham, but don't you see that this could get you in a lot of trouble with the Glicks?"

He furrowed his brow. "I did what I thought was right. I don't care what happens to me."

Emma didn't know why, but the tone of his voice made her choke up and brought tears to her eyes. Protecting her was more important to him than the consequences of smacking Perry Glick. Who could ask for anything sweeter?

Out of the corner of her eye, Emma saw Mahlon and Moses Zook sprinting toward them from the empty field on the other side of the chain-link fence. Both boys hurtled the fence between the field and the restaurant in a single bound.

"Is everything okay?" Mahlon asked, panting as if he'd run three or four miles.

Moses wiped the sweat from his brow. "We was cutting across the field and saw Perry Glick go down."

Mahlon nodded. "Thought you might need some help."

Red heat crept up Abraham's face. "We . . . we don't need any help. *Denki.*"

Moses looked at Emma. "Are you okay? We saw what Perry did and took off running. Abraham beat us here."

"Abraham is strong enough to take two Perrys with one hand," Mahlon said.

Moses chuckled. "Three Perrys." His gaze flicked between Abraham and Emma. "I'm glad you have someone watching out for you, Emma. Abraham is a *gute* man."

The back door opened and slammed against the wall behind it. Raymond Glick stood in the doorway looking like a thunderstorm. "Emma Wengerd, I'm not paying you to meet boys behind the restaurant. Stop flirting and come help my wife with the dishes."

Emma hadn't done anything wrong, but she felt the shame of his rebuke all the way to her toes. She picked up her lunchbox, the bucket, and Perry's broken plate.

Raymond glared at Mahlon and Moses. "Don't you have better things to do than loiter outside my restaurant?"

"*Nae*, Raymond," Mahlon said, looking as embarrassed as Emma felt.

Raymond saved his nastiest expression for Abraham. "Abraham Petersheim, I would have a word with you inside. Now."

Abraham gave Emma a reassuring smile and followed Raymond into the building.

Emma was definitely going to be sick.

Chapter Twelve

Mamm didn't yell at him, which was a pretty *gute* indication that she thought he was hopeless. Of course he was hopeless. He'd lost one of their biggest buyers. They had two extra cases of Petersheim Brothers' Peanut Butter and nowhere to sell it. Abraham couldn't regret hitting Perry Glick, but Emma had said there would be consequences. Abraham hadn't thought that maybe those consequences would flow over to his whole family.

The peanut butter business had always supplemented their farm income, but in the last couple of years, peanut butter had proven to be a *gute* source of income for the family. Alfie and Benji would need braces, and Dawdi's medicine and doctor's visits were expensive. And Abraham had messed it all up.

The problem was, he didn't know what he would have done differently, because he refused to let Perry Glick keep smearing his lips all over Emma. Not now, not ever. But he shouldn't have let his righteous indignation get the better of him. If he didn't find another buyer for the peanut butter, they wouldn't be able to afford Dawdi's medication.

But Mamm didn't yell. She'd kind of given up on Abraham.

She still yelled at Austin and Alfie and Benji. They were her last hope.

Abraham finished milking the cows and let them out to pasture. Mamm was standing in the barn staring at the milk when he got back. "Is Snowball drying up?"

"I don't think so. It's been the same amount for three years."

Mamm nodded, as if even his milking skills were a lost cause. "I want you to go to the gathering tonight."

What was she talking about? "What? Why?"

"You did something very nice for Emma today. She might want to thank you."

Abraham turned and walked out of the barn. "She already thanked me."

"Well, let her thank you again. You deserve it."

"Mamm," Abraham said, expelling a deep breath from his lungs, "the Glicks aren't going to buy any more of our peanut butter. I don't deserve anything."

Mamm pressed her lips together. "Well, then. You owe it to me to go to the gathering. I hardly ever ask you to do anything."

"You ask me to do things all the time. I make peanut butter. I sweep the floor. I milk the cows and plant corn."

"I gave birth to you. You'll never be able to pay me back for that."

She had a point there, and maybe Emma would smile and wave to him tonight and he wouldn't feel like such a failure. Or such a wicked man. The Amish believed in nonviolence, and he had hit someone. Maybe doing something for his *mamm* would make up for a few of his mistakes.

But now that he and Emma were friends, he hated gatherings. He hated watching her talk to other boys. He hated seeing her laugh when they said something funny. He hated being on the outside looking in on Emma's life.

He'd never, ever tell her, but he wanted more. She liked him because she said he didn't expect anything from her, and that was true. He never expected her to talk to him at gatherings. He never expected her to want to be anything more than a friend. But that didn't mean he didn't want it with all his heart. He didn't expect more from Emma, but he for sure and certain wanted it. If that didn't make him pathetic, he didn't know what did. And maybe that made him a hypocrite too, because if she really knew what was in his heart, she wouldn't want to be friends with him anymore.

"I guess I could go and play basketball," he said, because *I really don't want to watch Emma flirt with other boys* would have sounded pitiful.

Mamm patted him on the shoulder. "There you go. It will be fun, and Emma will get a chance to thank you."

"She already thanked me."

"I don't care," Mamm said as she strolled into the house.

Alfie and Benji darted around the corner of the house as if they had been waiting for Mamm to go away before appearing. "Abraham," Alfie said, smiling as if he'd found another dog in the forest, "we heard you socked Perry Glick today."

Benji nodded and swiped the back of his hand across his nose. "Willie told us."

Abraham should have known his *bruderen* would find out. Willie Glick was Perry's cousin. "I shouldn't have done it. Don't ever hit anyone."

Alfie's eyes sparkled with delight. "Willie says you made Perry's lip bleed."

Abraham didn't regret hitting Perry, but he had been a poor example for his *bruderen*. "I was wrong to hit him."

"I don't think you were wrong. He kissed Emma. You had to protect her."

Abraham frowned and squatted to be eye level with his *bruderen*. "Violence never solves anything and usually makes things worse. Raymond Glick won't buy our peanut butter anymore, and my hand hurts something wonderful."

"It's cuz you did it wrong." Alfie made a fist and showed Abraham. "Willie says you'll break your thumb if you do it like this." He curled his fingers around his thumb and swung his fist back and forth.

"Did you break your thumb?" Benji said.

Abraham growled softly. "It doesn't matter where I put my thumb."

"*Jah*, it does," Alfie insisted. "If you keep your thumb on the outside of your fingers and squeeze as tight as you can, your hand won't hurt when you hit somebody."

Benji nodded. "And if you put a roll of pennies in your fist, it will hurt even worse . . . the person you hit, I mean."

Abraham put one hand on Alfie's shoulder and one on Benji's. "It doesn't matter, because you are never going to hit anyone. Do you understand?"

Benji's smile drooped. "But Willie gave us lessons."

Maybe Alfie and Benji shouldn't hang out with Willie Glick so much.

Abraham rubbed his aching hand. Maybe he should have taken lessons.

After dinner, Abraham hitched up the buggy, and he and Austin went to the gathering, which was at Kaufmann's house. They didn't have a basketball court, but they had a basket and backboard nailed to their shed with a good-sized cement pad to play on. It wasn't perfect, but six people could play without bumping into one another too much.

Abraham didn't even look for Emma when he and Austin strolled into the backyard. He didn't want to feel worse than he already did tonight. He took his basketball to the cement pad and started shooting baskets.

"*Hallo*, Abraham," Tyler said, getting the rebound and throwing the ball to Abraham. "I heard what you did to Perry Glick today. It's about time."

Ach. It shouldn't have surprised him that Tyler knew about the whole thing. Mahlon Zook was Tyler's best friend.

Abraham kept shooting. He hoped no one but his little *bruderen* and Tyler and Willie Glick knew about it. And the Zook brothers. He didn't want Emma to be embarrassed.

Matt Gingerich stole the ball and took a shot that

went wide. He grinned at Abraham. "Why didn't you tell us you and Emma are dating?"

Abraham's heart skipped a beat. "Who told you that?"

"I don't remember. Everybody's heard it. Mahlon Zook says Perry kissed Emma and you got mad."

That was true enough, but Emma wouldn't be happy if the rumor started that she was interested in Abraham. "Perry thinks people like him when they don't," he said bitterly. It was true, but it wasn't nice. Why was he so spiteful all of a sudden? Perry had gotten what he deserved and that was the end of it.

Lizzy, surrounded by three other girls, sidled near and stood with her toes on the edge of the cement. All four girls were chewing on their fingernails and looking very concerned, Lizzy especially. "Psst, Abraham," she said, as if it was possible to get his attention without anyone else knowing. "I need to talk to you."

Abraham tossed the ball to Matt and tried not to look too worried, especially since some of the other boys were watching. Something was wrong, and he had a feeling it was his fault. He followed Lizzy to the nearest tree and away from the game. Lizzy's friends gave her some space but probably not enough that they wouldn't be able to hear the entire conversation if they listened carefully.

Lizzy glanced at her friends and walked around to the other side of the tree. Abraham followed. She was as somber as a sixteen-year-old girl could get. "Emma is wonderful upset."

Abraham swallowed the lump in his throat. Whatever it was, it was his fault. "What happened?"

Lizzy gave him a sharp look. "What did you say to Raymond Glick?"

"Raymond Glick?"

"What did you say to him after you punched Perry?"

Abraham drew his brows together. "I . . . I only remember saying about five words. He yelled at me for hitting Perry and then told me they would no longer buy Petersheim Brothers' Peanut Butter."

Lizzy's frown dug deeper into her face. "*Ach*. I'm sorry."

"I expected it."

Something like amusement flashed in Lizzy's eyes. Then she slumped her shoulders and seemed to lose all hope of happiness. "Before Emma could even tell me about Perry, Raymond fired both of us."

Abraham took in a sharp breath. "He fired you?"

"He said Emma tricked Perry into coming outside so you could attack him and that he wouldn't stand for such wickedness at his restaurant. Even Martha, who never says anything to Raymond, tried to talk him out of it, but he wouldn't listen. He made us hand over our aprons and get out."

"*Ach*, Lizzy. I can't believe it. I'm sorry."

A tear rolled down Lizzy's cheek. "I'll never get a husband if the boys think I'm wicked. But I didn't do anything wrong and neither did Emma."

"It was me. I take all the blame. I never thought you would get in trouble for something I did."

"You didn't do anything wrong either. If Perry Glick had kissed me, I would have set one of Emma's hens on him and let her scratch out Perry's eyes."

That was a little harsh, but Abraham understood the sentiment. The good news was that chickens didn't scratch out people's eyes as a general rule. "I'm wonderful sorry you lost your job. Maybe I should talk to Raymond Glick and tell him you had nothing to do with it."

Lizzy adamantly shook her head. "I wouldn't work for him if he paid me a hundred dollars a day. He's strict and never tells us '*Gute* job,' and he thinks we sneak food when he's not watching. Martha sometimes gives us tastes, but we don't sneak and Martha always says it's okay. And I hate Perry spying on Emma all the time. I wouldn't work there again even if Raymond begged me. He treated Emma like a dirty dishrag. I've told all my friends to tell all their friends not to work there."

Abraham's heart swelled. He loved Lizzy's righteous indignation, especially on behalf of her sister. "She must have been wonderful upset. Where's Emma now?" He didn't know why he asked. Emma didn't like him talking to her at gatherings. There wasn't much he could do to comfort her now. Or maybe what he needed to do was apologize. It was his fault she'd lost her job, and the Glicks were no doubt spreading rumors about her.

"She's over by the eats table," Lizzy said. "Our cousin Ben gave us a ride to the gathering tonight, and he'd already heard about what happened at the restaurant today. He said you and Emma are sweethearts."

Abraham widened his eyes. "Ben thinks we're sweethearts?"

Lizzy fidgeted with her *kapp* strings. "I made it worse because I laughed and said, '*Jah*, they are sweethearts.' I meant it as a joke, but Ben believed me. Emma said you weren't sweethearts, but Ben just laughed. He said you told Mahlon Zook that you and Emma are sweethearts and Mahlon told Tyler and Tyler told Ben."

Abraham widened his eyes. "Ben thinks I told Mahlon we are sweethearts?"

Lizzy wiped a tear from her cheek. "When we got here, Sarah King said that some of the boys were mad at Emma because she's been flirting with them when she already has a boyfriend. Now none of the boys will talk to her, and she's standing over there eating an oatmeal cookie and she hates oatmeal cookies."

Abraham couldn't see the eats table because he and Lizzy were hiding behind a tree. He sidled to one side of the trunk to look around it but couldn't see Emma anywhere. He needed to talk to her, to tell her it wasn't true. Just because he wanted to be sweethearts didn't mean he'd told anybody. His heart knocked painfully against his chest. Would she believe him?

He wanted to make things right, but if people saw them talking together, it might make things worse. "What do you think, Lizzy? Will people think we're dating if I go talk to her?"

Lizzy looked at him as if he'd asked her to add two high numbers in her head. "But you are dating. You've come to our house a dozen times. That counts, doesn't it?"

Abraham folded his arms across his chest. "It doesn't count, Lizzy. We're not dating."

Lizzy looked at him sideways. "But you do like her. I know that for sure and certain."

Ach. How many other people could tell that he was crazy about Emma just by looking at him? He had tried not to follow Emma around like a little puppy, but maybe people had seen it just the same. He truly was pathetic. A ten-pound piece of coal settled at the bottom of his stomach. He'd never come to a gathering again. He'd probably have to stop going to church or at least move to another district. "It doesn't matter how I feel."

"I guess," Lizzy said. "Emma is always worried about what other people think, especially the cute boys. But you're the only one Emma can talk to. You listen to her. She likes to tell you things. Even if she doesn't want to be seen with you, she needs you."

Okay. He'd talk to her, but just this once and only because she was really upset and he wanted to make it better. "*Denki*, Lizzy. I'll see what I can do."

"*Gute*." Her tears dried up, and she gave Abraham a wide smile. "I'm *froh* you put Perry Glick in his place. Everybody thinks so. I don't care what Raymond Glick says. The Petersheims are not a wicked family. And neither are the Honeybee *schwesteren*. The Glicks hate the Honeybee sisters even more than they hate the Petersheims. They can squawk all they want. It won't make anyone like you less."

Abraham's stomach dropped to the ground. Raymond could say anything he wanted about Abraham, but Raymond shouldn't drag Abraham's family into his grudge. There were no better people than Mamm and Dat and Andrew and Mary. Even Mammi and Dawdi.

Abraham glanced around to make sure no one was watching before he made his way to the eats table. It was going to be impossible to get there unnoticed. It seemed that every eye was on him as he ambled across the grass, trying not to draw attention. Seven or eight girls waved, and more than one boy grinned at him as if they were in on the secret. Oh, *sis yuscht.*

Emma stood facing the crowd of young people, holding an uneaten cookie in her hand and staring off into the distance as if she wasn't really at the gathering. He could tell she saw him approach because she sort of turned away from him. She didn't run, though she probably wanted to, but running away would draw more attention than standing quietly at the table talking with someone who may or may not be her boyfriend.

Abraham got close to her but turned his back to everybody else and pretended to be choosing one of the many treats at the table. "I'm sorry, Emma."

She kept her gaze riveted on something hundreds of miles away. "Why did you tell Mahlon we were sweethearts?"

He meant he was sorry she got fired, but the sweethearts rumor was a good place to start. "I never told anybody we were sweethearts."

"Now everybody thinks I'm a flirt and a liar. They think we've been dating."

"I never told anyone we were dating."

"Boys like to brag. I didn't think you were that kind of boy."

"I'm not."

"Mahlon and Moses saw you hit Perry, and now they think you and I are more than friends. What did you tell them?"

Abraham picked up a lemon bar, then thought better of it and put it back. Lemon bars were *appeditlich,* but they had too much powdered sugar, and he couldn't have a serious conversation with powdered sugar all over his lips. "I didn't tell them anything."

Keeping tight hold of her cookie, Emma folded her arms. "You shouldn't have hit Perry. Mahlon and Moses thought you were protecting your girlfriend, and people believe the rumor that we're sweethearts. Now they think I'm a flirt. They think I tricked them. No one will talk to me."

He didn't know how many times he should say sorry, but he said it again. "I'm sorry, Emma, but I couldn't stand there and let Perry do that."

"You didn't have to hit him. If he'd heard your voice, he would have backed off. He's afraid of other boys."

"I should have handled it differently."

Emma took a step to the side, as if that would put enough distance between them to make a difference. "I got fired. Now Raymond Glick is telling everybody that I'm a lazy worker who stole money from him."

Abraham's blood started a slow rolling boil. "He accused you of stealing?"

"He said I sat out back and talked to boys when I should have been working—he said my eating lunch was stealing money from his business."

"That's not fair. We should tell everybody the truth."

"Not *we*," Emma said. "I'm going to tell everybody the truth, if they'll believe me."

Abraham couldn't ignore the little stab of pain her words gave him. "Emma, I didn't tell anybody we are sweethearts."

She sniffed. "It doesn't matter now anyway. Everybody hates me."

"Nobody hates you. They just heard a rumor. I can fix it."

She turned on him, as if she'd just realized he was

standing there. He dropped his cookie in surprise. "You can't fix it. You've made it worse. I just want to have fun and spend time with my friends. Is that so bad?"

She had once told him she wanted to be friends, but she was obviously talking about her other friends. Her real friends. Another stab right to the gut.

She set her uneaten cookie on the table. "I don't want your help with the chickens anymore. And please keep that dog away from my coops." She let out a sigh that came out more like a sob, turned her back on him, and walked away.

There had never been pain like this. He felt it like a hot coal at the center of his chest. In an effort to protect Emma, he'd ruined everything for her. Her friends had rejected her, the boys thought she was a flirt, the district believed she was a thief. He didn't know what to do, but he knew he had to get out of there, to go somewhere no one could find him. Not that anyone would care to look.

Might as well face the truth about himself. Most people thought he was nice, but nobody really cared one way or the other about him—except for Mamm and Dat and his *bruderen*—and he was beginning to wonder about his *bruderen*. Austin was too wrapped up in himself, and Alfie and Benji hid more things from him than they told.

He'd told Mamm he'd go to the gathering, but he hadn't promised to stay.

Abraham walked out of the yard without telling Austin. Austin would figure out he'd left. Probably. Abraham started in the direction of home even though he didn't want to go home. Maybe he could spend the night with Tintin in his hideout. Tintin would never lecture him or be disappointed. Tintin would never be ashamed to talk to him at gatherings. Tintin was his friend.

Everyone needed a friend like that.

Chapter Thirteen

Alfie clutched the full pillowcase tightly in his fist and knocked on Bitsy's door while Benji tried to keep Tintin from pulling his leash right out of Benji's hands. Tintin jumped and pranced around Bitsy's porch like there was a party waiting for him on the other side of Bitsy's door. Tintin loved coming to Honeybee Farm, probably because it smelled like cats and flowers.

Bitsy opened the door. She wasn't holding her shotgun, but she leaned on it like a cane. Her hair was a normal reddish-brown color, but there was a little picture of a flower on her neck, like someone had painted it there, and she wore round gold earrings that looked like a pair of canning lids.

"So," Bitsy said, "it looks like you caught your dog."

Benji wrestled with Tintin and the leash. "I like your earrings."

Bitsy shook her head so Alfie and Benji could hear how her earrings tinkled. "If you're trying to soften me up, don't bother. I'm not letting that dog in my house. He'll stink up the rug and shed on the sofa."

Alfie squinted into Bitsy's house. "But don't you have four cats?"

"Four too many."

"Cats shed more than dogs."

Bitsy shook her head. "I don't need more animal hair in the house, and don't pretend you know more about cats than I do."

Benji got that really sad look on his face that made grown-ups feel sorry for him. "But, Bitsy, we have to bring him in or he'll run away."

It didn't work on Bitsy. She took Tintin's leash and hooked it around her doorknob. "He'll be fine out here, and I just pulled a loaf of apple bread from the oven. Would you like a piece?"

Alfie looked at Benji.

Benji looked at Alfie. "He'll probably be okay out here."

Benji was a *gute* partner. And smart when it was really important.

After making sure Tintin's leash was tightly hooked to the doorknob, they followed Bitsy into the house. Benji had to hold Tintin back long enough for Bitsy to close the door. Tintin was a little sad at being left out, but Alfie promised to save him a piece of apple bread and Tintin seemed to cheer up.

Alfie gently set his pillowcase on the floor next to his chair, then sat at the table next to Benji while Bitsy sliced the bread and poured them two glasses of milk. She brought their snacks to the table. The bread still had steam rising from it.

"*Denki*, Bitsy," Benji said, taking a big bite and then another without even swallowing the first one. "We wanpoo halk to oo."

Bitsy handed Benji a napkin. "Eat your bread, then we can talk."

Benji swallowed and took a drink of milk to wash it down his throat. "This is better than our bread at home."

Bitsy raised her eyebrow. "I'm sure your *mamm* makes excellent bread."

"She does," Alfie said. "But Mammi bought some special bread for us at the store."

Benji nodded. "It's supposed to keep us regular, and I don't even know what that means. Mamm throws it in the garbage when Mammi is away shopping."

Alfie finished off his apple bread in about four bites. He wanted to ask for another piece, but he didn't want to be rude, especially since they needed to stay on Bitsy's good side. He wiped his mouth with the napkin, like boys with good manners were supposed to. Good manners would make Bitsy like them better. "We sure like our new dog," he said, trying to ease into the conversation.

Bitsy sort of smiled, cleared her throat, and then frowned. "Does your *mamm* know about your new dog yet?"

Benji smiled wide. "For sure and certain she doesn't. Tintin has a hideout in the woods."

"Abraham helped us buy dog food with the money you gave us." Alfie swallowed hard. "We sure were grateful for the money."

Unfortunately, Bitsy wasn't *dumm*. She leaned back in her chair. "So. You need more money."

Benji squished his lips upward toward his nose. "We're almost out of dog food, and Abraham and Emma almost love each other."

Alfie nodded. "She played games with us one night, and she kept smiling at Abraham. Then Abraham bought her some Silkies, and she smiles even more."

Benji leaned closer to Bitsy. "Silkies are chickens with fur."

Bitsy got that funny look on her face again, like she was going to laugh and then growl at them. "It sounds like things are coming along well, but it wonders me why you picked Emma Wengerd. Abraham is the salt of the earth, and Emma is a little too impressed with her own popularity."

"What does that mean?" Alfie said.

Benji licked the crumbs off his napkin. "We picked Emma because Abraham stared at her all the time, but he was too afraid to talk to her. Tintin brought them together."

"That's a *gute* reason." Bitsy propped her elbow on the table. "I heard Abraham had a fight with Perry Glick."

Benji nodded so hard his hair flapped in the breeze. "Because he loves Emma now, and it's all Tintin's fault."

Bitsy wiped her hand across her mouth like she was wiping away a smile. "*Ach, vell* then. It sounds like Tintin's done a *gute* job."

Alfie hopped from his chair, retrieved his pillowcase, and reached his hand inside. "We need money for dog food, but we aren't asking for charity. We have things to sell."

Bitsy wiped her hand across her mouth again. Why didn't she use a napkin like anybody with *gute* manners? "I don't know that you'll have anything I want to buy, but I'll take a look."

Alfie pulled out the carton of eggs they'd bought

from Emma a few days ago. "We can sell you these eggs for four dollars."

Bitsy narrowed her eyes. "A dozen eggs for four dollars is pretty steep."

"*Ach, vell,*" Alfie said. "It's only eleven eggs."

Benji took his last drink of milk. "We dropped one."

"Four dollars is a lot of money for eleven eggs."

Alfie squirmed in his chair. He had been hoping Bitsy wouldn't notice they'd added three dollars to the price, but she was too smart for that.

Benji raised his pointer finger. "It's one dollar for the eggs and a three-dollar delivery fee." Alfie beamed at Benji. Sometimes he was a wonderful *gute* partner.

Bitsy's eyebrows crept closer together. "That sounds reasonable. It's a trial having to go fetch my own eggs. I'll buy them. Put them here on the table."

Alfie set the egg carton on the table and then pulled a bird's nest from his bag. He hated to give this one up, but Abraham and Emma weren't married yet and it was no time to be stingy. "This is the best nest from my collection. It still has two little blue eggs in it."

Bitsy peered into the nest. "Did you knock it down, young man?"

"*Nae.* We found it a year ago. It fell from the tree, and I think the mother bird just flew away. The eggs never hatched."

"I can see that." Bitsy held out her hand, and Alfie handed the nest to her. He hated to do it, but he didn't want to be sleeping in the cellar for the rest of his life. "How much?" Bitsy said.

"Twenty dollars," Benji said.

Alfie gave Benji the stink eye. They'd agreed on

ten dollars. Bitsy would never pay twenty dollars for a bird nest, even with two eggs in it.

"Okay," Bitsy said, "but only if you keep it at your house. I'm afraid my cats would try to eat those eggs and then the house would really stink. Right, Farrah Fawcett?"

Farrah Fawcett the cat looked up when she heard her name but seemed very uninterested in robin eggs. Alfie tried not to smile. It would be just like he'd never sold his nest. He could still keep it with his collection until all of Bitsy's cats died. And that could be years from now. This was the best day of his life.

"What else have you got?" Bitsy said. "And put that nest back in your bag. I don't want you to leave without it."

Benji pulled the Tic Tac box from his pocket. This was sure to earn them at least five dollars. He handed it to Bitsy. "Look," he said.

Bitsy held the box up to the light of the window, gasped, and nearly dropped the box. She shuddered. Maybe they'd get six dollars out of it. "Is this a spider?"

"Don't worry," Benji said. "He's dead."

Bitsy set the box on the table and frowned. "This is a black widow spider. Do you know they're poisonous?"

Alfie swallowed hard. "We know."

"We found him in the cellar, but he was already dead," Benji said. "Now Alfie sleeps with the lights on, even if it uses all the battery."

"This is why Abraham needs to get married. We're going to get killed in that cellar, and no one will even care."

"I care. I promise I'll come to your funeral." Bitsy pushed the spider away from her. "I'll give you three dollars to take that box out behind the barn and bury it."

Benji scratched his cheek. "You don't want to keep it?"

"Three dollars is my final offer."

"Okay," Alfie said. He knew a *gute* deal when he saw it. He pulled the last thing out of the pillowcase and rolled it around in his hand. "This is a real gold rock Mamm bought me at Wisconsin Dells last summer. She paid three dollars for it, but I can sell it for two."

Bitsy took the rock and held it next to her eye. "This looks just like something I need to decorate my bookshelf. I'll take it. I owe you twenty-nine dollars."

Alfie couldn't help but smile. They'd have enough money to buy Tintin a huge bag of dog food. Maybe they'd get out of that cellar after all.

Bitsy went to her bookshelf. She set the gold rock on top and pulled out her Bible. "Here is thirty dollars," she said, pulling some cash from between the pages and handing it to Alfie. "Keep the change, and tell me what your plans are for Emma and Abraham?"

Alfie pressed his lips together. Their plans were top secret, like in a spy movie. "We can't tell you."

Benji nodded. "But we might do something with blood."

Bitsy waved her hand in the air. "Actually, I don't want to know. That way, your *mamm* won't blame me when something burns down." She put a hand on Alfie's shoulder. "Whatever you're doing, keep up the *gute* work. I want to see fireworks at the wedding."

"We will," Alfie said, clutching the thirty dollars in his fist.

"And please get your slobbery dog off my porch. I'm going to have to spray the whole thing with hand sanitizer."

Alfie opened the door and took Tintin's leash off the knob. "Bye, Bitsy. *Denki* for the money. You won't regret buying that nest. It's always been my favorite."

Bitsy picked up the Tic Tac box with two fingers. "For goodness' sake, don't leave without burying the spider. I paid good money to be rid of it."

Chapter Fourteen

Hannah Yutzy was the most good-natured girl Abraham had ever met, next to Emma. She was loud and funny and made everyone comfortable. She had also been Austin's best friend since they were kids.

Hannah and her family ran a fruit and vegetable and doughnut stand in Bienenstock that was open from early May until September or whenever it got too cold to make doughnuts outside. They also sold fresh produce and Amish jams and jellies. The Glicks held a grudge against a lot of families, and they didn't like the Yutzys because Raymond Glick said the doughnut stand stole business from Glick's market and restaurant. Once he asked the bishop to make the Yutzys close down because people in the same *gmayna* shouldn't compete against one another.

Sometimes Abraham wondered if Raymond had any friends left.

Abraham walked to the Yutzys' doughnut stand on Monday morning, deciding he didn't deserve the buggy. He'd already caused everybody enough trouble. Hannah and her *bruder* James were at the stand, making doughnuts using a deep-fat fryer powered by a gas generator.

Hannah was dribbling some frosting on a hot doughnut when she caught sight of Abraham. She practically exploded into a smile. "Abraham Petersheim, it's been ages, absolutely ages since I saw you. *Vie gehts*? I heard you gave Perry Glick something to remember last week." She didn't wait for a reply. "As a member of the *gmayna*, I can't approve of your actions. As a girl who knows what it's like to be cornered by Perry Glick at the library, I couldn't be happier. Everybody's grateful, you know."

Nae. Most people thought he was wicked. Or they thought he had punched Perry because Emma was his girlfriend. Abraham expelled a deep breath. "Hannah, I'm here to ask you two favors. One is very big, and one is even bigger."

Hannah grinned and widened her eyes. "Sounds exciting. Tell me the big one first so I can prepare myself for the bigger one."

"The Glicks won't sell our peanut butter at their store anymore, and I was wondering if you might be willing to sell it here. I know you don't have a lot of space. . . ."

"Of course," Hannah said, clapping her hands as if he'd just given her a million dollars. "We've wanted to carry Petersheim Brothers' Peanut Butter here, but we're trying not to make the Glicks mad. Now that they've stopped buying your peanut butter, we can in good conscience carry it here."

"The Glicks will still probably be mad."

"Of course they will. That makes it all the better."

Abraham felt a little guilty that the thought of

making the Glicks mad brought him a little thrill of
pleasure. He shouldn't wish for anyone's misfortune
or unhappiness. "How many bottles do you want?"

"Give me a dozen to start with, but for sure and
certain, we'll need more once people know we've got
your peanut butter here. Some folks go to Glick's
Market just for your peanut butter."

Abraham swallowed past the lump in his throat.
"*Denki.*" At least he could start to right that one mistake.

"That wasn't a really big favor. What's the
bigger one?"

Abraham almost chickened out. This was a *dumm*
plan. He'd end up offending Hannah, Austin, and
probably every girl in the *gmayna*. But he had to make
things right for Emma. This was the only way he
knew how. "Can I drive you home from the gathering
this week?"

Emma lay on her bed and stared at the ceiling.
She had never been so profoundly unhappy in her
life. It was an unfamiliar feeling, and she didn't know
what to do with it, didn't know who to blame or
how to fix it.

Ach, vell. She knew who to blame, but she didn't
want to think about him. It just made her sadder.

Lizzy barged into the room and threw herself across
her bed. "Emma," she said, using that I'm-so-excited
voice she'd used on Emma all week, as if she could
cheer Emma up just by acting enthusiastic enough.
Lizzy was trying too hard, and Emma just didn't
have the stomach for it. Lizzy propped her chin in
her hand and smiled as if Emma's life hadn't been

ruined by Perry Glick and Abraham Petersheim. "The gathering starts in half an hour. Mamm says we can take the buggy. Doesn't that sound fun?"

"I'm pretty tired."

"I'll help you feed the chickens before we go."

Emma pressed her head into her pillow. "I'm not in the mood."

Lizzy rolled onto her back and let her head dangle over the side of the bed so she was looking at Emma upside down. "Emma, you're always in the mood to be with your chickens."

"Not tonight."

Lizzy rolled over again, got on all fours, and leapfrogged onto Emma's bed, landing on top of Emma. "Come on, Emma. You've been moping for over a week."

Emma tried to take a deep breath with Lizzy pressing on her. "It's not my fault I lost my job and have no friends. It's not my fault I'm so miserable."

Lizzy got off Emma, sat up, and pulled her feet underneath her. "You think it's Abraham's fault."

"Who else?"

Lizzy puckered her lips. "Well, I'm sure it's Abraham's fault, though probably not in the way you think it is."

Emma wasn't in the mood for Lizzy's games, but she asked anyway. "What is that supposed to mean?"

"You were wonderful mean to him."

"I was not."

Lizzy kneed Emma in the arm. "You were. And now you feel bad about it. You feel so bad that you don't even want to see your chickens."

"That is so unfair. Abraham told Mahlon we were dating. Now the boys ignore me, and the girls think

I lied or at least kept a big secret from them." Emma rolled over and turned her back on Lizzy. "Nobody likes me anymore."

Lizzy sighed as if she was barely putting up with Emma. "This is *dumm*. Come to the gathering tonight, and we'll fix it. I'll spread it around that you and Abraham are not sweethearts, and you can go to each boy individually and explain yourself. You're pretty, and they're already inclined to like you."

"What if Abraham is there?"

"Then you can ignore him like you always do. But after how you treated him, he'll probably stay as far away from you as possible."

"You keep saying that. I wasn't mean. I just told him how I feel. I should be able to tell him how I feel."

"I guess so, but you never tell any of the other boys how you feel—how you really feel," Lizzy said.

Emma pretended she didn't understand what Lizzy meant. But her heart hurt all the same. "Do you really think I could fix it with the *buwe*?"

"We can fix it together," Lizzy said. "You know how fast news travels in the *gmayna*."

Emma caught her bottom lip between her teeth. She wouldn't be able to fix it if she stayed away. And wouldn't *die youngie* gossip about her *more* if she wasn't there? "I guess I could go."

Lizzy jumped off Emma's bed and threw her hands in the air. "Wear your pink dress. I love the pink dress."

Emma curled one side of her mouth. "It accents my eyes."

Emma ran outside and fed her chickens, then Dat let them take the buggy to the gathering. Emma's heart somersaulted over itself. She was usually so excited for gatherings. Tonight, she was wonderful nervous. She wasn't used to facing rejection or even indifference. What if she couldn't fix it?

Lizzy took her by the hand and pulled her into the house where Ruth and Lisa Hoover were helping their *mamm* make pretzels for *die youngie.*

"Lizzy! Emma!" Ruth hugged both of them gingerly because she had sticky dough all over her fingers. "We're making about a thousand pretzels. *Buwe* love them. They gobble them up as fast as we can bake them."

"Girls eat almost as much as the *buwe* do," Lisa said. She smiled at Emma as if she didn't hate her at all. "It is *gute* to see you."

"You too. I never see you at gatherings anymore."

Lisa laughed. "I'm twenty-nine. Too old for gatherings." She sprinkled salt on a pretzel. "I heard you had a bit of a scrape last week."

Ruth raised an eyebrow. "Perry Glick should be sent to obedience school, like the dogs."

Lisa glanced behind her to make sure no one was listening. "His lip was as fat as a ping-pong ball at *gmay*. Did you see it?"

Jah, Emma had seen it. Word was that Perry's *dat* had made Perry go to *gmay* so people would see how wicked Abraham Petersheim was. Emma had been surprised they hadn't asked Abraham to make a kneeling confession, but maybe Raymond hadn't wanted anyone to hear why Abraham had punched Perry in the first place. Emma's heart beat an unruly rhythm. Abraham had hit Perry to protect her. How could she be anything but grateful?

And yet she was acting so ungrateful.

Emma pressed her lips together and tried to clear

her thoughts. If she wanted to be popular with the boys again, she couldn't worry about Abraham.

Lisa and Ruth's *mamm*, Esther, wiped her hands down her cream-colored apron. "I'd like to give Abraham a whole plate of pretzels. He's a brave boy, even if it's wrong to hit people."

Ruth smiled. "What a blessing he chose you as his sweetheart."

Lizzy jumped in so quickly, Emma didn't have a chance to say a word. "*Ach*, Abraham and Emma aren't sweethearts. Abraham was just being nice."

Ruth drew her brows together. "I thought for sure and certain I heard you were sweethearts." Her eyes sparkled with mischief. "All the girls are so jealous of you."

"There's nothing to be jealous about," Emma said, nearly choking on her words.

This news made Ruth very excited. "I might have to go play basketball with the *buwe*. That would get Abraham's attention. I'd even let him drive me home if he asked."

Lisa patted the pretzel dough on the cutting board. "You should hope he doesn't ask tonight. You're already home."

Lisa, Ruth, and Lizzy laughed as if that was the funniest thing they'd ever heard. Emma couldn't even manage a smile. Abraham was shy. If all these girls suddenly wanted to show their gratitude, he might feel like he was being attacked. And why was Ruth suddenly interested now? Abraham was as tall and handsome as he ever had been. The girls shouldn't be clamoring for his attention just because he did something nice for Emma. He was just as nice as he had always been.

Something like guilt and regret pressed on her chest.

"Would you like to help us finish the pretzels?" Lisa asked.

"Emma would," Lizzy said. "But I need to go outside and talk to some of *die youngie.*" She gave Emma a significant look. Lizzy was planning to single-handedly squash a rumor.

"We have the volleyball set up," Esther said.

Lizzy was already halfway out the door. "Okay."

All Ruth and Lisa could talk about was Abraham while they finished the pretzels. They were appalled at Raymond Glick's behavior, and even more shocked that Emma had been fired. They were impressed at how unselfish Abraham had been to protect Emma, even knowing what kind of trouble he'd be in. By the time they were done making pretzels, Emma felt thoroughly wretched and could barely remember why she'd been so mad at Abraham in the first place.

Just in time, she thought about all the boys who would avoid her tonight because of Abraham's rumor. That was enough to stoke her righteous indignation.

She carried a plate of hot pretzels to the eats table and was surrounded by four boys who each wanted one.

Adam grabbed a pretzel before she set the plate on the table. "*Denki*, Emma. You were always so nice."

Matt Gingerich used a napkin to hold his pretzel between his fingers. "You should come play volleyball, Emma. I want you on my team."

He did? Didn't he care that she already had a

boyfriend—or rather didn't he believe the rumor? "I would like that," she said, blooming into a smile.

"*Nae*, Emma," Mahlon Zook said. "You want to be on my team. My team always wins."

Okay, this kind of attention was what she was used to. Girls who already had boyfriends did not get this kind of attention. Lizzy had been busy.

Mahlon and Adam walked off to play volleyball, urging her to join them as soon as she could. Lizzy ran up and grabbed her hand. "You'll never guess." She pointed to a concentrated group of boys and girls. Abraham stood in the middle of them, easy to see because he was taller than everybody. "The girls met him like a swarm of bees the minute he got here. He told everybody first thing that you and he weren't sweethearts and that you weren't interested in him." She got a funny look on her face. "I like that he tries to be honest."

Emma could only fake a smile. "*Ach*. That's wonderful nice of him."

"Linda Eicher and Anna Schrock were too eager, like mosquitoes zooming in for an attack. I don't think Abraham expected it. The girls don't believe you and Abraham are a couple anymore. All the boys know too. Abraham fixed it before I had a chance."

Emma could barely breathe past the heaviness in her chest. "That's nice of him . . . but . . . but I still don't have a job." That was Abraham's fault. There was still something she could blame him for.

"Abraham says Bitsy Weaver might be able to get us jobs at the care center in Shawano. They have a van that picks up employees."

Emma couldn't make sense of it. "Bitsy Weaver?"

"She knows a lot of Englischers. Abraham talked

to her about finding us a job." Lizzy could barely contain her excitement. "The care center pays better than the restaurant, and Perry Glick doesn't work there, and Mayne says they're wonderful nice. And they like Amish girls. I think we should try it out."

"*Ach.* That's wonderful nice of Abraham."

Lizzy looked as if she was trying very hard to contain her laughter. "*Jah.* Abraham is wonderful nice. Ben told me there might be a job at the harness shop, and Scilla might be able to get you a job at the library. Nobody believes we're dishonest. Except Raymond Glick."

Emma should have been ecstatic. The boys were talking to her, and she might actually be able to start earning money again. "I'm . . . I'm so excited," she said, adding a little squeak so Lizzy would think she was sincere.

She was excited about getting a job—probably overjoyed—but she just couldn't feel anything but crushing guilt and overwhelming sadness. She couldn't remember the words she'd said to Abraham, but she remembered the look on his face and the despair in his eyes, and she remembered trying to talk herself into feeling justified in what she'd done.

Ach. She was so selfish.

Emma held her breath as Abraham waved goodbye to all his admirers. Was he leaving so soon? He peeled himself away from the crowd, and Hannah Yutzy went with him. Emma couldn't take her eyes off the two of them as they disappeared around to the front of the house. Only incredible determination kept Emma from following them. Where were they going? And why were they together? Hannah and Austin Petersheim had always been friends, but why was she with Abraham? Maybe she didn't feel well and needed a ride home, and Abraham had offered to drive her.

That was it. Lord willing, Hannah would get better soon.

Would Abraham come back?

Mandy Mishler, one of Lizzy's best friends, came running at Emma as if to warn her of a coming tornado. "Did you see that? Abraham asked Hannah if he could drive her home right there in front of everybody, and Hannah said yes. She didn't even act surprised."

Emma was definitely going to choke. Abraham liked Hannah Yutzy? That couldn't be. Abraham didn't like anybody but Emma. Her mouth went dry. Her throat ached with longing. And suddenly, it was all wrong. Nothing in her life was how it should be. She didn't want any of these other boys. They didn't know her. They didn't really care about her. They gave her the attention she craved, but not the closeness she needed.

Mandy snatched Lizzy's hand. "Isn't it romantic? I never would have guessed." She sighed longingly. "I wish he would pick me."

Lizzy glanced at Emma. "We're too young. Abraham would never pick us."

Tyler Kaufmann passed them carrying a handful of M&M's. "Emma," he said. "Come play volleyball. You can be on my team."

Mahlon and Moses Zook found Emma next. "*Hallo*, Emma," Mahlon said. "How are you feeling today? You didn't look so *gute* last week. I'm sure you were shaken up."

Emma yanked her thoughts away from the front yard and Abraham's buggy. "*Ach.* I am fine, *denki.*"

"You know we would have taken care of Perry if we had gotten there first," Mahlon said.

Emma gave him a curt nod. "*Denki.*" What else was there to do but thank him for the thought, even if she was pretty sure Abraham was the only one who cared about her enough to take such a risk. She caught her breath. Abraham was the only one, and he had been for many weeks.

"If you ever need us, you know you can always come to us for help," Mahlon said, but Emma was barely listening.

Would Mahlon Zook have taken her to Green Bay to buy a chicken? Would Adam Stoltzfus have refinished her roof or installed a solar heater for her Silkies? Would Matt Gingerich have made her Pigs-in-a-Blanket or been *gute* at Pictionary?

"Emma, are you okay?" Lizzy said.

Emma couldn't speak. She patted Lizzy on the shoulder, trying to send some sort of message, then turned and fled into the house. Lisa and her *mamm* were cleaning up the kitchen. Emma ran past them into the bathroom and locked the door. She pulled some toilet paper from the roll as she burst into tears.

Was Abraham really interested in Hannah? Emma had been proud and blind enough to think that she was Abraham's only friend. Maybe he'd been interested in Hannah all this time. It seemed reasonable, but Emma couldn't believe it. Or maybe she didn't want to believe it.

While crying her eyes out, she finally realized what she truly wanted. It wasn't the shallow attention of two dozen different boys, but the deep affection of just one. She didn't want to associate with boys who only cared about her because she was clever or pretty. She wanted to share her life with a boy who loved her for just being herself. She wanted a boy who liked chickens and didn't care if she ate every last hot dog on the plate. She wanted a boy who would listen to what she had to say instead of a boy who just wanted to flirt.

How could she have been so blind? How could she have taken Abraham for granted like that?

She knew the answer without having to think about it. She was selfish and proud and thought she was too important for someone as quiet and unassuming as Abraham Petersheim.

But Abraham Petersheim was the only boy she wanted, the only boy she knew she could love with her whole heart. The only boy who could love her with his. Abraham would never be ashamed of her chickens, even if she had been ashamed of them herself. Abraham would never abandon her like she had abandoned him. Abraham was the only one, and she'd stabbed him in the heart. *Ach*, how she wanted to take back every selfish thing she'd done, every unkind word she'd said.

And what if he truly didn't want to be friends anymore? She couldn't blame him, not after how she'd treated him. What if he really loved Hannah Yutzy? What if Hannah really loved him? Emma certainly wouldn't get in the way of that, no matter how much she longed for Abraham. Even if Abraham loved Hannah, Emma had to make things right between her and Abraham. She took a shuddering breath and thought of Hannah's smiling face. There might not be a way to go back and make it right.

After a gut-wrenching cry, Emma blew her nose and looked in the tiny mirror Josiah Hoover used for shaving. Her eyes were red, and her nose wouldn't stop dripping. She stuffed her handful of toilet paper into the garbage and left the bathroom.

The kitchen was empty when she returned. She sighed, left by way of the front door, and walked home. Even if Abraham couldn't love her, she could still make it right, though she knew in her heart it would never be right again.

Chapter Fifteen

Abraham sat on the floor leaning his head against the barn wall. He wasn't sure how he'd managed to milk the cows with this dull, throbbing ache in his chest, but a full stainless-steel milk bucket and a smaller pail sat near his feet, so he must have accomplished it somehow.

The days were getting hotter, and he welcomed the cool of the barn, even if it smelled of manure and hay. He'd have to take the milk in soon or Mamm would get worried and come out to find him. Mamm had been nothing but worried about him for two weeks. She hadn't yelled at Alfie and Benji hardly once, even when Alfie had used the clean peanut butter jars as bowling pins and a full jar of peanut butter as the bowling ball.

Abraham would have done anything to make Mamm stop worrying, but he was a failure as a son, and he didn't know what he could do to make things better. She'd be worrying for the rest of her life.

The door to the barn creaked open. *Ach.* He'd waited too long to bring in the milk pail. Mamm had decided to look for him. "You in here, Abe?"

Much as he didn't want to hear a lecture or watch Mamm tiptoe around his fragile feelings, he also didn't want to play hide-and-seek with his *mater*. She knew he was there. He might as well get it over with. "Over here."

He heard Mamm's light steps on the cement. She tapped the milk pail with her toe. "Is Snowball drying up?" She always asked that when she didn't have anything else to say to him. He was pretty much useless to everybody.

"*Nae*. Still producing the same as far as I can see."

She studied his face. "The gathering starts in an hour, and you've been working outside all day. You should take a shower or nobody will want to get near you."

Abraham propped his arms on his bent knees and closed his eyes. "Mamm, I know you're disappointed in me."

"You know no such thing."

"I know you're disappointed, but please don't make me go tonight. I just don't have the heart for it. Can you understand?"

The lines around Mamm's mouth deepened. "I heard you and Hannah Yutzy were coming along."

"We're not."

"What happened?"

Abraham let out a deep breath he felt like he'd been holding for days. "You won't like it."

"Don't assume I'll feel a certain way until you ask." There was a spark of irritation in her voice that gave Abraham encouragement. Mamm only got irritated if she didn't think you were a lost cause.

"A rumor started that Emma and I are sweethearts.

I wanted to stop the gossip, so I asked Hannah if I could drive her home."

Mamm squatted next to him. "Young man, you're making no sense whatsoever."

"Do you remember when I hit Perry?"

"How could I forget? It was one of your finest moments, next to the time you stole that dog."

She might as well have smacked him on the forehead. "You know about that?"

"Of course I know about that. You boys think I only have half a brain in my head, but I see a lot more than you think I see. I've got five sons. I have to stay on my toes." She sat next to him and leaned against the wall. "So what does hitting Perry have to do with Hannah Yutzy?"

"After I hit Perry, someone started a rumor that Emma and I were sweethearts. It made her wonderful upset, especially after it was my fault she lost her job."

Mamm shook her head. "That girl can't see past the nose on that pretty little face of hers. Austin has the same problem. But it's not fatal."

Abraham didn't want to talk about Emma. He'd let himself believe something about her that wasn't real. He'd been so in love, so naïve. He'd finally seen who Emma really was and hated himself for being such a fool. Mamm never needed to know. She already thought he was hopeless. "I told Hannah what happened and asked her to let me drive her home so *die youngie* would see that Emma and I are not sweethearts. Hannah was in on the plan from the beginning, and we told Austin too so he wouldn't think it was strange when I drove his best friend home from the gathering. I didn't want to hurt Hannah's chances with another boy, so I only drove her home twice. I'm not going to do it again. And I'm not going to go to the gathering tonight or ever. I know you're disappointed in me, Mamm, but I was meant to be a bachelor. The other boys will give you plenty of grandchildren."

Mamm growled and pushed herself from the wall. "If you say I'm disappointed in you one more time, I'm going to beat you with my spatula."

"It's okay, Mamm. You don't have to pretend. I am at peace with the person I am." He wasn't really, but maybe it would keep Mamm from worrying.

She narrowed her eyes. "What kind of hogwash is that?"

"I just want you to know I'm at peace."

"Abraham, I've only heard one person say she was at peace with herself and that is Bitsy Weaver. She sometimes uses Englisch phrases that don't make a lick of sense. Would you like to explain yourself?"

Mamm truly did know everything. He had been talking to Bitsy Weaver, and she'd made him feel much better about his choice to be a bachelor. Of course, right before he'd left Bitsy's house, she had told him to say *hallo* to Emma. Maybe she hadn't been altogether serious about this "making peace with himself" thing. "I don't need to get married to be happy. Mamm. Convincing a girl to marry me sounds like about the most horrible thing in the world. Too painful and too humiliating. I'd rather be single."

Mamm placed her hand on Abraham's knee. "Emma broke your heart."

He turned his face away. "She wasn't a *gute* kind of friend."

"Okay," Mamm said. "She was not a *gute* friend. You love her, and she disappointed you."

"I don't love her."

She put her arm around him. "Love is not a weakness, Abraham."

"It is when it makes you hurt this bad." A dam of pain broke somewhere in his heart. He covered his face as a sob parted his lips.

Mamm pulled her to him, and he cried into her shoulder. She let him cry for a few minutes while she smoothed her hand down his hair. "I'm never making caramel popcorn for Emma Wengerd again."

Abraham sat up and wiped his eyes. "I'm never buying chickens for any girl again, no matter how pretty she is."

"Alfie is forbidden to buy her eggs."

"I will never reroof another chicken coop."

"I will never make you go to another gathering. But you can always choose to go tonight so Emma knows she can't get away with treating you like this and so the other girls will know you're available. Diane Shrock told me her daughter thinks you're handsome."

"Mamm."

"What?"

"I'm not going to the gathering."

"I never said you had to."

Chapter Sixteen

"Do you see her? Over."

"Why can't I get up in the tree and you come down here with the ants? Spatula."

"Because I climb trees better than you, Benji. You're better at eating broccoli. Over."

The walkie-talkie crackled for a few seconds before Benji said anything. "My fingers hurt. Spatula."

"Don't you think my fingers hurt too? We had to do it. Over."

"Maybe we didn't have to do it. What if Tintin gets in real trouble this time? Spatula."

Benji was a *gute* partner, but he worried too much. Alfie sat up a little straighter on the branch. "We had to do it, Benji. Abraham and Emma haven't spoken to each other for thirty days. Or seventeen. I can't remember. But it's a long time, and this is an emergency. Over."

Benji didn't say anything for a few minutes, and Alfie hadn't even ordered radio silence. "A van is driving down the road. Spatula."

Alfie's heart sped up. "That's her. She doesn't take the bus anymore because she has a new job."

"You didn't say *over*. Spatula."

Alfie groaned softly. Benji was a *gute* partner, but it was time to cut him off. "Over and out," he whispered.

Emma hated gatherings. Why had she gone to the gathering last night? It had been such a waste of time. Nobody cared about anything but flirting and playing volleyball and eating pretzels. And Abraham hadn't been there. His girlfriend Hannah was there, but Abraham hadn't even made an appearance. Not that Emma would have done anything if he'd come, but at least she could have seen him, seen if he was happy with his new girlfriend, seen if he still liked playing basketball.

Emma and Lizzy slid out of the van that took them to work every morning and brought them back every night, three days a week. Emma liked her new job at the care center, she really did, but nothing brought her joy anymore. Not even her chickens.

"Bye, Mr. Long," Lizzy said. "Thanks for the ride."

The toothpick in Mr. Long's mouth bobbed up and down. "You girls be good."

Lizzy giggled. "We will. You be good too."

"I'm too old to make trouble. I have a bad knee."

Lizzy practically pranced to the house. "Mrs. Belmont said I'm the best Uno player she's ever seen."

"Mrs. Belmont cheats."

"I know," Lizzy said, skipping up the steps, "but when you get that old, Gotte forgives you for everything. And I like trying to catch her."

Emma trudged up the porch steps after Lizzy. "Do you want to wash dishes tonight or dry?"

Lizzy stopped short, and Emma almost knocked

her over. "For goodness' sake, Emma, just go and talk to him."

"Talk to who?"

Lizzy narrowed her eyes and pursed her lips. "Stop it."

"Stop what?"

"Stop pretending. Quit moping and go apologize. He'll forgive you. He doesn't have one petty bone in his body."

Emma didn't have to ask who Lizzy was referring to. He was the only person she thought about nowadays. "I can't apologize. Everyone will say I'm trying to steal Hannah's boyfriend."

"Why do you think they'd say that?"

Emma slumped her shoulders. "Because I want to steal Hannah's boyfriend."

Lizzy blew air from between her lips. "*Ach*, Emma. You've got it bad. Go talk to him."

"He doesn't want to talk to me. After the way I treated him, I wouldn't be surprised if he picked up and moved out of town just so he doesn't have to live close."

"It's not that bad," Lizzy said. "And Abraham wouldn't do that. He likes you. Maybe even loves you."

Emma plopped herself down on the top step. Lizzy sat next to her. "He installed a solar heater for me, Lizzy. A solar heater. And I blamed him for getting me fired, then got mad at him for starting a rumor he didn't start. And to top it off, I'm shallow, insensitive, and proud. If he liked me once, he doesn't anymore."

Lizzy put her arm around Emma. "I hate to say I told you so, but I told you so."

"You did not."

"You said he was harmless. I told you he was deep. You liked him. You were fighting it, but you liked him."

Emma wrapped her arms around her knees. "What does it matter now?"

"Because you need to go apologize. And maybe he still likes you."

Emma shook her head. "He has a girlfriend."

Lizzy tilted her head to one side. "Maybe he does. Maybe he doesn't. He didn't come to the gathering last night, and Hannah was there. Does that sound like true love to you?"

"He was busy."

Lizzy raised her eyebrows and got a serious look on her face. "You're never too busy for the woman you love. I read that in a fashion magazine at the library."

Emma didn't even allow herself to hope. Until she was sure about Abraham and Hannah, she'd stay away. It was the least she could do to make up for all the damage she'd done. Abraham would be happier if he didn't have to bother with Emma.

"Go talk to him," Lizzy said, in that growly voice she used when she didn't get her way.

Emma sighed. "Okay." But maybe it would be a letter and maybe it would be after a few years had passed. It hurt too much to face him today. "Tell Mamm I'll be in for dinner as soon as I feed the chickens."

Chapter Seventeen

"Rebecca, where are the cookie sheets?" Mammi said.

Mamm looked at Abraham, and he could tell she was trying very hard not to sigh in frustration. "Abraham, I think those cookie sheets are in the cellar next to Alfie and Benji's bed. Would you go find them?"

Abraham tromped down the stairs. The cellar was dark and damp and smelled like mold and dirty socks. Abraham felt sorry the boys had to sleep down here, but then again, it was cool in the summer with plenty of spiders to keep them company. It was like having their very own cave.

The cookie sheets Mammi had bought for the family were stacked next to Alfie and Benji's air mattress, and the boys were using the stack as sort of a nightstand. A dirty plate with two forks sat atop the cookie sheets, along with a used Band-Aid, a Popsicle stick, and some bug spray.

Abraham stuffed the Popsicle stick and the Band-Aid in his pocket and put the bug spray on Benji's pillow. He picked up the cookie sheets with the plate still on top and carried them upstairs.

Mammi was always eager to be helpful, and she came home with something new from the store every week for Mamm. One week she bought a bookshelf from Walmart because she said the family didn't read enough. That was about the time she instituted family reading hour. That was also about the time Andrew and Mary got married. Andrew didn't get married just to get out of family reading time, but that might have made him eager to push up the date.

Mammi had bought special soap and special cleaning rags and rose water for the boys to spray on themselves whenever they left the house. Andrew had hidden some *gute*, strong deodorant soap underneath the trash can liner in the bathroom so they didn't have to use Mammi's special soap when they showered. It smelled like roses and manure.

Mammi had also bought nine metal cookie sheets, not for making cookies but for the family to use as placemats when they ate dinner. Mammi said they would help keep the table clean, but they were really more work because each cookie sheet had to be washed after they ate. It seemed a lot easier to just wipe off the table.

Mamm stored most of Mammi's "gifts" in the cellar because she didn't have any room upstairs, and Mammi tended to forget about them. Abraham wasn't certain what had sparked Mammi's memory today, but it looked as if they'd be using the cookie sheets tonight.

"Where are those boys?" Mamm said, glancing at the clock.

The twins still had ten minutes. Plenty of time.

Abraham set the cookie sheets on the table, then set plates, silverware, and cups on the cookie sheets.

"The fork goes on the left, Abraham," Mammi called from the living room.

Abraham looked at the table. Every fork was in its correct place. "Okay, Mammi."

Someone tapped loudly and urgently on the front door. Mamm narrowed her eyes. "That sounds like trouble."

Abraham went into the living room and opened the door. His heart lurched. He hadn't expected to see Emma standing on his porch ever again. He hated how pretty she was, and he hated that he still loved her, even though she was shallow and proud. She was also extremely upset. Her cheeks were bright red, and he could see the trail her tears had taken down her face.

"Emma?"

"You . . . you need to come to the coop right now."

He frowned. "What is it?"

Mamm came out of the kitchen and caught sight of Emma. Her mouth hovered between a smile and a frown. Mamm could be grumpy and strict, and she was fiercely loyal to her boys. She probably wondered if Abraham would like it better if she was welcoming or cold. "*Ach. Hallo*, Emma." She had decided to be welcoming. "Won't you stay for dinner?"

Emma squeezed the edge of her apron in her fists. "I need Abraham to come with me."

Mamm eyed Emma suspiciously. "Be nice." Sometimes Mamm just couldn't resist.

Abraham grabbed his hat from the hook by the door. "Don't wait dinner on me."

Emma had turned and run down the steps before

Abraham even shut the door behind him. She moved fast, but with his long legs, he caught up to her before she reached the edge of the grass. "What happened? Is it the dog?"

Emma breathed heavily. She'd obviously run all the way to his house, and she certainly wasn't slowing her pace on the way back. "It's Queenie." A sob escaped her lips.

"Is she sick?"

"Just come."

They ran all the way to Emma's house. Emma stopped at the big coop and leaned against the fence. "Look. Just look."

At first he didn't see anything out of the ordinary. The hens seemed to be happily scratching the dirt, just as calm and empty-headed as they usually were. Then he realized. "Queenie's gone."

Emma erupted into fresh tears. "Not gone. Dead."

"Dead?"

"Look over there."

Abraham's mouth went dry. A few feet from the coop, he saw a single purple feather. Then another. Then another. He followed the trail of purplish gray feathers to the big oak tree. At the base of the tree sat a pile of purplish gray chicken feathers smeared with blood. Queenie had very possibly met her end right there under that tree.

It felt like someone had tied a millstone around Abraham's neck. Queenie was dead, Emma was completely distraught, and now he was going to have to get rid of the dog. His *bruderen* would be heartbroken. Did this story have a happy ending for anyone?

He squatted next to the feathers, took off his hat, and paid his last respects to Queenie. She had been a beautiful chicken. It made him sad to think how this hurt Emma. She loved all her chickens, but Queenie had always been her favorite. He gazed at Emma, who was still standing by the coop crying. "I'll take care of this," he said, because he didn't know anything else to say that would make her feel better.

She nodded and swiped her hand down her cheek. "I . . . I didn't know who else to tell."

"*Jah.* Okay." With a lump in his throat, he stood and put his hat on. "Someone will bring over some money. It won't make up for losing Queenie, but maybe you can buy another Lavender Orpington."

"I don't want any money."

He ambled back to the fence. "All the same, you'll get some."

He turned to go, and she reached out and wrapped her warm fingers around his arm. "I'm sorry, Abraham."

He had a feeling she was talking about more than just the chickens. His heart shattered into a million pieces. "I'm sorry too."

Emma turned over in bed and looked at the clock. 5:00 a.m. The bedroom she shared with Lizzy was at the back of the house, and she could hear that little Silkie rooster crowing. She might have to rethink owning a rooster. Hens were noisy enough, but roosters never seemed to shut up.

She got dressed, went downstairs, and lit the propane lamp. It was early enough to make cinnamon rolls for breakfast. She got to work. Mamm came downstairs while the rolls were rising and kissed Emma on the forehead. "Feel better this morning?"

Emma nodded, even though she didn't feel better at all. Losing Queenie was hard, but losing Abraham was the most painful experience of her life. *Ach*, how she'd wanted him to take her in his arms yesterday and tell her everything was going to be okay, tell her he loved her and forgave her for every stupid, unkind thing she'd ever done to him.

Instead, he had treated her like an acquaintance or just some girl in the *gmayna* who had come to complain about his *bruderen*. There was no affection in his voice, nothing in his expression that gave her any clue as to how he felt about her. Was he indifferent? Did he care for her at all? Had he ever cared more than a friend? She wanted to believe he had cared once. She took a shuddering breath. He might have liked her, but she had ruined it all because she had thought she knew what she wanted and for some reason, she had believed Abraham stood in the way of all her dreams. She hadn't realized he was the one she'd been looking for all her life.

But now she'd lost him, and no matter how badly her heart hurt, she wouldn't steal another girl's boyfriend.

The family ate breakfast together, and Lizzy talked enthusiastically about their new job. Emma stayed silent and took two bites of her cinnamon roll. Since Queenie's death, everybody expected her to be sad, so she didn't even have to put on a happy face for her parents. They need never know that her sadness had more to do with their neighbor three houses down than the dead Lavender Orpington hen whose feathers were scattered all over the backyard.

After breakfast, Emma and Lizzy did the dishes and Emma went outside to be with her chickens. The

Silkies were growing every day. Emma wanted to raise some to sell. Everyone in the neighborhood should own a Silkie. They were such delightful chickens.

After gathering eggs, Emma cleaned the coops and put down fresh straw. She picked up all the purple feathers in the yard, keeping three of the biggest ones to put in her drawer as remembrances of Queenie. She really had been a beautiful chicken.

Just as she left the coop and closed the gate, Alfie and Benji Petersheim came from the shortcut behind her house and ran across the grass toward her. Benji carried a cardboard apple box. It was bulky, but must not have contained any apples because he was able to run with it, even though it was a little awkward for him.

"Emma!" Benji screamed, pumping his little legs as fast as they would go. Both boys had wet faces, as if they'd been crying for three days straight. They stopped right in front of Emma, and Benji set his box on the ground. "Emma," he said, sobbing with all the emotion of a broken heart. "We didn't mean to do it. You've got to save our dog."

Alfie wiped a plump tear from his cheek. "Please, Emma. We're sorry. We was trying to help Abraham. We didn't think . . . we didn't think . . ." Alfie disintegrated into a puddle of tears. Emma didn't know what they didn't think, but she probably wasn't going to get more information from Alfie.

She knelt down to be eye level with the *buwe*, pulled a tissue from her apron pocket, and started on Benji first because he seemed to be the most distraught. "Now, now, it's okay. Tell me what's wrong, and I'll try to help you."

Benji sobbed all the harder. "You're so nice, Emma. I'm sorry we did it. You stopped coming over, and Abraham won't let us come over, and we have to do family reading hour again, and I hate *Martyrs Mirror*, but don't tell Mammi."

Ach, Benji had said something about the dog. Her heart dropped to her toes. Emma took the boys' hands and pulled them to sit on the ground next to her. "Tell me what happened."

Benji took Emma's tissue and blew his nose. "You tell her, Alfie."

"Dawdi had a stroke," Alfie sobbed.

Emma frowned. "Another one?"

"*Nae*, the same one. Mammi and Dawdi had to move in with us, and Mamm put us in the cellar. But there are spiders down there, and we're going to die and Mamm doesn't even care."

Emma was pretty sure this story was going somewhere, but she couldn't follow it very well at the moment. "But what about the dog?"

Benji dabbed at his face with Emma's tissue. "Bitsy said girls like dogs."

"We wanted to find Abraham a wife so he'll move out of the house and we can have our room back," Alfie said.

Benji nodded. "We wanted Abraham to marry you because you're nice and you have chickens."

Alfie spread his hands. "Free eggs."

Emma swallowed the lump in her throat. Maybe she wanted Abraham to marry her too.

Benji's voice shook. "Alfie had a terrible idea."

Alfie all but exploded. "It was *not* terrible."

"He had this terrible idea to blame Tintin for

breaking your eggs, and that would make you come over to our house."

Alfie narrowed his eyes. "It worked, didn't it?"

Emma raised her eyebrows. "You broke my eggs?"

Benji nodded. "Not Tintin. But we bought the eggs first, so Alfie said it was okay if we broke them and left them in your coop. Then we carried Tintin's poop all the way to your house and put it in your coop so you would think Tintin did it."

"It wasn't a terrible idea," Alfie said, more to Benji than to Emma. "She came over and played games."

"Then Alfie said you and Abraham would get back together if one of your chickens died and we blamed it on Tintin." Benji's voice cracked, and he started crying all over again. "It was a terrible idea."

Emma felt as if she'd had the wind knocked out of her. "You . . . you killed Queenie?"

"*Nae*. We just pretended Tintin killed Queenie." Benji lifted the lid off the box at his side, reached in, and pulled out a very alive, very calm Queenie.

Emma squealed and snatched her hen from Benji's arms. She pressed Queenie to her breast and nuzzled her face against Queenie's head. "Queenie. Oh, Queenie. I love you so much." She smoothed her hand down Queenie's back and pinned the boys with a very serious eye. "You faked Queenie's death?"

Benji nodded.

"That was a very naughty thing to do. You should be ashamed of yourselves."

Both boys seemed to feel her scolding very deeply. Benji's lips drooped and trembled and tears rolled like rain down his cheeks.

Alfie swiped his hand across his nose and sniffed

back tears that flowed anyway. "I'm sorry, Emma," he said. "We just want to get out of the cellar."

Emma kissed Queenie's head, then drew her brows together. "How did you do it? There was blood and everything."

Alfie shrugged. "There was always lots of feathers in the coop. I took them home every time just in case we needed them."

"We piled all the feathers and dripped blood on them to make it look real," Benji said.

For the first time since the boys had come over, Emma noticed they had Band-Aids wrapped around each finger and thumb. "Your blood?" she said.

Benji nodded. "We poked my finger first, and I squeezed out all the blood I could. Then we poked Alfie."

"We poked all our fingers because we wanted a lot of blood. We had to make it look real."

Benji was still sobbing. "Alfie wanted to poke our toes too, but I can't run away with poked toes, so we decided just to do our fingers. It's hard to hold a walkie-talkie."

Emma was struck momentarily dumb. The boys had poked their fingers and bled all over the feathers to fake Queenie's death. She was *froh* they hadn't poked their toes. There had been plenty of blood.

Those naughty, incorrigible, clever boys. They needed a *gute* spanking—and a dozen cinnamon rolls for coming up with such a shrewd plan. She hadn't doubted for a minute that Queenie was really dead. *Ach!* She should run right over there and tell their *mater*. They'd be in big trouble for sure and certain, and it was nothing less than they deserved. But it was clever, nonetheless.

Alfie whimpered softly, "Are you mad at us?"

Emma opened the gate and set Queenie in the coop. She closed it again and propped her hands on her hips. Her anger was tempered by the fact that Queenie was back, but the boys didn't need to know that. "Of course I'm mad at you. Do you know how sad I was when I thought Queenie was dead?"

Benji frowned at Alfie. "I told you it was a terrible idea."

Alfie pressed his lips together and folded his arms. "We have to get out of that cellar, and I'm the only one who even has ideas."

"But it was a terrible idea." It had been bad before, but now Benji wailed like a lonely cat. "Abraham took Tintin to the pound this morning, and they're going to gas him."

Emma caught her breath. "Abraham took him to the pound?"

"This morning," Alfie said. "And we just bought a giant bag of dog food."

Benji sniffed. "He said we weren't taking *gute* care of Tintin because he kept getting into your coop, but we were taking *gute* care of him. We were the ones getting into your coop. Abraham wasn't taking good enough care of us."

No matter how much Alfie and Benji had put her through, Emma wouldn't be able to live with herself if their dog got gassed. She had enough guilt on her head already. She didn't need to compound her sins with Tintin's death, even if that dog had been a wonderful nuisance. Emma took a deep breath. She was probably the last person Abraham wanted to see, but she had to save Tintin. "Okay," she said. "I'll go talk to Abraham right now."

Alfie shook his head. "It's too late."

"Maybe Abraham can get Tintin back from the pound."

Benji's face brightened. "He would do it if you asked him to."

She wasn't near as confident as Benji. "Will you boys take these eggs into the house and give them to my *mamm*? Try not to drop them."

"We'll be careful as a newborn *buplie*," Alfie said.

Emma didn't have time to ask if they would be as careful as a newborn baby would be or if they would be as careful as if they carried a newborn baby. She probably didn't want to know. She said good-bye to the boys and took the shortcut behind the houses, running all the way to Abraham's. An extra minute or two might mean the difference between life and death for Tintin. Her heart felt as heavy as an anvil, and her throat was dry. *Please, dear Heavenly Father, let it not be too late.*

A truck was parked outside the house. Emma didn't even have time to be curious. She knocked frantically on Abraham's front door, just like she had yesterday. It was almost becoming a habit. It seemed to take forever, but Rebecca finally answered with an orange spray bottle in her hand. A man in some sort of official-looking uniform stood behind her holding a large metal canister and a spray nozzle.

"*Ach*, I'm sorry to interrupt," Emma said.

"I'm having the cellar sprayed for bugs," Rebecca said. She was understandably aloof, not even attempting a smile. For sure and certain Abraham had told her how Emma had treated him. She didn't deserve any kindness from Rebecca. Rebecca squinted, and her glasses sort of lifted from the bridge of her nose. "Are you okay, Emma?"

Emma probably looked a sight. No doubt her face was red from running, and strands of her hair had escaped her bandanna. She didn't even pause to catch her breath. "Is Abraham home?"

Rebecca frowned. "Is there something I can do for you? Abraham is wonderful busy. He's so nice that it wonders me if people don't take advantage of his kind heart just so they can get things done around their farms."

Ach. She deserved that little dig. She had treated Abraham very poorly. No wonder Rebecca thought the worst of her. There wasn't time, but she should at least apologize to Rebecca if she couldn't apologize to Abraham. "I'm sorry. I've made too many mistakes to count, and I've been proud and *deerich* and shallow, but I wasn't nice to Abraham just to get a new roof or a solar heater in my coop."

Rebecca furrowed her brow. "He installed a solar heater for you? He's even more generous than I thought."

"He is generous. Generous and kind and *wunderbarr,* and I don't deserve all those things he did for me. But his friendship is very important to me, even though I haven't always shown it." Emma almost choked on the word *friendship.* She didn't want to be Abraham's friend. She wanted so much more, but right now, it was the best she could hope for. "Can you forgive me for being less of a friend than I should have been? I want to make it right. It wonders me if I couldn't talk to him." She wouldn't mention that she was in a wonderful big hurry and that Tintin's life depended on it.

Rebecca hesitated and lowered the orange spray bottle as if she just realized she'd been pointing it at Emma. "I suppose Abraham is old enough to make his own mistakes. He's in the barn with the vet giving shots to the cows."

Emma didn't even wait for Rebecca to shut the door. She sprinted toward the barn and slid the door open. It took a few seconds for her eyes to adjust. Abraham and an Englischer stood on either side of a cow that was tied in one of the small stalls they used for milking. The Englischer was holding a needle the size of a turkey baster. Emma's first inclination was to warn that cow to run away as fast as she could.

Instead, she focused in on Abraham, tall, handsome, earnest Abraham, who had all sorts of muscles but would never hurt a fly—except for Perry Glick and that poor cow about to get a shot. "Abraham," she said as quietly as possible, wanting to get his attention without spooking the cow.

Abraham looked up, and a deep line formed between his brows. Emma suddenly found it hard to breathe. He wasn't happy to see her. He didn't want to see her. It was plain he didn't even like her anymore. She swallowed the lump in her throat and trudged forward. Even if he didn't like her, she had to save the dog.

"I-I need to t-talk to you," she stuttered.

.He looked away, as if eager to see if mold was growing on the wall. "I can't right now. Barry is showing me how to give inoculations."

"It's wonderful important."

He pressed his lips together, as if resisting the urge to say something he wanted to say but shouldn't.

The Englischer nodded. "We're almost done here. Another five minutes."

"Okay," Abraham said, as if being almost done was the most disappointing thing in the world. "Why don't you wait outside, and I'll come as soon as we're finished."

Emma wasn't altogether sure Abraham wouldn't sneak out the back and try to avoid her, but she had no choice but to trust his *gute* heart. A shard of glass lodged in her chest. She had taken his *gute* heart for granted, and now she'd lost him. The thought was almost more than she could bear. She backed out of the barn and waited about three feet from the door so she would be the first thing Abraham saw when he came out, if he didn't go out the back way.

The cow shuffled her feet and made a fuss, then Emma heard the Englischer's soft voice through the closed door. He was obviously giving Abraham some sort of instruction and taking too long. She'd told them it was important, and the Englischer had said it would only be another five minutes. Emma's heart hadn't stopped racing since Benji had pulled Queenie out of that box, but now it was galloping like a skittish horse.

Just as she decided to steal the Petersheims' horse and ride bareback to the pound, Abraham came out of the barn. Emma was so relieved, she didn't even ask what the Englischer was doing all by himself in the dark barn. She didn't even care if he listened in on their conversation. Tintin's life was all that mattered.

Well, all that mattered at this very moment.

Abraham's forgiveness mattered very much. His

love mattered even more. But those things would have to wait.

Abraham stared at her with an unreadable expression, a mask to hide whatever he was really feeling.

She pushed back the self-pity and ignored her beating heart. "You've got to get Tintin back."

"What?"

"Go to the pound and get Tintin back right now."

He didn't change his expression. It was more than frustrating. "I thought you wanted me to get rid of him."

"Not like this. I wanted him to stay out of my coop. I never wanted you to take him to the pound."

"You don't have to worry about him. I told you I'd take care of it, and I did."

A sob worked its way from Emma's throat. "It was Alfie and Benji the whole time. They faked Queenie's death because they were trying to . . ." She took a deep breath. It didn't matter now what they were trying to do. "Queenie is alive."

She finally got a reaction out of him. "Alive?"

"Alfie and Benji stole Queenie, piled up some feathers, and poked their fingers so there'd be blood. They also broke some eggs and put dog poop in the coop to make it look like Tintin had been there. I should have known Tintin couldn't have gotten in by himself."

Abraham rubbed his forehead and paced back and forth. "I've been too easy on those boys."

Nae, he hadn't. He had been a *wunderbarr*, kind *bruder*—someone who'd make a *gute* husband and *fater*. The best kind of *fater*. *Ach*. She was going to cry. She blinked back the tears and tried to concentrate on why she'd come. "You've got to go to the pound right now and get Tintin back. What the boys did was naughty, but Tintin doesn't deserve to die for it."

The lines around Abraham's mouth seemed to be etched into his face. "They've got to learn their lesson."

The tears wouldn't be stopped. "You can teach them a lesson, but Tintin's just an innocent dog. Don't take it out on him."

Abraham watched her closely as he pulled a tissue from his pocket and handed it to her. "I thought you hated Tintin."

"Hate him?" Emma wailed. "I love that dog. He's big and friendly and loves everybody, even when they don't deserve it. Tintin is the most lovable dog ever, and I treated him badly because I just didn't want to see it." She grabbed a fistful of Abraham's shirt. "Can't you see how heartbroken those boys would be if they lost Tintin? You've got to get him back."

Abraham hesitated, then slowly stepped away from her. She took a deep, shuddering breath and let go of his shirt. "We used to be friends," he said. "You should know me well enough to realize I'd never take Tintin to the pound, not even for you."

Relief tinged with pain flooded Emma's chest. In his mind, Abraham and Emma only *used* to be friends. His meaning left her gasping for air. "But . . . but Benji said you took Tintin to the pound."

"I took Tintin away. He's at Bitsy Weaver's house, no doubt harassing her cats and bees. I'm keeping him there until Bitsy and I can find him a *gute* home. She thinks an Englisch friend in Shawano might take him."

"You can't take Tintin away from the boys. They love that dog."

Abraham shrugged. "Mamm was bound to find out about him. Might as well find him another place now. It will be less trouble for the boys."

Emma wouldn't accept it. Those boys needed their dog, and she didn't need any more guilt on her shoulders. "But wouldn't you rather they were mad at your *mamm* instead of you? Wait until she finds out and let her take care of it."

Abraham actually thought about that for a second. "But it will be that much worse when Mamm does find out."

"Maybe you can cross that bridge when you come to it."

He actually cracked a smile. It was a half-hearted, I'm-not-convinced smile, but it made Emma's heart skip a beat. "Mamm wouldn't be happy if she knew you suggested I let her take the blame for getting rid of Tintin."

"Like you said, she's going to get rid of him anyway. Might as well let her be the mean one."

Abraham's smile got a little bigger. "I'll fetch Tintin home today, but it's not going to be long before Mamm finds out."

"Then the boys will have a few more days of happiness."

"I guess." And just like that, he turned to go back into the barn.

She couldn't let him go without even a good-bye. And she really couldn't let him go without apologizing, even if she'd told herself she wasn't ready. Even if he had a girlfriend. Even if she made a fool of herself. She reached out and wrapped her fingers around his arm. "Abraham, I'm wonderful sorry for all those things I said and the way I treated you."

Something raw and painful flashed across his face before he hid behind that mask again. "It's over and done with."

"Not for me. I regret it every minute of every day. How shallow was I to be worried what other people would think about you and me? To think that those boys at the gatherings were more important than you are?" Her voice cracked. What would he do if she told him how important he really was to her? But she couldn't. It wouldn't be fair to Hannah.

"It's okay, Emma. You like to have fun at the gatherings, and I know I'm not much fun."

"But you are," Emma said. "You're the boy I have the most fun with."

He shook his head slowly. "I don't believe you."

Emma's heart lurched. "I don't blame you for doubting me. I've been proud and silly, and I'm ashamed of myself. But I've changed. I didn't really understand what was important to me. I hurt your feelings because I was more concerned about things that don't even matter, like what the other boys think. I should have done better. I'm going to do better."

He lifted his chin and stared into the distance. "Maybe I'm glad you said all those things to me."

"Why?"

"It makes it easier."

Emma wrapped her arms around her waist. She didn't want to know why, but she asked anyway. "Easier?"

He looked at the ground. "Doesn't matter."

"Tell me."

He glanced in her direction, then let his gaze fall again. "I liked you a lot, Emma." He looked up and met her eyes. She couldn't look away from his intensity, like a moth to a flame. "But the way you acted, the things you said, I saw the kind of person you really are. I don't even want to be your friend anymore."

The pain was harsh and sharp and so richly deserved.

There were too many tears to blink back anymore. They rolled down her face like water from a leaky faucet. Abraham drew his brows together, but he made no attempt to comfort her. Aside from taking back every word, there wasn't much he could do anyway.

Speaking was well nigh impossible, but she tried anyway. "I've been horrible to you . . . just . . . horrible. But can't . . . can't you give me another chance?"

He stuffed his hands in his pockets. "What for?"

"Because I've been a very silly girl, even sillier than Lizzy. I wanted the boys to like me, so I pretended to be someone I wasn't. There's no excuse for it except that I want people to like me. I didn't think they'd like me if they knew who I really was."

"Everybody likes you."

"Maybe they wouldn't if they knew I love chickens and eat like a horse and am very bad at Pictionary."

"Of course they would. People don't like you because of how much you eat, they like you because you make them feel important, and you're nice to everyone, even Perry Glick."

Emma couldn't help when one side of her mouth

curled up. "I'm not nice to him anymore." She sniffed back a fresh wave of tears. "You're the first boy I ever introduced to Queenie."

"Me?"

"Because you make me feel comfortable, like I don't have to pretend around you. You are one of the few people who really knows me. We spent hours together playing games and cleaning out my coops. I ate an outrageous number of Pigs-in-a-Blanket right in front of you. I showed you my chickens. We went to Green Bay together and threw cookies into a puddle. We made each other laugh. That is the person I want you to remember when you think of me."

His eyes shone as if he was lit from the inside. "That's the person I want to remember too."

"Will you . . . will you give me another chance to be your friend?"

He took a deep breath and let it out slowly. "I don't know."

Emma's heart clenched with longing. "I guess maybe it's hard with Hannah." It was almost better if he was thinking of Hannah, because if he wouldn't be friends because he really didn't like her anymore, she didn't know if she could bear it.

"*Jah*," he said. "Maybe it's better if we go back to the way it was."

The way it was—when Emma was self-centered and Abraham never said a word to her. How could she ever go back to that? The thought was unbearable.

But she couldn't argue—didn't even know how. "*Ach.* I . . . don't know if I can."

"It's better this way," he said, almost as if he were trying to convince himself. But that couldn't be true. It was painfully obvious he wanted nothing more to do with her.

His piercing gaze almost made her turn away, but she held her ground as he finally turned around and disappeared into the barn, leaving her holding the pieces of her shattered heart.

Chapter Eighteen

Emma used to love *gmay*. When the sermons were boring, there had always been boys she could stare at across the aisle or look forward to flirting with after services. That kind of thing used to excite her. But who cared about stupid *buwe* when the one person she loved wouldn't even look at her. He sat on the other side of the room avoiding her gaze while the minister droned on and on about the Parable of the Sower.

And it broke Emma's heart every time she looked at him.

The worst part was knowing she had no one to blame but herself. Abraham had been so kind, and she'd been too stubborn to admit she'd fallen in love with him until it was too late.

More singing, another sermon, more singing, another prayer. Finally services ended. Emma and Lizzy went to the kitchen to help get the fellowship supper on the table. Lizzy and Mamm had made two loaves of bread, and Emma had thrown together a tub of peanut butter church spread. It was all so predictable and so depressing. She was quite sure she'd never feel happy again.

Alfie and Benji found her in the kitchen while she was stirring the spread. Three *fraaen* scolded them for being underfoot, but they seemed determined to talk to Emma.

Benji grabbed her hand and almost made her drop her spoon. He still had Band-Aids on every finger. Emma winced. Poor boy. Those fingers were victims of Alfie's terrible idea. "Emma, come outside. We have something to tell you."

"Two things," Alfie said.

Benji nodded. "Two things."

"Can't you tell me now? I'm helping with the fellowship supper."

Alfie glanced around the room and wrinkled his nose in disgust. "All these old ladies will spy on us."

Emma sighed. She wasn't doing anything that important. How hard would it be for Lizzy to take the spread and the loaves to the table? She motioned to her sister. "Lizzy, I have to go outside for a minute. Will you take care of this?"

Lizzy grinned at Alfie and Benji. "*Hallo*, boys. Kill any chickens lately?"

Alfie glanced around the kitchen again and laughed nervously. "That's a funny joke. We never ever killed a chicken."

Lizzy messed up Alfie's hair. "Well, be careful out there. You never know who's watching."

Benji scrunched his lips to one side of his face. "It's usually us. We have binoculars."

Alfie shoved Benji into the nearest cupboard. "Benji, be quiet."

Benji frowned, clamped his lips together, and shoved Alfie back.

"Okay, okay," Emma said, before the twins started a fistfight. "Lead the way."

She followed Alfie and Benji into the mudroom, out the back door, and down the porch steps. Some of the men were in the yard stacking the church benches into tables. If the boys wanted privacy, they'd have to pick another place. Alfie motioned for her to follow them around to the side of the house. Nobody was setting tables up on this side. There was no shade, and it had to be about ninety degrees. Lord willing, the boys would make it quick.

"So," Emma said, propping her hands on her hips, "what are the two things you have to tell me."

Benji poked his toe around in the grass. "Well, we don't really have two things to tell you. It's one thing to tell you and one thing to show you."

Emma raised an eyebrow. "Okay."

"The first thing we want to tell you is that Abraham didn't take Tintin to the pound."

Alfie smiled. "He took him to Bitsy's house, and Bitsy didn't gas him."

Benji picked up a dandelion and blew the little parachutes off the stem. "And he brought Tintin home and told us to keep him at the hideout or we'd be in trouble. Then he told us we could start buying eggs from you again. He made us stop when we pretend-killed Queenie, which we didn't really kill her."

Alfie chewed on his fingernail. "But then he said if we pretend-killed one of your chickens again or even stepped on your grass, he'd tell Mamm about Tintin and she'd take him to the pound. So we're not ever going to sneak in your coop, or Abraham will be too mad to spit."

Benji nodded. "That's what Willie Glick always says."

The one thing they had to tell her had turned into about five things, but Emma didn't mind. It was nice just to hear Abraham's name. "I would really appreciate if you never pretend-killed one of my chickens again."

"We won't," Benji said. "It was a terrible idea."

Alfie stuck out his bottom lip. "It was not."

"So what was the thing you had to show me?"

Benji slid his hands into his pockets, turned around, and ambled around the corner of the house. Alfie smiled tentatively at Emma. "We have to wait here."

Benji returned almost immediately, but it didn't look as if he'd brought anything with him to show Emma. He held out his hand to the side as if he was introducing a special guest. Hannah appeared around the corner with a plate of cookies and a wide smile. "Isn't this just the biggest secret?" she said, giggling as if she found the whole situation very funny.

Emma couldn't share her amusement. Abraham liked Hannah. Emma couldn't muster happiness for either of them.

Hannah took two suckers out of her apron pocket and handed one to each of the boys. "*Denki*, Alfie. *Denki*, Benji." Alfie's sucker was inches from his mouth when Hannah added, "Don't eat those before supper."

Alfie groaned and stuffed his precious treat into his pocket. He nudged Benji with his elbow. "Come on. Hannah wants some privacy."

Benji looked at Hannah. "What's privacy?"

Hannah giggled. "It means Emma and I want to be alone."

The last person Emma wanted to be alone with was Hannah Yutzy, Abraham's girlfriend. Well, maybe not the last person. Perry Glick would always be the last person Emma wanted to see.

Hannah handed Emma the plate of cookies. They were heart-shaped and pink, with beautiful frosting swirls on top, more a work of art than something to eat. "These are for you. My *mamm*'s special recipe."

Emma furrowed her brow in confusion. "For me? Why?"

"If I were you, I'd be harboring some resentful feelings toward me, and I don't blame you one little bit. Abraham is definitely worth the trouble."

Emma almost choked on her own tongue. Hannah was one of the nicest girls in the *gmayna*. It wasn't like her to gloat, but here she was with her heart-shaped cookies and her big, toothy smile and her claim on Abraham's affections. Emma was going to be sick.

Hannah tugged on Emma's arm and guided her to sit on the grass. "We need to talk."

Ach. No doubt Hannah had heard about Emma's last conversation with Abraham where she'd practically confessed her love to him. It wasn't right to try to steal another girl's boyfriend. Emma probably deserved a *gute* scolding, but she'd rather not hear it, all the same. She set her plate beside her on the ground. "I'm sorry, Hannah. I didn't mean to—"

Hannah patted Emma on the knee. "I'm going to tell you something that only two other people in the whole world know, so please don't tell anyone I told you, especially Abraham."

Emma swallowed hard. It sounded serious.

Hannah looked into the sky. "Maybe four people in the whole world know." She counted something in her head. "Like as not, it might be seven." She threw up her hands. "I don't know. Some people can't keep a secret." She smiled at Emma, then seemed to think better of it and drew her brows together. "Emma, Abraham and I are not dating. I don't even like Abraham." She thought about that for a minute and waved her hand back and forth. "I mean, I like Abraham but not as a boyfriend."

Emma lost the ability to breathe. "But . . . does Abraham know?"

Hannah laughed as if Emma had told the funniest joke in the world. "It was Abraham's *dumm* idea, but I went along because he was so sad and I wanted to help him out."

"What do you mean?"

Hannah smoothed her hand down her dress. "Abraham said somebody started a rumor that you two were sweethearts. He felt wonderful bad about it and asked if he could take me home from the gathering so *die youngie* would think me and him were sweethearts."

Emma scraped her chin off the ground. "You're not dating Abraham?"

Hannah shook her head. "Don't be mad at Abraham. He didn't drive me home to be mean or trick anybody. He wanted to make sure the boys knew you weren't interested in him so you could have fun at gatherings like you used to. He wanted you to be happy again."

Emma had to work hard to blink back the tears. Again. She was turning into a watering pot. Abraham always did the unselfish thing, no matter the consequences to himself.

And he and Hannah weren't dating.

Emma could have done a cartwheel. While crying.

Hannah had no idea the tornado she'd set off inside Emma's head. She looked up and started counting to herself again. "I think he told his *mamm*, and we had to tell Austin because Austin would have known we were playing a trick. And Alfie and Benji probably know too. Benji hears everything."

"*Denki* for telling me," Emma said, when she was calm enough for rational speech.

Hannah grinned. "It wouldn't have mattered except I could see it was bothering you, and I kept asking myself why it would bother you. Then I realized." She took both of Emma's hands. "You love him."

Emma half laughed, half sobbed. "I do."

Hannah pulled Emma in for a big hug. "Abraham sort of sneaks up on you, doesn't he?"

"For sure and certain."

Hannah nodded as if she'd known all along. "You stopped coming to gatherings, and I was thinking, 'Emma is jealous of me.' She's not interested in those other boys, and she's jealous but she can't tell Abraham how she feels because she's nice enough not to steal another girl's boyfriend. So I'm here to tell you, don't be jealous. Just go get him."

"Do you think I can?"

"Of course. He doesn't have a girlfriend anymore."

Emma felt ecstatically happy for about five seconds, then her happiness popped like a balloon. "But he told me that the way I treated him made it easier for him to give up on our friendship. He doesn't even like me. He won't give me another chance."

Hannah picked up one of Emma's cookies and took a bite. "Abraham is so in love with you, he can't think straight."

"But he said it would be better if we went back to the way it was."

"That sounds like Abraham. He's never been in love before, and love hurts. He thinks he'd rather be a bachelor. That's what he told Andrew." She started counting again. "Maybe Andrew and Mary know about him driving me home. Anyway, Abraham is just protecting his heart by making up a list of all the reasons he doesn't love you. It's getting him nowhere but miserable."

Hannah was the nicest girl in the *gmayna*, and Emma loved her like a sister. This sublime feeling felt a lot like hope. "So what do I do?"

"I don't know about you, but when I have a serious problem, I find all the help I can get."

Emma pressed her lips together. "You're right. I'm going to pray with all my heart."

"*Ach, vell,* Gotte is the best place to start, but I was thinking of something a little less divine." Hannah leaned closer. "Do you know Alfie and Benji have walkie-talkies?"

Chapter Nineteen

Emma Wengerd was proud and snobby and trying to fatten him up, for sure and certain. Abraham stared down at the plate of peanut butter bars Emma had sent over. "I hope you can come. 2:00 p.m.," the note said. It was the fourth plate of goodies this week and the fourth invitation to a "chicken" party at her house this afternoon.

Abraham balled the note in his fist and threw it as far as he could. It bounced off a tree and came to rest at the edge of the grass. He'd always had a *gute* arm. Not that it mattered or anyone cared, but he was a *gute* athlete.

He looked down at the paper plate. He never should have told Emma that peanut butter bars were his favorite dessert, but how was he to know four weeks ago that he should have been wary? Abraham sighed and ambled to the tree to retrieve the note. He shouldn't leave trash in the yard. Mamm wouldn't like it.

Mamm opened the front door. "Are you going?"

"Going where?" It was easier to play dumb than argue with Mamm.

"To Emma's house. She invited the whole family."

"I've already seen her chickens."

Mamm stepped out onto the porch. "You installed a solar heater for the coop. You could show everybody how it works."

The last thing Abraham wanted to do was talk to a group of *die youngie* about solar-heated chicken coops. He got tongue-tied in a group. Lord willing, he'd never draw the lot for minister. His sermons would be the shortest in the history of sermons. But he was probably safe. Gotte wouldn't saddle any congregation with a failure for a minister. "Emma can show them," he said.

Mamm threw up her hands. "Suit yourself. I'm going over with the boys as soon as the Pigs-in-a-Blanket come out of the oven. Emma asked me to bring them especially."

Abraham frowned. It felt like a betrayal. After how Emma had treated him, maybe Mamm shouldn't be so nice to her. "You work too hard, Mamm. Emma has plenty of friends who can bring something for her chicken party."

Mamm scrunched her lips together and glared at Abraham. He didn't deserve the stink eye. "I believe in forgiveness, young man, and I didn't raise you to hold a grudge. You'd do well to think on your own sins, like moping around the house when you could be popping popcorn or selling peanut butter by the side of the road."

"You want me to sell peanut butter by the side of the road?"

Mamm puckered her face like a dried apple. "It's just an expression. My point is, Emma is doing her best to make it right, and you won't let her. She brings cakes and cookies and eggs, and you run away whenever she comes to the door."

"I don't run away. I have stuff to do like milking cows and cutting hay." And he didn't want to talk to Emma. He loved her too much, and he'd make a fool of himself without even trying.

"All I'm saying is that it's time to forgive Emma and quit feeling sorry for yourself."

He couldn't forgive Emma. She'd hurt him too badly. He was going to feel sorry for himself for the rest of his life.

"But if you can't do that, at least bring those peanut butter bars into the kitchen so I can have one. She made them with Petersheim Brothers' Peanut Butter."

Why was Mamm so testy? What did she care if he didn't forgive Emma Wengerd? Abraham furrowed his brow. Mom hadn't used her "nice" voice. She really was mad at him. He smiled to himself. Maybe she didn't think he was so hopeless after all.

Abraham peeled the plastic wrap back from the plate and picked up a peanut butter bar. Nice and heavy. The sign of a good peanut butter bar. He shouldn't have taken a bite. The taste only softened him toward Emma. She was a *gute* cook and she had gone to a lot of trouble to make him peanut butter bars. But why? For sure and certain she didn't want to be friends, did she? Being his friend had nearly messed it up for her with all the other boys. Why would she want to risk that again?

She probably wanted him to forgive her so she wouldn't feel guilty anymore. Hadn't she said she felt "horrible" for how she'd treated him? The peanut butter bars should have been enough to convince

Abraham to forgive her, even if the sugar cookies, the German chocolate cake, and the cinnamon rolls hadn't.

But if he forgave her, he'd have to let go of her, and if this hurt and anger were the only ways to stay connected to Emma, he'd hold on to them for the rest of his life.

Benji came crashing through the bushes, his eyes wild and his face bright red. "Abraham, Tintin is gone."

Abraham frowned. "Are you sure?"

Benji took a deep breath. "He's not at the hideout. You've got to help me find him."

Abraham's heart raced. A few weeks ago, he would have told Benji that Tintin had probably run away and they shouldn't waste time looking for him. Unfortunately, Abraham had grown to love that stupid, adorable dog as much as the twins did. "Where's Alfie? Did Alfie take him for a walk?"

"We need to find him." Benji spied the peanut butter bars. "Oh. Can I have one?"

It always marveled Abraham how easily distracted a nine-year-old was. At this moment, he should be too upset to even think about eating. "Sure. Then I'll go put this plate on the porch, and we can go look."

"Bring it with us," Benji said. "We might need it."

Abraham had no idea what Benji meant by that, except maybe they might need something to eat if they got lost in the woods. "It'll slow us down," Abraham said.

"That's okay."

Never try to understand a nine-year-old.

They jogged to Tintin's hideout. Sure enough, there was no sign of him. The rope the boys used to attach Tintin's leash to the tree was still there. "Did you tie a *gute* knot?" Abraham asked.

"We always tie the double clope hitch," Benji said. "Willie's Englisch friend Max is a Boy Scout."

"Maybe he's lost in the woods," Abraham said, already looking around for paw prints. It was a *dumm* idea. There were paw prints everywhere.

"Where do you think he would have gone?" Benji gazed expectantly at Abraham, as if he already knew the answer.

Of course he already knew the answer. If Tintin ever went anywhere, it was to Emma's house. It would be just like Tintin to want to go to Emma's chicken party, or whatever she was calling it.

Abraham hesitated barely a second. He would rather clean up dog poop for the rest of his life than go to Emma's house, but they had to find Tintin before Mamm did. She'd be there any minute with her plate of Pigs-in-a-Blanket. "Let's check Emma's," he said, hoping against all hope that Tintin had maybe decided to go back to Bitsy's.

Abraham took off through the trees. Benji couldn't keep up with his pace or his long legs. He stopped and waved Abraham on. "That's okay. I'll catch up."

At the edge of Emma's yard, Abraham slowed down so he wouldn't make noise as he came from the woods. The last thing he wanted was to attract attention.

Ach. A lump the size of an egg formed in his throat. A group of *die youngie* gathered around Emma's coop—seven or eight boys and five girls. Emma stood in front of the big coop talking to them. He could go unnoticed if he slid around the edge of the grass and did a brief look in Emma's yard. Tintin didn't appear to be anywhere. Abraham breathed a sigh of relief. He'd go look at Bitsy's.

"Abraham, how nice of you to come," Emma called just as Abraham was about to duck back into the cover of the trees.

All *die youngie* turned to look at him.

He debated if he should just pretend he hadn't heard her, but Benji came up behind him, grabbed his wrist, and pulled him toward Emma. "Come on, Abraham. We have to look for Tintin."

Abraham wanted to protest that Tintin wasn't in this direction, but Emma was smiling at him with that beautiful smile that she usually reserved for boys at gatherings, and he couldn't look away.

"Abraham put shingles on this coop," Emma said, pointing inside the chicken run. "And he set up a solar-powered heater for my new Silkies. They look furry, but they get cold in the winter."

Matt Gingerich patted Abraham on the shoulder. "Looks *gute*. Our barn has a solar heater too."

Matt's sister Mandy smiled. "You're so nice, Abraham."

Linda Eicher giggled. "Nice to Emma."

Abraham nudged some blades of grass with his toe. "It wasn't hard. Emma loves her chickens."

"*Jah*," Emma said. "Abraham never thought it was strange of me to raise exotic chickens."

"I don't think it's strange," Mahlon Zook said.

Tyler Kaufmann nodded. "Neither do I."

Emma didn't seem to be soaking up the attention like she usually did. "Abraham hired a driver and took me to Green Bay and bought me two Silkies."

Abraham glanced around at the faces turned toward him. Emma shouldn't tell anybody he had taken her to Green Bay. They'd get the wrong idea. He'd have to drive Hannah home three more times to squelch the rumors.

Moses Zook sort of looked at Abraham funny, like he wasn't sure what to think. Then it seemed everybody was looking at him sort of funny, like they had finally figured out the secret. But there wasn't any secret to figure out. Emma didn't want to be his friend. Why was she telling them all this stuff? And would people quit staring at him?

He realized that even after running through the trees, he still had the plate of peanut butter bars in his hand. He nudged the plate toward Moses and offered him a bar. It was the only polite thing to do, and it might distract everybody from the subject of Emma and Abraham.

Moses took a peanut butter bar and then Mahlon. Soon the plate was empty. Abraham sort of regretted doing that. He'd only gotten one.

"Did your *mamm* make these?" Linda said. "They're *appeditlich*. I need this recipe."

"Emma made them," Benji said. "And she gave them to Abraham because she likes him."

So much for distracting *die youngie*. Abraham looked at Emma. If anybody was going to kill these rumors, it would have to be her. He'd already driven Hannah Yutzy home twice and socked Perry Glick. That was more attention than he wanted in a lifetime.

Emma didn't do one thing to contradict Benji. She could have at least snatched her plate from Abraham's hand or run crying into the house or listed all the reasons she didn't like Abraham. Instead, she gave Abraham the most dazzling smile he had ever seen in his life. He almost fell over. Why did she have to do that? He was trying very hard not to betray any feelings for Emma. If he melted into a puddle of milk chocolate right here on her lawn, everyone would know how he felt about her.

Benji tugged on his shirt from behind and grinned. "I told you we might need those."

Wait a minute. How did Benji know Emma had made those bars?

Benji pulled a walkie-talkie from his pocket. "Ready," he said. "Spatula."

Abraham's brows came together so fast, he might have heard a click. "Where did you get that, and who are you talking to?"

Before Abraham could get any answers, four cats, one squirrel, and at least a dozen chickens came tearing around the side of the house being chased by one very large chocolate-brown labrador. The four cats, that looked suspiciously like Bitsy Weaver's, scattered in four directions as soon as they got to the backyard. The chickens—and there were definitely more than twelve—squawked and spread their wings and ran around as if they'd had their heads cut off. There was a very *gute* reason for that saying.

Tintin jumped and ran and barked as if this was the most fun he'd ever had on a Saturday afternoon. He chased a chicken until his attention was diverted by another one. A fat Plymouth Rock rooster turned around, flapped his wings, and went right at Tintin. Tintin whined and turned his efforts to one of Bitsy's cats.

Some of *die youngie* in Emma's yard gasped. Others laughed. Some of the girls squeaked and squealed. Mandy Gingerich ran this way and that, changing directions every time she encountered a cat, a chicken, or a dog. Mahlon and Moses Zook wasted no time in trying to round up the chickens, but they wouldn't be able to catch the chickens until the dog was rounded up.

At least Tintin wasn't lost anymore.

Abraham was about to try to catch Tintin when someone grabbed his hand and pulled him in the opposite direction. That someone turned out to be Emma. If she didn't want anyone to think she and Abraham were sweethearts, she shouldn't be holding his hand.

She pulled him into the chicken run and shut the gate. Taking a few deep breaths, she gave him a dazzling smile. "Finally, we can be alone," she said, as if the chain-link fence would give them any privacy.

And maybe it did. Everybody was running around trying to catch chickens, except for Benji, who had the *gute* sense to try to catch the dog. Nobody was paying Emma and Abraham any attention.

Emma took a few steps closer and backed Abraham against the fence, making sure neither of them was going to step on any exotic chickens. He didn't mind it, really, except nobody was going to believe she didn't like him after this. *Ach, vell.* It was her own fault. "Abraham, when I thought you'd taken Tintin to the pound, you told me you wouldn't do that, not even for me. What did you mean by that?"

Abraham coughed. "I meant . . . I meant that . . . well . . . I wouldn't take him to the pound. Not even for you."

She gave him a wry smile and started to giggle. "You are incorrigible, Abraham Petersheim."

"I just meant that—"

"I hope it means that maybe you care for me just a

little bit." She blew air from between her lips. "Oy, anyhow. This is harder than I thought, especially when rejection might be seconds away." Her smile made his legs go weak. "I love you, Abraham, and if you don't love me back, I think I'll sell my chickens and move to Mexico."

His heart pounded so hard, he thought he might end up with a broken rib. "Why Mexico?"

"They don't have chickens in Mexico."

"For sure and certain they have chickens in Mexico."

Emma sighed in mock dejection. "Then I'll have nowhere to go, because every chicken will remind me of you."

He pressed his lips together and studied her face, trying hard not to let his desires run away with his reason. "Do you really love me, or are you just saying that?"

"Why would I just be saying that?"

"I don't know. I want to be sure."

She slumped her shoulders. "I know I'm not *gute* enough, but who is? If you're waiting for a girl worthy of you, you'll be waiting a long time."

He was the one who wasn't good enough, but he didn't want to ruin his chances by pointing that out. "Do you really love me, Emma?"

"I've taken you for granted, and I've been proud and silly and mean. But I love you so much, if you don't love me back, I think I'll quit the Amish and join the military."

"Why the military?"

"There are no chickens in the military."

Abraham chuckled. He didn't know enough to

contradict that statement. "Emma, I love you so much that if you don't love me, I think I'll buy a sheep and start knitting wool sweaters."

Emma's smile was like the sun at midday. "I would never condemn you to a life of knitting."

The chain-link fence was a real problem, because even if no one happened to be looking in their direction, it wasn't proper for him to take her in his arms and kiss her until they both ran out of air. Kissing would have to wait, even though he didn't know how he was going to contain all this happiness. He couldn't resist taking her hand in his and caressing the back of it with his thumb. She smiled at him. It would have to be enough.

Abraham glanced around at *die youngie* trying to catch chickens. "Do you think they know we're sweethearts?"

"They will if you drive me home in your buggy," Emma said.

"You're already home."

"Maybe you could drive me around the block."

The chaos outside the chicken run seemed to have gotten worse. No one had managed to catch Tintin, and now the rooster was threatening anyone who dared get within ten feet of him. One of Bitsy's cats, the ugly tom with the split ear, was having a standoff with one of the White Leghorn hens. The cat hissed at the hen, and the hen flapped its wings and showed its claws.

The squirrel had disappeared.

It was probably time to stop holding Emma's hand and fix this mess. Abraham and Emma stepped out of the chicken run, making sure that none of Emma's chickens escaped. They didn't need more flying feathers.

Mamm couldn't have chosen a worse time to show up at Emma's chicken party. She strolled around from the front of Emma's house with a heaping plate of Pigs-in-a-Blanket. Tintin must have smelled all that hot dog goodness. He ran at Mamm with no thought for the consequences and bowled her over like a wobbly yard sign. Mamm's eyes nearly popped out of her head in surprise as she went down on her backside and the Pigs-in-a-Blanket flew in the air. The Pigs-in-a-Blanket thudded on the ground like fat raindrops, and Tintin went to work gobbling them up. Three chickens in the vicinity swarmed around Mamm and pecked urgently at the treat.

"Mamm!" Benji yelled, racing Abraham to get there first. "Mamm, are you okay?"

Mamm was up before either Abraham or Benji could help her. "That dog is a menace," she said, throwing her empty paper plate on the ground in disgust. The chickens immediately started pecking at it. Mamm glanced at Emma. "Emma, it's nice to see you again." She narrowed her eyes and studied Abraham's face. "Nice to see you too, Abraham."

Why was Mamm looking at him like that? Did he look different? He felt different, as if his whole body was filled with light. Maybe he was glowing.

Word traveled fast around the flock. Every last chicken ran for the food at Mamm's feet. At least they were now gathered in one place. It might be easier to catch them. Abraham counted seventeen chickens. Where had they all come from?

All the cats by Farrah Fawcett ran for the Pigs-in-a-

Blanket and joined the chickens in the feast. Farrah Fawcett, Bitsy's snobby white cat, sat against the tree and pretended she didn't know any of the other cats.

Mamm shooed away a chicken and picked up one of the half-eaten Pigs-in-a-Blanket. "Benji Petersheim, I worked very hard on these. You and Alfie will be washing walls and cleaning toilets until Christmas."

Benji somehow found a whole Pig-in-a-Blanket on the ground and popped it into his mouth. "But, Mamm, what did we do?"

"Don't play innocent with me, young man. And don't talk with your mouth full. That dog didn't just decide to stroll over here on his own. Look at this mess. You're going to scrape every spot of chicken poop off Emma's grass."

"That's really not necessary," Emma said. "It's *gute* fertilizer."

Mamm cocked an eyebrow. "Believe me, Emma, it's not about fertilizer. It's about the consequences of letting that dog run wild."

Abraham narrowed his eyes. What did Mamm know about Tintin and his relationship to the boys?

Bitsy Weaver, with bright pink hair, and Alfie came running around the corner of the house. It looked as if Alfie had a walkie-talkie in his pocket, an exact match for the one Benji clutched in his fist.

"Alfie Petersheim," Mamm said. "What do you have to say for yourself?"

Alfie shrugged. "I was just—"

"I don't want to hear it." Mamm's patience was about an inch long. She looked over her glasses in

Bitsy's direction. "What do you know about these chickens?"

"All I can say is that if you don't want people interfering, you shouldn't have raised such adorable children. I can't resist brown eyes and freckles."

"That has nothing to do with chickens," Mamm said.

Bitsy watched as the chickens pecked at Mamm's Pigs-in-a-Blanket. "There's not much to explain. Benji asked me to bring my chickens, so I did. Most of them are *bottelhinkels.* Worn out and ready for the stewpot."

Mamm scrunched her lips to one side of her face. "Bitsy, you've got to learn not to fall for the mischief these boys cook up. They might very well burn down your barn or accidentally kill all your chickens."

Bitsy shook her head. "I'm smarter than I look— thank Derr Herr. I don't let them get away with anything but what I agree to. Besides, it was for a higher purpose. I never stand in the way of a higher purpose."

Mamm was too busy talking to Bitsy to notice, but Abraham watched Alfie and Benji out of the corner of his eye and pretended not to pay attention to their conversation. The twins grinned at each other, and Alfie draped his arm around Benji's shoulder. "Did it work?" Alfie said.

Benji nodded. "She held his hand and then he held hers."

For sure and certain they were talking about Emma and Abraham. What were those boys up to? Abraham wasn't sure he even wanted to know.

Mamm pointed at Alfie and Benji with one hand and the chickens with the other. "Round up every last one of these chickens and get them back to Bitsy's house this minute."

Alfie gave Mamm that not-guilty look that only fooled the most gullible adults. "How are we supposed to do that?"

Mamm was the least fool-able person in the world. "I saw the cardboard boxes in the front yard, young man. Get those chickens in their boxes and take them back. And don't you dare ask Bitsy or Abraham for help. You got yourselves into this mess. You can get yourselves out."

Alfie slouched and Benji wilted as they trudged toward the front of the house to retrieve the boxes.

Mamm propped her hands on her hips. "Just a minute. I'm not finished."

"But you just said—"

"I know exactly what I said, young man, and you are in no position to contradict me. I'm not about to forget my ruined Pigs-in-a-Blanket." Mamm gave Alfie and Benji one of her looks and grabbed Tintin's collar. "When were you going to tell me about your secret dog?"

Emma gasped. Abraham's heart skipped a beat.

Benji's mouth fell open. "We . . . we . . ."

Alfie attempted a smile, but no one could have expected more than a grimace. "We wasn't never going to tell you."

Mamm harrumphed loudly. "What have I told you about keeping secrets from your *mater*?"

"To don't," Alfie said.

Benji drooped like a thirsty flower. "Because you always find out."

"That's right. I always find out."

Alfie glanced at Abraham resentfully. "Abraham said he wouldn't tell."

Mamm puckered her lips like she'd just eaten a lemon. "Abraham didn't tell me, though I'm a little peeved about that. Bitsy didn't tell me and neither did your *dawdi*, and don't think I don't know you almost dumped him out of his wheelchair."

Benji poked his toe at the grass. "We wanted to show him our dog."

Mamm folded her arms. "And you didn't think to show your own *mamm*, the woman who gave birth to you and fixes you three meals a day?"

"We didn't want you to gas him," Benji said.

Mamm wrinkled her forehead. "Gas him? Why in the world would I do something like that? I took him to the vet to get his shots while you two were at school."

Abraham's *bruderen* had never looked so surprised. "You did?" Alfie said. "We thought you didn't like dogs."

"I don't like dogs. They're messy and loud. It's impossible to hide a dog, especially one that barks at every squirrel that comes near that hideout of yours. I found him weeks ago, and I wanted to make sure he had his shots so the two of you didn't come down with rabies or heartworm."

"But what about . . ." Alfie had the courage to ask the question. "But can we keep him?"

Mamm grunted her disapproval. "Heaven knows I'd rather have a wart than a dog, but now that we've got him, we might as well let him stay."

Alfie and Benji jumped up and down and hugged each other as if it was the best day ever. For them, it probably was. Benji knelt down and wrapped his arms around Tintin. He was now part of the family.

Abraham smiled. Mamm hated dogs, but she was also the best *mater* in the whole world. She'd never do anything to break Alfie or Benji's heart. Abraham should have known that. Keeping the secret had been way more trouble than it was worth.

Austin joined the conversation. "Wait, Mamm. I've been asking for a dog ever since I turned five. Why didn't you let me have one?"

"Because Alfie and Benji are my favorites," Mamm said.

"Hey," Austin protested.

Alfie grabbed Tintin's collar from Mamm. "We'll take Tintin to help us with the chickens."

"Just a minute," Mamm said. "I have a few conditions."

"What are conditions?" Benji said.

Mamm straightened her glasses. "First of all, that dog does not come in the house."

"But, Mamm, he'll freeze in the winter."

Mamm held up her hand to halt any objection. "Remember, that dog's position in our family is precarious at best."

Benji scratched his head. "What's 'precarious'?"

"He stays outside or we give him to another family that doesn't care about dander."

"Oh," Benji said, even though he probably had no idea what Mamm was talking about.

"You can move his shelter closer to the house, and Abraham will install a solar-powered heater like he did for the chickens."

"Okay. That would work," Alfie said.

"Of course it will work." Mamm pulled one of Alfie's suspenders and let it snap back. "You boys have to pay for dog food, but I'll let you earn extra money selling produce and peanut butter."

Alfie pumped his fist in the air. "We get to keep Tintin."

"Just a minute, young man. I have one more condition. I get to name your dog."

Alfie drew his brows together. "But, Mamm, we already named him. It's after my favorite explorer, and he comes when we call."

Mamm smirked. "Ha. That dog doesn't even look up when you call. I want to name him after my *dat*. We're calling him LaWayne."

The look of horror on Alfie's face was priceless. "But, Mamm . . ."

"No buts."

There was Mamm's firm voice and then there was her don't-argue-with-me-unless-you-want-Brussels-sprouts-and-cow-eyeballs-for-dinner voice. This was the second type. Alfie closed his mouth.

Austin, bless his heart, brought around five cardboard boxes from the front yard, and Alfie and Benji started loading chickens in boxes. Fortunately, the chickens were too busy pecking at Mamm's Pigs-in-a-Blanket to get too upset about the boxes. Hannah Yutzy, Matt Gingerich, and some of the other young people helped stuff chickens in boxes. It didn't take long. The chickens were full and happy and, as always, very stupid.

Once the boxes were loaded, Benji and Alfie, plus Matt and Hannah, each picked up a full box of chickens and headed toward the road where Bitsy had parked her buggy.

"One more thing," Mamm said, as if she was saving the worst for last. Benji and Alfie both stopped in their tracks. "Don't ever prick your fingers on purpose again. If you get an infection and die, you won't get any sympathy from me."

At this point, nobody expected any sympathy from Mamm ever again.

Chapter Twenty

"What are they doing now? Spatula."

Alfie shifted carefully on his favorite branch and adjusted the binoculars. "Nothing. They're talking. He isn't even holding her hand. Over."

"Do you think they're talking about love or chickens? Spatula."

Hopefully, they were talking about love. Alfie and Benji were never getting out of that cellar if Abraham and Emma were talking about chickens. "Wait. He's reaching out." Alfie pumped his fist and nearly fell out of the tree. "He's holding her hand. I think they're talking about love. Time to send in Tintin. Over."

"Don't let Mamm hear you call him that. Spatula."

"I can call him whatever I want. Over." But that was just a brag for Benji's benefit. Alfie would never call the dog "Tintin" in front of Mamm. She'd make him scrub toilets.

"Okay. I'll send in LaWayne. Did you sneak that bacon into Abraham's pocket? Spatula."

"Of course. I'm a master spy. Over."

Alfie gazed into the binoculars. Abraham was still holding Emma's hand, and Emma had her back to the fence that surrounded her chicken run. It was perfect, especially if Tintin followed instructions. Of course, Tintin was a dog, so he didn't really follow instructions, but that was why they had the bacon.

Abraham was talking and talking and talking. He'd probably never talked so much in his whole life put together. If Tintin didn't come right quick, Emma would probably fall asleep from boredom.

Benji was a wonderful *gute* partner. Tintin tore out from behind the trees and ran straight for Abraham. He jumped right at Abraham's back. It wasn't enough to knock Abraham over, but it was enough to make him fall into Emma. He sort of reached out his hands to her and she reached out her hands to stop him and sure enough, they ended up in a hug. Abraham's back was to Alfie, so he couldn't see Abraham's expression, but Emma got the biggest smile on her face as Abraham leaned in.

"Go, go, go," Alfie whispered, even though he thought kissing was disgusting and hoped a girl would never try to kiss him.

Abraham was pretty smart. He usually took an opportunity when he saw it. He put his arms all the way around Emma and kissed her, right on the lips.

"Yessss," Alfie hissed.

But it was a short kiss because Tintin, also known as LaWayne, jumped on Abraham, again trying to find that bacon, and knocked the two lovebirds apart. Abraham laughed—what a stupid time to laugh—and gave Tintin a pat on the head. Tintin licked Abraham's pocket, and Abraham finally figured out there was something Tintin wanted in there. He reached in and pulled out the thick slab of bacon Alfie had put in there just minutes before

Abraham had left the house. You had to be sneaky about these things.

Abraham laughed again, fed Tintin the bacon, and leaned in for another kiss, and Tintin hadn't even needed to give him a nudge.

Sometimes Abraham was smart like that.

Alfie smiled to himself. They'd be out of that cellar by harvest time.

Now if he could just get down from this tree.

Rebecca's Pigs-in-a-Blanket

1 can refrigerated crescent dinner rolls
8 beef hot dogs, cut in half (They have to be
   beef. Any other kind is not *gute* enough.)

Heat oven to 375 degrees. Separate dough into triangles and cut each triangle in half. Wrap dough triangle around each hot dog. Place on ungreased cookie sheet. Bake at 375 degrees for 12 to 15 minutes or until golden brown. Serve hot with mustard, ketchup, or mayonnaise.

Emma's Peanut Butter Bars

1 cup butter, softened
1 cup brown sugar
1 cup sugar
2 eggs
½ tsp. salt
1 tsp. baking soda
1 tsp. vanilla
⅔ cup peanut butter, creamy or crunchy
2 cups flour
2 cups quick oats
1¼ cups semisweet chocolate chips

½ cup sifted powdered sugar
¼ cup peanut butter, creamy or crunchy
2–4 Tbs. evaporated milk (enough for a drizzly
consistency)

Preheat oven to 350 degrees.

Cream together butter, brown sugar, and sugar.

To that mixture add eggs, salt, baking soda, vanilla,
and ⅔ cup peanut butter.

Stir in flour and oats.

Spread in a greased jelly-roll pan or a large greased
cookie sheet. Bake at 350 degrees for 20–25 minutes.
Do NOT overbake.

While the mixture is baking, combine powdered
sugar, ¼ cup peanut butter, and evaporated milk.
Set aside.

Remove bars from oven, and sprinkle chocolate
chips over the top. Let stand for 5 minutes. Spread
the melted chocolate evenly over the bars, then
drizzle the peanut butter mixture on top.

Cool and cut into bars.

Connect with

Visit us online at
KensingtonBooks.com
to read more from your favorite authors, see books
by series, view reading group guides, and more.

for sneak peeks, chances to win books and prize packs,
and to share your thoughts with other readers.

facebook.com/kensingtonpublishing
twitter.com/kensingtonbooks

Tell us what you think!

To share your thoughts, submit a review,
or sign up for our eNewsletters, please visit:
KensingtonBooks.com/TellUs.

Books by Bestselling Author
Fern Michaels

__**The Jury**	0-8217-7878-1	$6.99US/$9.99CAN
__**Sweet Revenge**	0-8217-7879-X	$6.99US/$9.99CAN
__**Lethal Justice**	0-8217-7880-3	$6.99US/$9.99CAN
__**Free Fall**	0-8217-7881-1	$6.99US/$9.99CAN
__**Fool Me Once**	0-8217-8071-9	$7.99US/$10.99CAN
__**Vegas Rich**	0-8217-8112-X	$7.99US/$10.99CAN
__**Hide and Seek**	1-4201-0184-6	$6.99US/$9.99CAN
__**Hokus Pokus**	1-4201-0185-4	$6.99US/$9.99CAN
__**Fast Track**	1-4201-0186-2	$6.99US/$9.99CAN
__**Collateral Damage**	1-4201-0187-0	$6.99US/$9.99CAN
__**Final Justice**	1-4201-0188-9	$6.99US/$9.99CAN
__**Up Close and Personal**	0-8217-7956-7	$7.99US/$9.99CAN
__**Under the Radar**	1-4201-0683-X	$6.99US/$9.99CAN
__**Razor Sharp**	1-4201-0684-8	$7.99US/$10.99CAN
__**Yesterday**	1-4201-1494-8	$5.99US/$6.99CAN
__**Vanishing Act**	1-4201-0685-6	$7.99US/$10.99CAN
__**Sara's Song**	1-4201-1493-X	$5.99US/$6.99CAN
__**Deadly Deals**	1-4201-0686-4	$7.99US/$10.99CAN
__**Game Over**	1-4201-0687-2	$7.99US/$10.99CAN
__**Sins of Omission**	1-4201-1153-1	$7.99US/$10.99CAN
__**Sins of the Flesh**	1-4201-1154-X	$7.99US/$10.99CAN
__**Cross Roads**	1-4201-1192-2	$7.99US/$10.99CAN

Available Wherever Books Are Sold!
Check out our website at www.kensingtonbooks.com

More by Bestselling Author
Hannah Howell

More from Bestselling Author
JANET DAILEY

Available Wherever Books Are Sold!

Check out our website at www.kensingtonbooks.com.